THE DEE VALLEY KILLINGS

By Simon McCleave

A Ruth Hunter Crime Thriller

Book 3

Your FREE book is waiting for you now

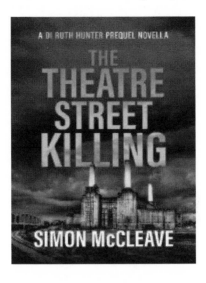

Get your FREE copy of the prequel to
the DI Ruth Hunter Series NOW
http://www.simonmccleave.com/vip-email-club
and join my VIP Email Club

For Dave, Jim, John and the fellowship

"The ends justify the means."
Niccolò Machiavelli

"No man is justified in doing evil on the ground of expediency."
Theodore Roosevelt

"To defeat evil, I shall become a greater evil."
Lelouch Vi Britannia

CHAPTER 1

8 *December 2018*

The picturesque market town of Bala lay at the heart of the Dee Valley on the outskirts of Snowdonia National Park. Dating back to Roman times, most of its inhabitants were Welsh speakers – until the tourists came in the summer months. To the north of the town was the imposing summit of Mount Snowdon, now covered in snow. Folklore said that Snowdon was the burial mound of Welsh giant and king, Rhitta Gawr, notorious in the fifth century for murdering kings, cutting their bloody beards from their faces and stitching them together to make a macabre, regal cloak to keep him warm from the cold. Rhitta would not be satisfied until he had the beard of the legendary King Arthur of England as the crowning centrepiece of his deadly shawl ... However, in a gruesome battle, Rhitta was killed by King Arthur and then buried at the top of Snowdon.

It was a bitter winter's day and the threat of sleet was in the air. It being early December, the town's high street was brightly festooned with colourful Christmas decorations. Shop windows twinkled and glistened with festive displays of green, red and gold. Further along the road, a small group from the Salvation Army, in smart black uniforms, sang 'Oh Come All Ye Faithful' enthusiastically while rattling their buckets, appealing to the season's charitable spirit.

A man in his forties, slim and athletic in build, slowed his car and parked in a space on the main road. He looked up and saw that the town's Indian restaurant had gold tinsel hanging in the windows. He smiled. The lead-up to Christmas was Andrew's favourite time of year. It was a happy and exciting time. However, as he turned off the ignition he was feeling a little nervous. He was meeting a blind date in the pub. Given how all his other 'encounters' had ended badly or dramatically, he had used an online dating website even though he'd sworn he never would. He was concerned. How safe were they? What if the person he was meeting was a homicidal freak? A maniac? He could always make his excuses and walk away. What if they took one look at him and left? Or laughed? He was having second thoughts. *Pull yourself together,* he told himself. A couple of drinks would take the edge off. It usually did. And maybe his date would be perfect. The kind of romantic night he had planned in his head all day.

Pulling down the sun visor, he checked his appearance in the small mirror. He knew he was boyishly handsome even with the scar that went horizontally across his left eyelid – the result of messing around in his garden as an eight-year-old. He and Dan Bagley had created a gigantic seesaw catapult with bricks and a plank of wood. They had marvelled at it and planned to launch all sorts of projectiles at various neighbours they disliked – namely flaming bags of dog shit at that cow Mrs Orwell from number seven. However, while Andrew examined the fist-sized rock they were about to launch at Mrs Orwell's greenhouse as a test run, Dan stamped on the other end, sending the rock into Andrew's face. It split his eyelid in two and he had to wear an eye patch to school for over a month. He heard every pirate joke going but was lucky to have kept his sight. And he now had a thick scar. But scars weren't wounds to him. Scars were the result of healing and becoming whole again. And Andrew could deal with the physical scars. They were like medals. Emotional scars were different. They could eat away at your very soul.

Taking a deep breath, Andrew got out of the car, pulled up the collar on his coat and headed across the road, which was becoming slushy underfoot. He could feel the tension in his stomach and groin. He had always been anxious, ever since he could remember. Andrew passed the statue of T. E. Ellis, a nineteenth-century MP and Welsh nationalist, that was now flecked with sleet. A small snowflake hovered, circled and then landed perfectly on the end of the statue's nose.

On the left was Bar Lounge, which he knew to be a popular hang out and restaurant. Strings of cream fairy lights hung magically from the dark green awning at its front. Approaching the door tentatively, he opened it, allowing a group of women who barely acknowledged him to exit. He was used to that. Invisibility was his superpower.

Scanning the room, his heart was beating hard. The air was warm and boozy. From somewhere there was the fragrant smell of spiced mulled wine. The sound of chatter, laughter and Dean Martin Christmas songs. And over in the corner, beside the brick fireplace and flickering wood burner, was his date. An olive-skinned man in his thirties; big, brown eyes, tasteful Norwegian jumper, nursing a large glass of red wine.

The man looked up, met Andrew's gaze and smiled. Andrew walked over, relieved that his date was handsome. Very handsome. He was feeling more positive already.

'Stefan?' Andrew asked, getting into his stride.

'Andrew? Let me get you a drink. What can I get you?' Stefan's voice was deep, soft and confident.

'Pint of bitter. Thanks,' Andrew said, taking off his coat and placing it on the back of the chair. He was wondering what Stefan had made of him.

As Stefan returned with the drinks, Andrew sat on a creaky wooden chair and took a moment to compose himself. *Keep it together, smile and don't say anything weird,* he said to himself.

'Cheers,' Andrew said as they clinked glasses.

'I'm a bit nervous actually,' Andrew admitted as he sipped his pint. *Phew, I've said it and it feels better already.*

'Me too. I'm not one for dating sites usually,' Stefan said.

'My first time. But you sounded lovely in your messages so I thought, *What the hell?*'

Andrew need not have worried. The next few hours were a whirl of chatter, laughter and alcohol. He knew within minutes that Stefan had everything he looked for in a man. A landscape gardener with his own business. A love of theatre and dance. It wasn't long before they were holding hands across the table, the candle throwing soft shadows over their faces. As far as Andrew was concerned, it was perfect. They were made for each other.

Andrew surprised himself when he asked Stefan if he wanted to go somewhere quieter. The booze had calmed Andrew's nerves and given him confidence. That's what alcohol did for him. It transformed him. In fact, the excitement was getting the better of him. It always did. Andrew suggested that they go back to his house. It wasn't far, and he had a car outside.

Despite only having had a few drinks, Stefan seemed to be incredibly drunk as they headed for Andrew's car. In fact, he had to help Stefan cross the road. Andrew didn't mind. In fact, he thought it was hilarious.

As they drove slowly out of Bala, Andrew watched the sleet turn to snow. Christmas lights looped from streetlight to streetlight and couples walked arm in arm below their glow. It was a winter wonderland, he thought to himself.

Andrew didn't want the evening to end. Up to this point it had been everything he had hoped for. 'Last Christmas' by Wham played on the radio and they sang along. Stefan's words slurred a little and Andrew thought it made him even more attractive.

Yet Andrew still had his doubts. What if Stefan was looking for a one-night stand? He would never see him again. He wanted something that would last. He didn't want him to go in the morning. The panic and paranoia began to set in. *No, no, no. Don't let those thoughts overtake you.*

As they sped along the A494 towards Corwen, the snow became heavy and Andrew slowed as visibility got worse. Stefan put his hand on Andrew's thigh and gave him a sexy wink. Something about Stefan's face unnerved him for a moment. Maybe it was just the glazed look in his eye? Maybe this was too good to be true?

Andrew knew for certain that Stefan would leave after they slept together. He could just tell. *No, you're not going to let that happen.* Andrew hated himself for his neediness but he was terrified of being left alone.

Suddenly, a metallic noise from the back of the car startled him. A clang or a bump. It completely unnerved him.

'What's that?' Andrew asked, pushing the brake and slowing the car.

Stefan frowned and then grinned. He was hammered. 'I didn't hear anything. Sorry, love.'

How did he not hear that? It sounded like they had gone over something.

'It came from the back. Hang on ...' Andrew carefully pulled the car over to the side of the road. 'I'm just going to check,' he said as he clambered into the snowstorm and went around to the back of the car. The snow blew into his face, making it difficult to see. There was nothing. Then he opened the rear door and peered in at the floor. 'I think it came from here, didn't it?'

Stefan turned and frowned. 'I'm not sure. I honestly didn't hear anything.' His voice was slurred and he looked as though he was trying to focus his eyes.

Andrew sat on the back seat behind Stefan and smiled. He would not let Stefan get away. He was perfect. Too perfect. *You're not going to leave me.*

With one swift movement, Andrew grabbed a thick rope from under the seat and wrapped it around his hands. He looped it around Stefan's neck, pulling him back against the seat with a violent jolt. He hoped this wouldn't take long.

'What ... the hell are you ... doing?' Stefan coughed, terrified and choking.

Andrew knew exactly what he was doing. He pulled the rope tight, pushing his knees into the back of the passenger seat to give him leverage. The rope was hurting Andrew's hands, but that was part of the thrill. He liked the burning sensation on his skin. The muscles in his arms were taut.

For Andrew, this was heaven. *Come on you beauty, just give in.* He watched Stefan struggling, fighting for his life. He clawed at the rope, trying to free it from his throat, but it was no good. His legs kicked and jolted as he tried to suck in air.

Andrew was getting aroused. He felt the movement in his trousers. This was such a rush. Power.

Andrew pulled with every ounce of his strength. *Squeeze the life out of him. Squeeze, and he'll be mine.* Then Stefan's foot hit the windscreen hard, and it cracked.

Bloody hell, thought Andrew. He would have to get that fixed tomorrow. It was a new car. What a shame.

A moment later, Andrew felt relief as the tension in the rope gave out and the life passed from Stefan's body. He smiled to himself and gave a little laugh. *That felt amazing. Wow.* He let out a sigh of relief. Now he could have the perfect, romantic evening that he had planned all along.

'I'll be home for Christmas' by Elvis played on the radio.

The rush of excitement was too much for Andrew. He moved across the back seat so he could look at Stefan's dead face. He unzipped his trousers and touched himself, and a few seconds later, orgasmed before slumping back onto the car seat with a sigh.

Bliss. I don't want this feeling to ever end.

CHAPTER 2

It was a Monday morning in Snowdonia, and despite the temperature being zero degrees, the sun was bright and the sky blue and clear. The serenity of the scene overlooked by the horseshoe of mountains was broken by a dark blue, unmarked Astra which came into view as it sped around the bend. Detective Inspector Ruth Hunter and Detective Sergeant Nick Evans of the North Wales Police were making their way into Llan Ffestiniog – also known as just Ffestiniog – a picturesque village in the heart of Snowdonia. It was famous as the starting point of the Welsh Highland Railway, the world's oldest narrow-gauge railway, which ran through Snowdonia Park and past the foot of Snowdon.

On their way, Nick had pointed out Llechwedd Slate Caverns, a big tourist attraction with a zip wire, high ropes and an underground trampoline adventure.

'I don't really do the whole outdoor-adventure thing,' Ruth admitted.

'You do surprise me,' Nick said sarcastically.

'Not many slate quarries in South London.'

'These caverns are meant to be haunted by a pair of Victorian miners who were last seen walking off together into the darkness of the shaft and were never seen again. The sounds of their pickaxes on rock can be heard echoing in the disused pit on the anniversary of their disappearance,' Nick explained in a faux scary voice.

'Ohh, thank you for that, Nick. Remind me not to go there any time soon. You know how much I love ghosts,' Ruth said sarcastically. That kind of thing really did spook her, which was strange as dead bodies at a crime scene didn't.

Ruth smiled as she looked out at the stunning landscape that stretched for as far as she could see. It certainly beat chasing drug dealers through the deprived estates of Peckham in South London. Despite transferring from the Met two years ago, she still counted herself as a virtual newcomer to North Wales. And despite thinking that she would enjoy a quieter, more peaceful time in the North Wales Police, her time there had proved to be anything but. Nearly two years ago, the Dinas Padog murders had broken her, and it was only four months since the Owen Ankers murder case and the shootings involving Callum Webb and one of her colleagues.

'Fairytale of New York' by The Pogues came on the radio and Nick reached over and turned the volume up.

'Oh, I love this song. My favourite Christmas tune!' he said with a grin.

'As a recovering alky, why isn't that a big surprise?' teased Ruth. She remembered the video with Shane MacGowan swigging Irish whiskey straight from the bottle.

Since she'd first met her sergeant, she had seen him ride the roller-coaster of alcoholism many times, but he was doing well.

'Three months sober today,' Nick said with an element of pride.

Ruth nodded. She should know how long he had been sober – she had picked him up from the police-funded rehab on the North Wales coast. She also knew that he hadn't been able to go more than a week or two sober for over a decade.

'What's changed?' Ruth asked. It was such a big achievement to go from being controlled by and addicted to alcohol, to putting it down for three months.

Nick thought for a moment. 'I asked for help, did as I was told and stopped thinking I could beat it on my own and my way.'

'So, a bit of common sense and humility?' Ruth asked, summarising.

'I guess so ... Yeah.'

Nick slowed the car and Ruth peered at the street names. She had some intel on a series of violent burglaries that had taken place across central Snowdonia in recent weeks. It was the elderly who had been targeted in particular and this angered her. The teenage burglars, who had worn masks, were brazen and callous enough to carry out the robberies with occupants in the house. They had restrained several pensioners, causing rocketing levels of fear in the community and causing one eighty-year-old man to have a heart attack as his home was ransacked. *Evil wankers,* Ruth thought. She would like to find and arrest the suspects, take them back to Llancastell Police Station and leave them in an interview room with Nick. He could explain North Wales Police Force's policy on those who tied up, tortured and robbed pensioners. She had seen Nick lose his rag a few times in the past, and it wasn't a pretty sight.

They slowed, and Ruth gazed out at a small, scruffy row of houses where an eighteen-year-old male suspect, Ethan Reid, who had a long record of petty crime, lived. *What did teenagers do in a place like Ffestiniog*, she wondered.

Opening the car door, the air was icy and bitter against her face. She could feel the breeze freezing her lungs as she breathed. The car dashboard had read zero degrees a few minutes earlier. The sound of the wind swirled noisily around her ears and she pulled up the collar on her woollen coat.

'This is it. Number twelve,' Nick said, pointing to a small dilapidated cottage. The grey stone had once been painted white, but was now worn and scruffy. Plonked in the centre of the facade was a large satellite that cast an oblong shadow on the flaky brickwork.

Ruth heard the reverberating sound of a motor. At first, she thought it was a lawn mower. Then suddenly from the side of the cottage, a black scooter and rider in a black helmet appeared at speed, screeching into the road and speeding away. Ethan Reid, she assumed.

'Shit!' Ruth said as they ran back to the car.

'Little wanker!' Nick growled.

As Ruth clicked her radio, the air was full of bitter exhaust fumes. 'Dispatch from three-six. We are in pursuit of a possible suspect. Eighteen-year-old male, Ethan Reid. Black Honda Scooter. Sierra-tango-five-nine, foxtrot-lima-alpha. Heading north out of Ffestiniog. Over.'

'Dispatch received,' her Tetra radio replied. 'Stand by.'

She jumped into the car. Nick had already turned the ignition, hitting the accelerator hard and spinning the wheels as they set off in pursuit.

'Let's get this bastard,' said Ruth. She could feel the adrenaline beginning to pump inside her as she buckled her seatbelt with a clunk. *Little bastards like Ethan Reid have no respect for anyone or anything.*

'Yes, boss,' Nick said as he hit sixty miles per hour. She knew he was enjoying the feeling of power from driving fast. *Typical bloody boy*, she thought. He was a good copper. And he was a much better copper now he had stopped drinking.

Ruth gripped the door handle with one hand and the front of her seat with the other as they screamed around the curves in the road. She had been in car chases with Nick before, and even though he was an excellent driver, the speed still terrified her. She tried to straighten herself in her seat before the next bend.

As they rounded the tight corner, the Astra's wheels squealed as they gripped the road, but the scooter seemed to have disappeared around the next sharp bend. Ruth sat forwards a little, peering through the windscreen. 'Where are you, you little bastard?'

The black scooter came into a view again, speeding up a hill about a mile ahead of them. *Got you, you fucker.*

'Central from three-six. We're still in pursuit of a possible suspect on black Honda moped. About two miles north of Ffestiniog on the A-three-four-three. Speed seven-zero.'

Ruth felt the Astra's back tyres losing grip again as they cornered another bend. Her stomach lurched.

Nick came hammering up a hill and pulled out to overtake a car towing a caravan, which went past in a blur. Ruth closed her eyes as they missed a car coming the other way by a matter of feet. *Jesus, please don't let me die!*

'Pussy!' Nick teased her.

'Unlike you, I don't have a death wish.'

The radio crackled again. 'Three-six. Unit tango-two-one is now heading east on B537 to assist,' the CAD operator informed them. CAD stood for Computer Aided Dispatch.

'Received,' Ruth said as she saw that now they were on the straight road the boy's scooter was no match for the Astra. They were gaining fast as the car ate up the road ahead.

'He's going nowhere,' Nick growled under his breath.

Within seconds, they were only fifty yards behind. Ruth watched as Nick pulled closer – it was getting dangerous. Reid could see them in his mirrors. Nick touched the brakes and they lurched back.

'Careful, Nick,' Ruth said.

Reid slowed the moped suddenly, reached up for his helmet and pulled it off. He turned and waved at them.

'Shit!' Ruth exclaimed.

'What a little wanker,' Nick muttered.

They both knew the chase was over.

Ruth had seen this tactic all too often in the Met with the increasing rise in moped gangs. Her fellow officers had been hindered by the current rules that stated that officers could *only* chase criminals on mopeds without helmets if the safety risk to them was proportionate to the crime. She had seen one officer in court for dangerous driving when a teenager without a helmet had come off his bike while being chased. The youth had been awarded damages for his injuries. It was crazy. But it meant that many police officers in the UK now followed an unwritten rule to stop chasing mopeds if the rider wasn't wearing a helmet. It was either that or risk their career.

Given that they only wanted to question Reid and had no concrete evidence against him, both Ruth and Nick knew that to pursue him helmetless wasn't a risk worth taking. And Reid knew it.

They pulled up to a reluctant stop.

'Maybe I should just run the little scrotum over anyway. No witnesses,' Nick said dryly.

Reid turned, his blonde hair blowing in the wind, grinned and gave them the middle finger. He then pulled the scooter to the middle of the road and turned down a single track before disappearing.

'Follow him?' Nick asked, but he knew the answer.

'No point,' Ruth replied. Sometimes she thought that the world had gone mad. She wasn't for a return to the heavy-handed or corrupt policing of the 1970s, when suspects could be 'fitted up' as long as there was a strong suspicion that they were guilty. However, when they had to suspend chasing a possible criminal who might be robbing and tying up pensioners because they had chosen to deliberately take off their helmet, that didn't sit comfortably with her either.

Her radio crackled. 'Three-six. This is Dispatch. We have reports of the discovery of a body at the foot of Snowdon. Halfway up Miners' Track. Uniform are on site.'

Nick looked over. 'Hope you're feeling fit, boss.'

'Why?' Ruth asked, not liking the subtext of his comment.

'That's a two-mile walk uphill in the freezing cold,' Nick said with a grin.

'Bollocks. At least the housing estates in Peckham had stairs,' she said.

IT WAS LUNCHTIME BY the time Andy Gates had settled his wife Kerry down in the comfort of their small sitting room. Gates had cared for Kerry for twenty years. She had multiple sclerosis, which had been diagnosed in her early twenties, a month to the day after she and Gates had married. He didn't mind. He loved her dearly. If it was God's will, so be it. However, the symptoms were getting worse and he was having to carry her around the house to wherever she needed to be more frequently. He could see that she felt guilty, but he reminded her that he had agreed, in front of God, to love and cherish her 'in sickness and in health.'

Gates, now in his mid-forties, was fit and healthy. He ran three miles a day and generally looked after himself. He wore thick-rimmed, tinted glasses to stop the migraines that he had suffered from since he was a boy. Gates didn't care that they made him look a bit odd. His migraines could see him retreat to a darkened room for a whole day, so anything that could stop them was welcome.

They lived in Llantysilio, a small, friendly hamlet a few miles to the west of Llangollen, on the eastern borders of Snowdonia. The Gates's home was cosy and tidy, if a little dark. There were a few religious pictures and paintings of the Snowdonia landscape on the walls. Gates thought it was perfect. They had lived in the bungalow for six years. Having a bungalow meant that Kerry didn't have to struggle with the stairs anymore. It also had an annexe building with a self-contained bedroom, bathroom and lounge. Gates kept promising that he would redecorate it so they could let it on, possibly on Air BnB. He had started work on it but kept getting distracted by other projects.

Sitting on the edge of the patterned sofa, Gates began to lace his trainers. His routine on his days off ran like clockwork because he enjoyed having structure. He loved his work as a freelance building surveyor and, as a side-line, he was developing a property over in Pentredwr. He would take a run via the spectacular Horseshoe Pass. Then he would go to the house where he would do some more work. He hoped to let out the property to give him and Kerry a reliable income. He worried how she would cope if anything ever happened to him. Although he knew that God was looking out for him. *Thy will be done.*

Gates reached over, took the remote and turned on the television. 'There you go, love,' he said, handing the remote to his wife. Her hand shook a little as she took it from him.

'Oh, a true-life movie. *She Led Two Lives.* Fantastic,' she said with a wry smile. She pulled her blonde hair back and made it into a ponytail. She reached for her glasses but her hand was now trembling too much to pick them up.

Gates smiled, and handed her the glasses. 'Here you go.'

'Thanks. That's better, I can see now.'

'Hammy acting, bad plots. Perfect.' Gates smiled as she gestured to the television. Afternoon movies were Kerry's guilty pleasure and she would no doubt tell him all about it later and make him laugh.

'Be careful out on the pass, will you?' she warned him. Her blue eyes seemed a little smaller behind the lenses of her glasses. That's what he first noticed about her. Piercing blue eyes and blonde hair. Every man's dream, wasn't it?

'Scout's honour.' Gates winked at her and made a Scout salute. He loved the fact that she worried about him so much. He felt truly blessed.

Despite Kerry's illness, Gates thought their little world was perfect. It was those 'out there' that were in true pain. It was his mission in life to help them. He grabbed his things and closed the front door behind him.

Twenty minutes later, Gates hit the Horseshoe Pass, or *Bwlch yr Oernant*, 'The Pass of the Cold Stream.' Stopping to catch his breath, he took in the spectacular view. He knew that local mythology told of an enormous wolf-like animal that inhabited the pass. It was a story that dated back to the eighteenth century. They said that a stagecoach travelling between Denbigh and Wrexham was attacked and overturned by an enormous black beast. It was described as being as big as the coach horses. The attack had taken place just after sunset, with a full blood moon on the horizon. The sightings and stories continued after that. In 1903, a nearby snow-covered field had been turned into 'a lake of blood' dotted with carcasses of sheep, cattle and even the farmer's dog. The tracks of an enormous wolf had been found. The sightings of large wolf- or cat-like animals in the area had continued into the twenty-first century. Gates was told that it was a family of pumas that had continued to survive out in Snowdonia for centuries. He wondered if he would ever see the beast on his daily run.

Now standing at 1,400 feet above sea level, Gates looked down into the pass that curved for over five miles in a horseshoe shape and was scattered with patches of snow. Disinterested sheep watched him. The ridges were clad with purple heather. As the wind picked up, black grouse and curlew flapped and rose into the sky. *What a fantastic way to spend an afternoon*, Gates thought to himself.

The clouds passed across the winter sun and cast dark shadows over the steep sides of the valley. The ground was hard underfoot and Gates lost his footing on part of the icy footpath. He didn't care. He drew in a deep lungful of fresh air. As he gazed out across the landscape, he felt like calling out, 'This is God's country, God's work, and it is a miracle.'

Running was Gates's time to think and plan. It was a form of meditation. Projects, ideas, the future. His important work.

By the time Gates arrived at his property development, the sun was completely hidden behind the thickening clouds and his rucksack had cut into his shoulders a little. He let himself into the house as his pulse began to slow. He liked how it smelt of drying plaster and paint. It smelt of progress and hard, honest work. It was redolent of the blissful times he had helped his *taid* paint and decorate when he was a boy. He would watch with sheer joy as his taid measured and rolled out wallpaper on the old wooden trestle table, before applying the rich-smelling paste and then hanging it with meticulous precision. That was before his taid had died suddenly when he was eight. It was a day he would never forget.

There was, however, another odour. At first, Gates thought it was the smell of sulphur or rotting eggs. Although it seemed more putrid than that. Maybe it was the drains? There had been a lot of rain and sleet in recent days and Gates had been working on the house's drainage and pipes in the garden.

Pushing through the protective plastic sheeting, Gates went to get brushes, paint and overalls. Pouring himself a glass of water, he gulped it down as he went to look for his paint-splattered radio. An afternoon with Classic FM would be just the thing. His plan was to finish the painting of the main bedroom upstairs. Then he would go home, shower and cook him and Kerry dinner. He had a bottle of white wine in the fridge. Kerry wasn't meant to have alcohol with her medication but she didn't have many pleasures left in life. He liked to see how the alcohol relaxed her and even made her a little giggly.

There was a knock at the door. A shadow appeared at the frosted glass. For a moment, Gates felt uneasy. He wasn't expecting anyone. He hated being disturbed.

Opening the door, he saw a man in his twenties standing on the doorstep. He was tall and skinny with spiky brown hair. He seemed awkward.

'Oh, hiya. I'm Steve from next door.' The man avoided making eye contact and gestured left to show which way he meant. 'Erm ... We've just moved in and there's a horrible smell. We think it's coming from your garden.'

Even though he felt a little defensive, Gates nodded. 'Yeah, I thought that when I arrived. I did some work in the garden about a month ago. Drains seemed okay.'

Steve shrugged. 'Maybe it's the cold weather? Doesn't take much to crack an old sewage pipe. Or it could be the pipe coming out of your boiler?'

Gates raised an eyebrow. 'You know your stuff?'

'I'm a plumber by trade. Do you want me to take a look?'

'Erm ... Okay. If you don't mind.' The smell had bothered him. Now that they were out of the house, it seemed worse away from the smells of the paint and plaster. But he wasn't sure he wanted a neighbour meddling in his business.

'Do you know where the access point is to the drain? Steve asked.

'Yeah, the manhole is just at the back.'

It started to spit with rain as Gates showed Steve down the side of the house and out into the untidy garden. There were rusty iron garden chairs, overgrown plant pots and the patio was covered in leaves and moss. It would need a lot of work before he could rent the property.

Around the cast-iron manhole cover, Gates could see that there were a few inches of opaque liquid, which was turning the patchy lawn into a muddy mess. There was definitely a problem. And the smell was now unbearable.

'Looks like the sewer is blocked,' Gates gasped, pinching his nose.

He watched as Steve took a broken piece of metal from the patio. 'Mind if I have a look?'

Gates wasn't sure, but he shrugged. 'Help yourself.'

Steve levered off the heavy manhole cover, crouched and looked down into the hole. He pushed the metal bar down into the sewer.

'There's stuff down here that must be blocking it.'

'Do you need a torch?' asked Gates.

'Hang on.' Steve used both arms to lever something out of the sewer. He pulled it out and plopped it down on the ground. It was white, pulpy and looked like a cross between lard and porridge.

'What on earth is that?' Gates said. The smell was overwhelming.

'God knows.' Steve fished around in the gloop. Something gold and metallic appeared. It was a gold ring.

'Looks like a wedding band,' he observed.

'I'd better call someone to come and sort all this out,' Gates said shaking his head.

The man pushed and prodded more. As Gates looked, he could see something emerge from the liquid. Dark and solid. It looked like some kind of meat.

'What the hell is that?' Steve exclaimed, clearly revolted.

Gates could now see the entire shape. He knew exactly what it was. 'I'd better call the police. I think it's a human heart.'

CHAPTER 3

The weather had worsened by the time Ruth and Nick began to make their way up Snowdon's Miners' Track to where the body had been discovered. Clouds had formed a low and claustrophobic blanket over the heathland, and none of the mountain tops were visible anymore. Grand buttresses of silvery rock rose slowly beside them, while Snowdon's majestic shadows darkened the two lakes that lay to the left.

As Ruth climbed, a stoat stuttered and loped across the scree to her right and then disappeared into a hole at the foot of the cliffs. She puffed as her heart thudded at the strain of getting up the path. It had been months since she had been for a run. When she thought about it, probably not since the summer. Sian, Ruth's partner and work colleague, had made her promise to quit smoking but she had only managed a couple of weeks before succumbing again. She put her foot firmly on the grey, rectangular stones that marked the pathway towards the top of the ridge. *Bloody hell, this is hard work*, she thought.

The walk gave Ruth time to think, but that wasn't always a good thing. She had always promised Sarah that she would take her to Snowdon and they would climb it together. And this was the first time since she moved to the North Wales Police Force from London that she had been on Snowdon.

Sarah would have loved it. But she left the ghost of Sarah – or at least tried to – behind in London.

It had been a few months since Ruth had had any kind of information about her girlfriend Sarah's unexplained disappearance in 2013. For several years, Ruth had been crushed by the lack of progress in the search for Sarah or any answers as to why she had vanished off the face of the earth. Ruth felt it was time for her to start doing some more investigating of her own.

Ten minutes later, the cloud had thickened further and visibility was down to about two hundred yards. Ruth could see that if you weren't careful, walking off an edge and falling down a crevice or steep, rocky slope was a distinct possibility.

Nick had already told her that there were several deaths a year on Snowdon. At this time of year, not only were the conditions and weather very dangerous, but the speed at which they could change made it even more deadly.

'Come on, Grandma,' Nick quipped as he stopped and waited for her.

'Oi. You need to remember that I'm in my forties,' Ruth grumbled.

'How much longer are you going to be in your forties?' Nick joked.

'Another month. So I'm milking it.' Ruth stopped. 'Bloody hell. How much further?'

Nick pointed. 'Just over that ridge.'

'Great,' Ruth puffed sarcastically. 'I could have done with a nice, long surveillance job in a warm car. Hot coffee and a ciggie.'

'Stop moaning. You're looking at the site of King Arthur's final battle,' Nick said.

'Yeah, and you must have mistaken me for someone who gives a shit,' Ruth groaned.

As they trudged on, Ruth saw the luminous jacket of a uniformed police officer on the brow of the ridge. Above their heads, a northern goshawk glided on the air currents looking for prey. It was a blue-grey colour with a large wing-span and tail. Suddenly it dived from the sky and disappeared out of sight.

Reaching the ridge, Ruth could now see an array of fluorescent jackets where the body had been found. The bright yellow of uniformed officers and the red jackets and white helmets of the Snowdon Mountain Rescue team. They crouched down beside a large stretcher made from lightweight steel tubes. Yellow police tape was being rolled out to mark off the area.

From behind them, they could hear a deep whirring sound. Ruth looked around, slightly startled, as a rescue helicopter began to slowly hover. Its enormous central propeller created a downward force that flattened the grass and heathland, and even scattered the small shards of rock nearby.

Ruth ducked a little against the wind as a uniformed officer approached. 'DI Hunter and DS Evans. What have we got, Constable?' Ruth shouted as she showed him her warrant card.

'Unidentified male. Looks like he fell down that ridge. Paramedics have confirmed the man is deceased.'

'Who found the body?' Nick said as they walked away from the noise of the helicopter.

'Middle-aged couple and their dog. I've got a statement and an address. The thing that bothers me is that the body looks like someone has hidden it, ma'am,' the officer said.

Ruth was confused. 'I thought the man had fallen down the ridge?'

'Yes, ma'am. But, I'm just not how the body would have ended up where it was found,' the officer explained.

Ruth thought it was a strange observation but, in her experience, uniformed officers had an excellent instinct for when things just didn't feel right.

'Any ID?' Nick asked.

'I'm not sure, sir. I thought I shouldn't touch anything until you guys got here,' the officer explained.

'Good. That's great,' Ruth reassured him with a smile. She had had overkeen wooden tops ruin a crime scene before, so she was pleased it had been left alone.

'Let's take a look.' Nick gestured for them to go.

As they went down the steep, rocky bank, Ruth placed her boots on the small rocks and tried to balance. She was a city girl, and this was not her idea of fun. If truth be told, heights terrified her, as did slipping and cracking open her skull. The descent seemed to take for ever. It was over seventy feet from the path to the bottom. She slid on the final loose rocks but eventually got down to where the ground was more level. She looked back up the ridge and wondered quite how she had got to the bottom without slipping. At least her journey back up would be more controlled.

The clouds broke for a moment and the winter sun poured down.

'Behind that rock, ma'am,' the officer pointed.

Ruth and Nick approached a huge grey boulder. It was grey dolerite and stood at about four feet high and six feet long, shaped like a ragged arch. However, because of how the ground undulated, it wasn't until they went around the back that a man's body, in a bright-blue Karrimor waterproof climbing jacket, became visible.

Ruth immediately saw that the body was lying face down. She then looked back up the steep ridge and then at Nick.

'What do you think?' Ruth asked. She hoped he was thinking the same as her. Normally he did. The sun disappeared again, and the wind picked up and chilled her face and ears, numbing them.

Nick frowned and looked up the sheer, stony incline. 'Unless he crawled there after he fell, there's no way that he fell down that and ended up behind this rock.'

'Not unless he defied gravity.' *Definitely something not right about this scene of crime,* Ruth thought.

'And if you wanted to hide the body from the path, you would pull it behind that rock out of sight,' Nick said, thinking out loud.

Ruth took a moment as she surveyed the surrounding area again. It just didn't add up. The body had been moved.

Nick walked closer to the victim and crouched for a moment. The man's ear and hair were matted with dark, congealed blood.

'Okay. I'm going to get SOCO here. This whole scene doesn't feel right, does it?' Ruth said.

'No, boss.' But Nick's thoughts were elsewhere. He had noticed a part of a dragon tattoo on the man's wrist and the first inch of his forearm.

'Boss?' Nick said quietly.

'Yeah?'

'I know the victim. He's an old friend. Harvey Pearson.'

CHAPTER 4

The mid-week AA meeting took place in a large, cosy room that was attached to the university hospital's detox unit. Two large scrolls that carried the 'Twelve Steps' and the 'Twelve Traditions' hung from the wall.

Nick had been to the detox unit itself four times in recent years, and despite the promise of a withdrawal-symptom-free life, it hadn't kept him away from alcohol.

Standing at the table, Nick surveyed the plastic cups, tea, coffee and biscuits. Caffeine was now his drug of choice. He made himself a strong coffee and surveyed the room but he was distracted. He couldn't get the image of Harvey Pearson's cracked skull out of his head. They had gone to school together and Nick had been an usher at his wedding. He hadn't seen Harv for a couple of years, except for a chance encounter by the booze aisle at a local supermarket. The usual laddish banter of 'Not a surprise to see you on this aisle, Nick' had ensued, but that was about the extent of their catch-up. He heard that Harv had got divorced and could be found every weekend 'on the pull' in town pestering women. Harv had always been 'a player,' even when he was married. That was common knowledge.

What troubled Nick more though was the likelihood that someone had deliberately moved his body out of sight of the footpath up on Snowdon. Why? Had someone killed

33

him? They were waiting for the post mortem and the forensic evidence back from the SOCOs. The whole thing had made him uneasy, and he had asked his Higher Power for some help with it.

'Nick?' an uncertain female voice asked from behind him.

Nick turned to see an attractive woman in her late thirties, dark hair, olive skin and big brown eyes. Amanda Wheeler worked for Llancastell Social Services and she and Nick had met at various times through joint operations. She was on the Child Protection team, which Nick knew could be harrowing work.

'Amanda?' Nick said quietly. He then gestured for Amanda to move to a more discreet area. What was she doing there? He knew how much courage it took to get through the doors of an AA meeting. 'Are you okay?' he asked.

'I'm here, so ... no, not really. But I'm so glad to see you here.' Amanda's voice was trembling, and she seemed jittery.

'Yeah. Good to see you too.' Nick nodded compassionately. However hard he tried, Nick couldn't help feeling a jolt of excitement. Amanda was attractive and whenever they had worked together, he had found himself fantasising about her afterwards. He had a quick word with himself. *Focus on how you can help her, you twat, not how you can get into her knickers.* 'You think you have a problem with drink?' he asked.

Amanda looked away for a moment and then nodded. He could see it was difficult for her. 'Yeah. I *know* I've got a problem with drink.'

'First meeting?' Nick asked. He was pretty certain it was.

'Yeah,' Amanda whispered with a frightened smile. She looked terrified.

'Don't worry. You're in the right place. Come on, I'll make you a coffee,' Nick whispered. He knew how important the first meeting was to a 'newcomer.' If they didn't find any identification with the group, they could go back out there and drink themselves to death. It was that serious. And over the years, Nick had seen hundreds come to their first meeting never to return. And he knew for a fact that some of them were dead, homeless or insane. As a police officer, he had seen them on the streets.

'How long have you ...?' she asked tentatively.

'I've been around for a few years. But I've only been sober for three months.'

'Only? Christ, sober for three days would be a miracle.'

'I'll talk to some of the women here and get you some phone numbers at the end. Try to get to as many meetings as you can. And just listen. You're going to feel scared, but no one is going to judge you. I promise. Everyone wants to help.'

Amanda nodded. 'Can I have your phone number then?'

Nick would have loved to have given her his number but he knew the score. He pulled a face. 'To be honest, the normal policy in AA is "men for men" and "women for women." Makes things less complicated.' Nick had seen sobriety destroyed by disastrous relationships or even casual sex that had started in AA.

'Yeah, of course.' Amanda seemed to be embarrassed.

'Come on. Come and sit with me,' Nick said with a friendly smile.

They sat down together and the meeting started. Nick had told the group leader that Amanda was a newcomer and she was made to feel welcome.

Nick listened to the main share, noting the points that would be useful for Amanda. Aware that it was Amanda's first AA meeting, various others shared their experience of their first AA meetings. Nick did the same, hoping it would help her.

The meeting ended with the Serenity Prayer and chairs started to be stacked away.

Nick felt the kind of peace that he always seemed to have at the end of meetings these days. Then impulse got the better of him – a dangerous indulgence for a recovering addict. He took some paper and scribbled down his name, mobile number and headed over to Amanda who was looking lost.

'What did you think?' Nick asked.

'I don't know. I didn't get some of it. But there was some stuff where I was thinking, "Yeah that's me. That's definitely me."'

Nick smiled and nodded. 'Well that's more than I got from my first meeting. But then again, I was hammered.'

'Really?'

'Oh yeah.' He handed her the piece of paper. 'Look, forget what I said earlier. I know how hard it must have been to come here tonight. And knowing someone will make it easier. So here's my number. Ring or text me if you want to know anything or if you want to chat. Okay?'

Nick looked at her, trying his best to not react to how bloody gorgeous she was. He knew it was the wrong thing to do, but frankly, he didn't care.

Amanda smiled and nodded. 'Yeah. Thanks, Nick.'

FOR RUTH, IT WAS THE perfect Christmas scene. Detective Constable Sian Hockney, Ruth's girlfriend, walked over and put another log on the open fire before continuing to help Ella put Christmas decorations around the room. 'Jingle Bells' by Michael Bublé was playing, and they were both singing along, '*Dashing through snow, on a one-horse open sleigh...*'

Curled up on the sofa, Ruth was on her laptop checking through emails and bills. She looked up as Sian playfully lobbed a Christmas bauble that bounced off Ella's head with a plop.

'Oi, what was that for?' Ella said in mock indignation.

Sian gave her the finger and grinned. 'Get me a drink, bitch!'

'What did your last slave die from?' Ella asked.

'Gonorrhoea,' Sian quipped as Ella disappeared into the kitchen.

Ruth loved that Sian and her daughter got on so well, even if when they were together, they turned into infants. Sarah's disappearance had taken its toll on her and Ella's relationship; Ruth had been a preoccupied, grief-stricken mess for a long time. It was a relief that Ella and she were so much closer now.

Sian had moved in six weeks ago and things were going well between them. Ella was in the spare room as a stop-gap until she found a new flat. As much as she loved having her daughter around, it wasn't ideal as the house was small. Ruth also wanted more time to be alone with Sian. She knew this was selfish, but Ella was now twenty-two, had a job and was living there rent free.

Putting those thoughts out of her head, knowing that in the grand scheme it was a minor thing, Ruth realised that she hadn't felt this content for a long time.

Ella came back into the lounge with a bottle of beer, which she handed to Sian, and a clean bath towel that she had grabbed from the utility room.

'Mum? Drink?' Ella asked.

'Not for me, darling.'

Sian frowned. 'Come on. Have a drink. Live a little.'

'That's the idea. And my liver is older than yours.'

Ella gestured with her towel. 'I'm going to have a long soak and read my new book.'

'Be careful. Don't fall asleep in the bath,' Sian said in a serious tone.

Ella rolled her eyes. 'Yes, Mummy.'

Sian pulled a face. 'Err, you can cut that out. That's just plain weird.'

Ella laughed, kissed them both and went upstairs. Sian spent the next twenty minutes in the kitchen clearing away and Ruth relaxed in the air of domesticity.

Until Ruth saw the date on her computer screen – 10th December.

It was, or it would have been, Sarah's fortieth birthday today. However illogical, Ruth felt guilty at having forgotten. She had remembered a few days ago, but the thought had got lost amongst everything that was going on. And of course, Ruth had no way of knowing if Sarah was actually turning forty today.

Overwhelmed by grief, and not wanting Sian to see her upset, Ruth went up to the small study. She didn't want to have to explain and for it to create an emotional distance between them. It hadn't been easy for Sian.

Closing the door, Ruth went to the folders and files that she kept under the desk. Sian didn't know about these. Ruth knew that was wrong but part of her felt that she owed it to Sarah, on her birthday, to reconnect in some way.

She began to flick through the file, even though it was heart-breaking. As she shuffled through, she came upon a photo. Her and Sarah photographed cheek to cheek on a blustery autumnal day in Battersea Park. The wind had caught Sarah's hair and blown it away from her forehead. They looked so bloody happy. Closing her eyes for a moment, Ruth could feel the tears. *Don't cry*, she told herself. *How are you going to explain that?*

Opening the door, Ruth went out onto the landing and looked down the stairs. There was no sign of Sian, and Ella was in the bath reading.

'I'm just going to sort out the washing,' Ruth called downstairs.

'Okay! I'm going to watch *Love Island* then, so I don't have to listen to you moan that it's vacuous shit!' Sian called back.

'Okay!' Ruth said.

Now feeling a mixture of guilt and anxiety, Ruth went back into the room and sifted through the photos, folders and newspaper cuttings. She wanted to show Sarah that she wasn't forgotten as she became lost in the events of five years ago.

On the 5 November 2013, Ruth's partner, and the love of her life, Sarah Goddard vanished into thin air. She had not moved out. Not quit her job. Not met someone else. Not decided to cut ties with Ruth. She simply disappeared and hadn't been seen again.

That morning, Sarah had left home and boarded the 8.05 a.m. train from Crystal Palace to Victoria. The CCTV footage showed her getting on the train, as she always did. But she never got off. They examined CCTV at Victoria station millisecond by millisecond. Every frame of CCTV on the line between Crystal Palace was scoured. Every station scanned. Two passengers remembered seeing her chatting to a man as the commuters were squeezed together in the compartment. The man was described as tall, blonde and well dressed. She knew that man was Jurgen Kessler, a German banker who had been working in London at the time.

Ruth came to some of the newspaper stories that she had collated in another file on Jurgen Kessler. She was convinced that he was in some way connected. Last year, police in Germany had linked Kessler to two murders in Berlin. He had disappeared but had been spotted entering the UK on a false passport in August. Since then, Kessler had vanished.

Ruth knew that the key to Sarah's disappearance was Jurgen Kessler. And however long it took, she was going to track him down.

CHAPTER 5

As Ruth entered the office, she could see that although the morning sky outside was icy and grey, inside there had been some half-hearted efforts to make Llancastell CID festive. Someone had pinned red-and-gold tinsel to some of the office dividers and a small Christmas tree had been placed apologetically in one corner.

The smell of coffee felt reassuring as Ruth sat down next to Detective Constable Luke Merringer. With his short ginger hair and goatee, he had acquired the nickname *Ginge* but Ruth didn't like it. Merringer was an excellent copper. Meticulous, hard-working, he really cared about the cases he worked on.

'How's your daughter doing? Katie isn't it?' Ruth asked. Merringer's ten-year-old daughter had learning difficulties.

'Yeah. She's doing great. We got her a place at that school, St Paul's. The staff there are amazing,' he told her with a beaming smile.

'Great. I've heard great things about St Paul's,' Ruth said. She was genuinely pleased for him. She needed reminding sometimes how lucky she was that Ella was fit and healthy.

Files and paperwork were passed between officers and there was general chatter.

Detective Chief Inspector Ashley Drake stood at the front of the room and had just begun to bring officers up to speed with ongoing CID operations. He was six foot, slim and black with a shaved head and a neat goatee. Normally Ruth took CID briefings, but every once in a while, DCI Drake would keep his hand in and remain a visible presence.

Ruth nodded to him as he continued. He was a good skipper. Fair, approachable with instinctive man-management skills. And his intuition as a copper was second to none.

DCI Drake went to the computer, clicked, and a photo of a man in his thirties appeared on the large monitor up on the wall. He had olive skin and dark hair. 'We have a missing person. Stefan Olsen. Thirty-six. Went missing last Saturday night. It's becoming suspicious as he missed a family Christening on Sunday and work meetings on Monday. He's close to his family and they're very concerned as it's completely out of character.'

It was difficult for Ruth to listen to any Missing Persons case for obvious reasons.

Drake looked over at Merringer. 'Luke, what have we got?'

'Boss.' Luke stood up and went over to the computer. 'Stefan Olsen runs his own tree-surgeon business. Clients are mainly residential. Nothing from his mobile phone, which is also missing. We've checked all hospital admissions. We did get some of his social media information. Stefan was meeting an unknown male at this bar, Bar Lounge, in Bala.' Merringer clicked and the exterior of Bar Lounge appeared. 'Staff remember Stefan having a drink with a man but the description is sketchy. No answer from his house and no sightings from the neighbours.'

'Okay, I'm not liking the sound of all this. Sian, can you go with uniform and get into his house? Check with relatives and neighbours to see if anyone has a key.'

Sian nodded. 'Boss. If not?'

'If not, it's a forced entry,' Drake replied.

Ruth caught Sian's eye fleetingly. It was a look of acknowledgement. Sian knew that cases like this were difficult for Ruth.

Drake continued. 'Let's pull any CCTV we can find on the high street. Banks, shops, pubs. Luke, can we look at traffic cameras in and out of Bala? ANPR. Contact the Missing Persons Bureau.'

ANPR stood for Automatic Number Plate Recognition and there were ANPR cameras on most major roads in the UK.

Luke nodded. 'Boss.'

The mention of Missing Persons took Ruth straight back to her hunt for Sarah over the years. In the first twelve months, Ruth had worked closely with the bureau.

'Ruth. Body found on Snowdon yesterday?' Drake said, breaking Ruth's train of thought. *Bloody hell, I was miles away!*

Ruth composed herself, got up to address CID and clicked a photo of Harvey Pearson that she had found on social media. 'The body of Harvey Pearson was found on a ridge below Miners' Track. Nick and I were there yesterday and we suspected that the body had been moved to hide it out of sight of the footpath. The PM is later this morning so we'll know cause of death. There was a severe injury to his head, which may have been caused by a fall. First estimates are that he died some time on Sunday afternoon or evening.'

'Witnesses?' Drake asked.

'Not at the moment. The weather wasn't great on Sunday so there won't have been many people up there. We'll need to do an appeal to the public and a press release.' Ruth's phone buzzed on the table and she glanced down to see who it was from. 'Right, I've got this through from Tech who have been looking at his phone.'

Ruth tapped her phone and linked it to the computer. A moment later an attachment opened. An image of Harvey Pearson, dressed in his blue climbing jacket, appeared on the screen. It was clearly taken on Snowdon and on the day he died. He was clean-shaven, handsome and confident looking.

Ruth scrolled down and there were another three photos of Harvey waving or with his thumb up at various stages of his walk up Snowdon.

'As none of these are selfies, by the look of things, Harvey Pearson was walking up Snowdon with whoever was taking these photos. There're no photos of this person. Where are they now? Were they involved with what happened to Harvey?' Ruth said.

Drake nodded and arched his eyebrow. 'And why did they fail to report it?'

RUTH AND NICK WALKED into the mortuary where Dr Tony Amis was just starting his preliminary post-mortem on Harvey Pearson. Ruth's shoes squeaked on the white tiled floor – the noise grated on her teeth. She was already feeling uncomfortable.

'These places give me the shivers,' Ruth admitted in a virtual whisper.

'You see, boss, they have to keep it very cold in here because of all the dead bodies,' Nick said, taking the piss.

'Very fucking droll, Nicholas. Maybe you should do stand up,' Ruth said, rolling her eyes. Dark humour was part of the coping mechanism of all experienced detectives.

Ruth often got spooked by mortuaries, which she knew was silly. She had been to dozens during her time as a police officer but they were too quiet, too sterile and too lifeless. The underlying hum of fans and the air conditioning added to the eerie atmosphere. The buzz of the enormous fridges at the other end of the room only served to remind Ruth of their grisly contents. Chiller cabinets for bodies.

She hated the sterile smell of clinical disinfectants and other cleaning fluids that masked the underlying stench of death. The lighting was cold and stark. The steel scales used to weigh internal organs were unsettlingly shiny and clean.

Ruth glanced up and saw that Nick was now staring at Harvey Pearson's cadaver, which was lying like a large white mannequin on the gurney. As a police officer, you could become immune to seeing dead bodies. The disassociation became instinctive, and by the evening, seeing a dead body would often be forgotten. However, when the body was someone you knew, the reaction was often different.

'What have we got, Tony?' Ruth asked. She was hoping for some clues as to what had happened to Harvey.

Dressed in pastel-green surgical scrubs, Amis came over. He adjusted his black rubber apron and turned off the microphone. He had been making a digital recording of his findings.

'Our victim has an epidural hematoma on the left side of the frontal lobe as a result of a fractured skull.' Amis pointed to where the skull had been cut away to examine the brain.

Ruth looked at the exposed pink-coloured brain matter that glistened under the light. 'If you look here, you can see that the blood vessels under the skull are torn. And that's consistent with a fall and the victim hitting their head on a rock.'

'And that's what killed him?' Ruth asked.

'That's what I assumed. But actually no, it didn't kill him,' Amis said, replacing a scalpel in the row of gleaming surgical instruments.

Ruth's was interested. 'Then how did he die?'

Amis pointed with his blue latex-gloved hand to some purple marks around his neck. 'Asphyxiation. You can see the bruising here on the neck.'

'He was strangled?' Ruth said, confused. She was a little thrown by the news that Nick's old friend had been murdered. Their assumption was that he had been killed by the fall. And she could see that Nick was visibly shocked.

'Er? I don't understand,' Nick said, his brow now furrowed.

'The bruising shows that the asphyxiation occurred after the fall,' Amis explained.

Ruth played out the events aloud to try to make sense of it. 'So, Harvey Pearson fell — or was pushed — down the ridge. He smashed his head on a rock and fell unconscious. And then someone strangled him as he lay there and hid the body.'

'That's pretty much it,' Amis said. 'But no fingerprints I'm afraid – they must have been wearing gloves.'

Ruth looked over at the body. There was a dark-blue oriental dragon tattoo across most of his chest and arms, which now had black stitching through the middle where the post-mortem had cut his torso wide open.

Amis rolled the body over a little to show them Harvey Pearson's back. It was covered in short, thick scars. 'I also found these.'

'Bloody hell,' Nick exclaimed, moving closer to inspect them.

'They look old?' Ruth said as she leant forwards. They were the kind of scars that she might expect to see on someone who had been whipped or beaten. What was that all about?

'Yes. Definitely historic. I would take a guess they were from childhood. They healed over a long time ago.'

Ruth looked at Harvey Pearson's body as something occurred to her.

'How much does he weigh?' Ruth asked.

Amis checked the paperwork. 'Two hundred and twenty pounds.'

'Nearly sixteen stone,' Ruth calculated.

'But the victim was six foot four, so that's normal,' Amis said.

Ruth looked at Nick. She could see that he was distracted by seeing his old friend lying there.

'You okay?' Ruth asked quietly.

Nick nodded and then cleared his throat.

'Moving a two hundred and twenty pound body would be bloody difficult,' Ruth observed.

'Very difficult. In fact, you would need to be fit and very strong,' Amis suggested.

And then Ruth had a thought. 'Or there would need to be more than one of you.'

CHAPTER 6

By mid-afternoon, Ruth was making her way over to the tiny hamlet of Pentredwr. She had left Nick at the station to continue with the Harvey Pearson case, especially now it had escalated to murder. Passing the signs to Valle Crucis Abbey – Valley of the Cross – which were the ruins of a thirteenth-century Cistercian monastery, she sang along to eighties Christmas songs on the radio.

The winter sun felt hot on Ruth's face through the windscreen. She pulled a cigarette from her bag, lit it, and wound down the window. The air outside was crisp and fresh. *Better than sitting in traffic on the South Circular,* she thought to herself. Even though she had been in the North Wales Police Force for a while now, there were moments where she flashed back to what she might have been doing if she were still in SE19.

An hour earlier, a call had come through to Llancastell CID that uniformed officers were at a property in Pentredwr. The owner had reported finding something unusual blocking the sewage pipe to the rear of the property. Now uniform were there, the intel was that officers suspected it was human remains that had been found. It sent a chill down Ruth's spine. She had made a call to SOCO who arranged to meet her there.

By the time Ruth arrived at the house, there were two patrol cars and the SOCO forensic van outside. She was pleased to see that the house was already beginning to be taped off as a possible crime scene. She spotted a couple of nosey neighbours chatting and trying to see what was going on. Nothing wrong with that. They usually proved to be useful witnesses.

Ruth got out of the car and approached the uniformed officers who were manning the police cordon and crime scene. She showed her warrant card.

'Detective Inspector Hunter, Llancastell CID. Are you the FOA, Constable?' Ruth asked the very young female uniformed constable who was holding her notebook but gazing into space. FOA stood for First Officer in Attendance and meant the officer first on the scene.

She nodded. 'Yes, ma'am.'

The constable looked pale and shocked. Ruth knew that finding human remains could unsettle and disturb the most experienced officers, let alone a rookie in her early twenties. *Poor girl.*

'Are you okay?' Ruth asked gently.

The constable nodded but it was unconvincing. She was a lighter shade of green. 'Yes, ma'am.'

'If you're struggling, we'll get a replacement officer down here. Finding that sort of thing is horrendous. There's no shame in feeling shaky.' Ruth didn't want her to feel that she was stuck at the crime scene.

Ruth still remembered her first experience of finding human remains, rather than just a dead body. Someone had dismembered a prostitute in Streatham and put her body parts in bin bags in an alleyway. The image of her severed left arm falling to the wet concrete was still burnt into Ruth's memory.

'I'll be all right but thank you, ma'am.' The constable gave her a smile.

'Okay, so what have we got?' Ruth asked. *If she wants to tough it out, then good for her,* she thought.

'There's a manhole cover down the side of the house. That's where the owner found the remains. SOCO are down there now,' the constable explained.

'Thank you.' Ruth smiled and put a reassuring hand on her shoulder. She had been a rookie once. 'Take care of yourself.' Ruth turned, ducked under the tape and made her way to the house.

Within seconds, a SOCO handed her a white forensic suit, mask, shoes and purple gloves. Turning down the side of the house, she could see they had erected a white forensic tent over an area in the garden. Lights had been set up, and photographs and a video were being taken. The generators for the lights juddered noisily in a haze of blue diesel smoke.

And then, over the smell of the generators, she caught the unmistakable waft of rotting human flesh. There is no smell quite like it. It is a thick, horrendous stench that can turn even the strongest of stomachs. Somehow, she had managed to get used to it over the years.

A tall man bounded over to greet her. As he pulled down his mask, she could see it was the chief forensic officer, Alexander Travis. Round glasses, floppy blonde fringe and thin lips. Travis was a little too jolly given the nature of his job, but he was good at what he did.

'Afternoon, Alex,' Ruth said. 'What have you found?'

'I'm afraid it's human remains. Actually, it's a veritable smorgasbord of stuff down there,' Travis explained with an eager raise of an eyebrow.

Ruth wasn't sure that *smorgasbord* was the appropriate term but that was Travis for you. 'Are the remains recent?'

'I'd say the oldest remains are weeks old, but some appear more recent. A couple of days, maybe. I can be more exact when we get back to the lab.'

'Anything else?'

'My guess would be that it's the remains of an adult male.'

Behind Travis, Ruth spotted a middle-aged man talking to a uniformed officer who was taking notes.

'Is that the owner of the property?' Ruth watched the man nodding as the officer asked him more questions.

'Yeah. Andy Gates. Says that he didn't notice the smell until the neighbour came around,' Travis explained.

'How many houses feed into this sewer?' Ruth asked, looking over the adjacent back gardens. If they could narrow that down, it would be a start.

'At a guess, these four,' Travis said gesturing up the street.

'And the remains could have originated from any of these houses?' Ruth asked.

'Looks that way.' Travis nodded and then looked back at the other SOCOs who had pulled something else from the manhole and were beckoning him over.

'You're being summoned,' Ruth prompted him.

'Excuse me. Back in a sec,' Travis said as he strode away.

Ruth wandered over to where Gates was giving his statement.

'Mr Gates? Is that right?' she asked.

Gates looked at her and nodded. 'Yes.' If she was guessing, then Gates seemed to be thrilled at getting the attention of a police officer of a much higher rank.

There was something distinctly peculiar about Gates's appearance, she thought. Maybe it was the large, tinted glasses; it seemed to her that he was hiding behind them. She had seen men like him before. Voyeurs, meddlers, creeps. It was an instant judgement, but her instinct was pretty sharp.

She showed him her warrant card. 'DI Ruth Hunter. And you're the owner of the property are you, Mr Gates?'

'Yes, that's right. As I was telling your colleague here, I don't actually live at the property. I'm renovating it as an investment. And that's why I didn't notice the smell, as I haven't been here for a few days,' Gates explained. 'It's horrible what we found in there. I couldn't believe it at first. We were shocked.'

'And it was you that rang us?' Ruth asked.

'Yes, of course. Straight away.' She could see Gates was eager to help. Maybe too eager? Sometimes that was a sign of guilt.

'Who has access to your property, Mr Gates?' Ruth asked. If it was only the four houses feeding into that sewer, they just needed to narrow down those who had access to the houses. It would speed up the initial investigation.

'I've had some builders in to do some structural work.'

'And when was that?' she asked.

'Last week. And the week before that.'

'Do you know the name of the firm you used and what exact dates there were at the property?' Ruth asked. Having builders in the property would increase the number of suspects and that was frustrating.

'Dai Morris Builders from near Corwen. I've got all the paperwork and invoices at home. I could get you all that information if you need it?' Gates said helpfully.

Ruth still wasn't sure about him. She fished her card out of an inside pocket and handed it to him. 'That would be great. If you could get me that information later today, that would be incredibly helpful, Mr Gates.'

'Andy, please. And of course. No problem.' Gates took the card and smiled as he read it.

Ruth noticed that Travis had appeared again and was looking her way. 'Inspector? Could I have a minute?' He sounded serious, which was a rarity.

Ruth looked at Gates. 'Excuse me.' She wasn't sure if Gates had anything to do with the remains, but his over eagerness and general manner made her feel uncomfortable.

Travis gestured for Ruth to come over to a more discreet spot.

'Can I have a word?' Travis said in a hushed voice.

'Everything okay, Alex?' Ruth knew something wasn't right.

'There's been a development.'

'What have you found?'

'The remains in that sewer don't belong to just one person,' Alex explained. The colour had drained out of him.

'You mean you think that there are two victims?'

Alex hesitated. 'Two, three, more. I'm not sure yet.'

IT WAS CLOSE TO FIVE o'clock as Nick made his way down to Interview Room One to talk to Jack Pearson, Harvey's younger brother. The family liaison officer, FLO, had broken the news to the family that Harvey's death was now being treated as a murder investigation. Until that point, they would have assumed Harvey had died from a fall on Snowdon.

The information from the duty sergeant was that Jack had come to the station to give a statement. He had been walking on Snowdon with Harvey on the day of his death. Nick was close to Jack, and given what he knew about Harv's death, he was worried about what Jack would tell him.

Nick walked in with his files and saw Jack sitting at the table. He looked tired and lost.

'Nick.' Jack got up and looked a little tearful. He and Nick went back years, and even though Nick had been an usher at Harvey's wedding, he was actually closer to Jack. They used to go drinking in Llancastell in the old days. They had planned Harv's stag do together. They had been on the same rugby and cricket teams. Jack was the best left-hand spin bowler he had ever seen.

'Mate, I'm so sorry about Harv,' Nick said holding out his hand. They shook hands and hugged. Seeing Jack really brought home the fact that someone had killed his friend Harvey. The sharp clarity of that fact shook him for a moment.

'Sit down. Do you want a cup of tea or anything?' Nick asked, regaining his composure.

Jack simply shook his head. He had shaved his hair since the last time he had seen him, back in the summer. He was tanned and handsome, and Nick guessed that he had been off travelling somewhere. That was Jack. A free spirit, and that's what Nick liked about him. 'So you were with Harv on Sunday?' Nick asked, getting out his pen.

Jack nodded. 'Yeah, I was.'

'What happened, Jack?' Nick asked as he shook his head and let out an audible sigh.

'I'd promised him we'd go up Snowdon before Christmas. It's something we did together a couple of times a year.'

Nick nodded and waited for Jack to elaborate. When he didn't, Nick asked, 'So what happened?'

'That's the thing. I don't know. We had a row, and I stormed off. I went back down, got in my car and went home. When I didn't hear from him, I assumed it was because he was still pissed off with me,' Jack explained.

Nick felt a slight relief from Jack's explanation. He had feared there had been a fight and that things had got out of hand. He had seen Harvey and Jack's fights before and there were no holds barred, especially when drink was involved. On Harvey's stag do in Dublin, Jack had a made a joke about Harvey's fiancée. Harvey broke his nose and spent the night in a garda cell.

'What did you row about?' Nick asked.

'Stupid stuff. Mum's not well. He wanted me to be around more to help out.' Jack seemed overwhelmed by grief again. 'I just thought he'd fallen or something.'

'I'm sorry, mate. It does look like someone killed him, though,' Nick said.

Jack screwed up his face as if he was trying not to cry. Taking a deep breath, he blew out his cheeks. He was clearly struggling with what had happened.

'Who? Who would have killed Harvey?' Jack looked distraught at the idea.

'That's what I'm trying to find out.' Nick was as baffled as he was.

'I should have been there, Nick. I left him and now he's dead. He'd be alive now if I hadn't gone off. I could have protected him.'

'You can't blame yourself, mate. We're going to get the bastard that did this to Harv, okay?' Nick reassured him.

Nick gave him a few moments. He could see how upset and guilty Jack felt.

Jack nodded even though Nick could see he was still coming to terms with it. There would be moments when it just wouldn't feel real.

'Where did you find him?' Jack asked.

'I can't tell you that. It's an ongoing investigation. Sorry, mate.' Nick felt awkward that he was having to be official.

'Come on, mate. It's me, Nick.' Jack looked at him.

Nick paused. 'There's a ridge about a third of the way up Miner's Track. He was at the bottom of a ridge there,' Nick explained and glanced at the interview room door. 'But I didn't tell you that.'

'Miners' Track? We weren't even on Miners' Track.' Jack was clearly confused.

'Maybe he came down that way? Did you see anyone that day? Anyone you knew or recognised?' Nick asked.

Jack shook his head, 'No. No one. Weather wasn't great so it was quiet.'

'Nothing out of the ordinary? Anything, however small, could help us.'

'No. It was quiet. Couple of other walkers, but I couldn't tell you who they were or what they looked like.' Jack shrugged.

'What about Harv? Was he okay? How did he seem?' Nick asked.

The key to who murdered Harvey would lie somewhere in what was going on in his life. Money problems. An affair. Business partner. Ex-wives and step-dads.

'He was all right. You know what he's like. Everything's a fucking joke,' Jack said. And then Nick saw that Jack had caught himself using the present tense, and the grief came again. 'You know ...'

Nick nodded as he turned the page of his notebook. 'What about Linda? The kids?'

'Linda's been living in Marford with the kids and her new fella. Been about eighteen months, two years maybe. Sometimes that would fuck him off. But he got used to it.'

'Anything else in recent weeks? Anything that was different? New friends or a girlfriend? Money stuff?' Nick asked.

Nick saw that something had occurred to Jack. 'Actually, he'd been on one of those old school websites. For St Patrick's.'

St Patrick's was a very old-fashioned boarding school near the North Wales coast. Harv had won a rugby scholarship there but had never settled.

Nick frowned. 'He hated it at St Patrick's, didn't he?'

Jack shrugged. 'Yeah, I didn't understand it. He was trying to track down some old friends and some of the teachers. It didn't make any sense when he told me.'

Nick frowned as he took in this information. Tracking these people down, after all these years, seemed completely out of character.

What was Harvey doing looking back into his past? Nick wondered.

IT WAS DARK BY THE time Gates left the small annexe at the back of his house. He had been doing some work. A little project that he couldn't tell Kerry about. She wouldn't understand. Well not yet.

Bless her cottons. She doesn't understand me and all my eccentricities, Gates thought as he went down the path.

Turning on a small torch, Gates heard the noise of an owl hooting from the darkness of the trees. It spooked him. He turned the handle of the back door. It was still loose. He needed to get some screws to tighten it.

Making his way through the back door, he noticed that one of the pans he had left simmering was now boiling over. He turned down the heat and then checked the carrots that were boiling on the next ring. Perfect. He was cooking dinner, as he did every night. He couldn't complain though. It was therapeutic, and it calmed him after he had worked so hard all day. Kerry loved his stew. It was just like his mother had made, although he didn't tell Kerry that. They hadn't got on when she was alive so there was no point raking up the past.

'Fancy a drink, love?' Gates called to Kerry. He had left her tucked up under a blanket on the sofa, watching TV. It was time for *The Chase* on ITV, which was their favourite. Sometimes Gates let Kerry answer the questions before he did because it made her happy.

'No, no, I'm fine,' Kerry called back.

'Go on. A little one. I'm having one and I don't want to drink on my own.'

'Oh, all right then.'

'Good girl,' Gates said. He smiled to himself as he took two wine glasses from the cupboard. Holding them up to the light, he checked they were clean. He grabbed the cold bottle of pinot grigio from the fridge and then reached into the medicine cabinet. Pulling out a strip of red capsules, he took one and broke it in half, tapping the white powder delicately into a glass.

This late-afternoon ritual gave Gates a warm glow inside. The nitrazepam and the alcohol would keep Kerry relaxed and half-asleep for the rest of the evening. That's how he liked her to be. Docile was the word, wasn't it? Compliant? Particularly tonight as Gates wasn't sure if he needed to go out later.

Before dicing up the beef for the stew, Gates went into the downstairs cloakroom. He looked at his reflection in the mirror and smiled back at himself. He was handsome. Filmstar looks. His mother had told him that daily. She told him that his eyelashes were like those of a beautiful girl. He pouted for a second at his own reflection.

He wanted to splash his face with water so he removed his tinted glasses and again surveyed his reflection. There it was. The scar across the lid of his left eye. He often forgot about it as the frame and tinted lenses of his glasses hid it from view.

He cleaned his glasses with a soft hand towel and put them back on. Stepping back into the warmth of the kitchen, Gates went back to the cooker. *All systems go,* he thought to himself. He then took Kerry her wine.

'There you go, my love. I've left my watch in the annexe. I'll be back in two minutes.' Gates didn't enjoy lying to her but he felt too compelled to go back. Something was making him anxious.

Kerry smiled. 'I don't know what you do over there. You seem to spend more and more time there, and less time here.'

'Sorry. I'll make it up to you. Put *The Chase* on and I'll be back in a minute. Promise,' Gates said, squeezing her shoulder gently. It did make him feel guilty that his latest project was becoming so time-consuming.

Gates returned to the kitchen, went to the large pot boiling at the back of the cooker and removed the lid. A cloud of thick steam rose and at once misted his glasses. He couldn't see a thing. Grabbing his shirt, he cleaned his glasses again.

Now that the steam had cleared, he could see that the human head inside was cooking and reducing down nicely. The black hair on top of the man's skull swished and moved in the boiling bubbles of the water, which was now permeated with human fat. It looked a bit like black spaghetti, Gates thought to himself.

And the smell. What did it remind him of? Pork. *A pot roast, that's it.* He gave a faint smile of amusement. He had done his research. Boiling a human head reduces it to about a third of its original size. That made it easier to get rid of or keep if Gates decided that's what he wanted to do. It's what Dahmer and Nilsen had done. He had read all the books.

Unbolting the back door, Gates slipped out and stood smoking a menthol cigarette. Kerry didn't like him smoking. When he had finished, he headed over to the annexe. Coming into the empty lounge, he glanced into the large mirror at the other end of the room. There he was.

The reflection of Stefan Olsen's face staring back at him. Stefan had a beautiful face. Except the eyes. His dead eyes had glazed over and were now colourless. Such a shame. They had lost their dark chestnut colour. It was annoying. Why did that always happen?

Gates walked over. Stefan Olsen's naked body was sitting in an armchair facing the fireplace. He had already removed his lovely hands with a hacksaw.

'Stefan, I would love to light a fire for you. I know it's chilly in here, my love. But you're safe here,' Gates whispered.

That afternoon, Gates had stripped and washed Stefan in the bath. He had powdered him in talc. He had examined every inch of his body, even rolling him over. Gates noticed how elated he felt to have such control over this beautiful body. A body that was now his possession. He ran his fingers over it, marvelling at the power and sexual excitement that killing now gave him.

CHAPTER 7

As Ruth entered CID Major Incident Room One, she noticed that, although it was still early, the room felt clammy and airless as the heating was on full blast. The sky outside was grey and formless, the room buzzing with chatter and the odd boom of male laughter. There were the usual wind-ups and piss-takes. Ruth had seen it all before. Every single murder case – and there were very few in Llancastell – added energy and anticipation to the incident room. Now it looked like there might be several. Around a dozen CID officers sat talking and preparing for the morning.

She glanced over at the two large whiteboards that had been set up. At the centre of one was a photo of number four Abbey Terrace, Pentredwr, which was Andrew Gates's house where the remains had been found. There were also detailed sewage, water and drain plans that had been obtained from Welsh Water. She hadn't worked on a case of discovered remains for a long time. It was always very grim.

The other whiteboard featured a photo of Harvey Pearson, smiling at the camera on Snowdon. His name and address were written in blue marker to one side, date of birth, *7/5/1983*, plus the approximate time and location of his death: *Miners' Track, Mt Snowdon – 4 pm, Sunday 9 December 2018.*

Ruth watched as Nick entered the room and settled himself. She spotted him looking over at the boards and the central photo of his old school friend. It reminded her of what an old Sergeant always told her about the job. You just never know what's coming down the pipe. Lives changed or were ended in a split second. That's what Ruth still found so hard-hitting about being a police officer: how the victim's relatives' or friends' lives were irrevocably changed too.

Ruth took a breath as she dwelt on this thought before watching DCI Drake as he manoeuvred to address the morning briefing. Drake gathered his files and then took a swig of strong black coffee. 'Good morning, everyone. I am sure that some of you are aware of the developments at number four Abbey Terrace, Pentredwr yesterday. The owner of the property, Andy Gates, called officers when he found what turned out to be human remains blocking the sewer in his back garden. Ruth?'

Ruth stood up. There was a slight touch of nerves as the room listened to her. She went over to the whiteboard. 'Number four Abbey Terrace is unoccupied at the moment. Gates is renovating the house to use it as a rental property. If you look at these plans of the underground pipes, the main household drains for numbers one, two, three and four, all feed into the municipal sewer pipe here. So even though the blockage was found in the garden of number four, it could be that the remains came from any of those houses. Forensics are inspecting the household pipes of each house for significant levels of human DNA in the hope that we can narrow down the remains to one of those houses. Everyone who has access to any of those four houses is a suspect at the moment. Luke, what about the builders at number four?'

Merringer nodded and looked at his notes. 'Gates emailed us last night with the name of the building company. A Dai Morris Builders from near Corwen. Mr Morris gave us a series of dates and times that the builders were there. He will also send over a list of names and numbers of the all the workmen who have been to Abbey Terrace. He had seen the news and put two and two together. He was at pains to stress that there were at least two or three workmen at the property when work was being carried out.'

Ruth nodded. That's what she liked about Merringer. Thorough, methodical and clear. 'Thanks, Luke. Let's start with standard background checks on them all. Then upgrade to enhanced if anything is flagged up.' The standard check would show up any spent and unspent convictions, cautions or final warnings. As the SIO, if Ruth decided to escalate to an enhanced check that would reveal any further information held by local police that was considered relevant.

Ruth gave Drake a look to say she had finished for the moment.

He stood up again, hand casually in his pocket. 'The main concern here is that SOCO believe the body parts belong to more than one victim. We're waiting for Forensics to confirm that and get DNA so we can see if we can make a match. I'll avoid using the dreaded phrase "serial killer" at this stage. It's premature. And I don't want to hear anyone else using it.' Drake moved over to the photo of Harvey Pearson. 'Nick, what's happening with the murder of Harvey Pearson?'

'Boss. I've interviewed his brother Jack. He claims that they were walking up Snowdon together. They had a row, Jack went home and knew nothing of his brother's death until his mother rang him,' Nick explained.

'What do you think?' Drake asked.

'This might be a conflict of interest, boss, but I've known Jack Pearson since I was ten. He's a peace-loving hippy. The idea that he shoved his brother down a ravine, went down and strangled him, and then dragged and hid his body behind a rock.' Nick shook his head. 'He hasn't got it in him to hurt anything. And he was close to his brother.'

Ruth could see that Nick was still caught up in the emotion of what had happened.

'Any other leads?' Drake asked.

'We're trying to find anyone else that was on Snowdon that day. Someone must have seen something. Also looking into Harvey's life but there's nothing at the moment that's worth pursuing,' Nick explained.

'Okay, everyone. Can we do the usual checks? Social media, bank accounts, work colleagues,' Ruth said looking around the room.

'I'm going to his flat today,' Nick said.

Drake nodded. 'Good. Okay, any other business for today?'

Sian looked up from a file she was holding. 'Boss. The missing person we're looking at, Stefan Olsen, who was last seen in Bala.'

Drake finished his coffee. Although he didn't say it, a missing person was the least of his problems today.

'I went to see his wife yesterday. She gave us his laptop voluntarily, so I gave it to Tech to have a look. Stefan Olsen had been using a gay dating site that's hosted in North Wales, *U'veGotMale-dot-com*. The Tech boys have hacked into his recent activity and emails. He emailed a friend to say that he had a blind date on Saturday night and had used a dating site to get it. I'm thinking it's the same one.'

'And no one's seen him since?' Drake asked.

'No, boss. He's vanished.'

'Okay. Go to where the site is hosted. Look at his account. See who he was talking to and who he arranged to meet,' Drake said.

AS NICK PARKED OUTSIDE Harv's apartment block, on the edge of Llancastell's town centre, the sky was bleached white with clouds tinged with grey. Closing the car door, Nick pulled the collar of his coat up as the sharp wind cut against his face. It was at this time of year he was glad he had a beard.

A moment later, he saw Jack standing outside the entrance. Jack's face showed he was struggling with what had happened to his brother. Who could blame him? Nick had felt like that when he had lost his cousin Megan several years ago. It had shaken him to the core.

They shook hands and hugged and went into the apartment block that was modern and tastefully decorated, aimed at professionals in the area.

Harvey's flat was on the first floor. Once they were in, Nick asked Jack to wait in the kitchen so as not to potentially contaminate the rest of the flat. It could end up being a crime scene and might need forensic examination. Wandering the tidy apartment, he looked for anything that could shed any light on what had happened to Harv and why.

Nick put on his purple latex forensic gloves and instantly inhaled the familiar waft of rubber from them. An old DS he worked with always moaned that he went home smelling like a giant condom, which made his wife suspicious that he was 'going over the side' – police slang for having an affair.

He went into the main bedroom and noticed that the bed was made neatly, a smart jumper folded on a chair and shoes lined up in a row. An expensive television had been mounted on the wall and a Bluetooth speaker stood nearby. Nick found the silence in the room unsettling. The sound of a car starting from outside broke the eeriness.

He walked over to the en suite bathroom, his shoes flattening the thick cream carpet as he went. The bathroom also revealed little. The air smelt of the remnants of shower gel and aftershave. No medications except some paracetamol. Nick thought about what a contrast it was to his medical supplies at home of Librium, diazepam, morphine and various other opiates. It was a supply that would have made Elvis proud, he thought, making a mental note that it might be time to ditch the lot. Nick had seen several alcoholics relapse after getting hooked on prescribed or over-the-counter medications. An addict is an addict, and if changing the way you feel was the goal, it didn't matter what substance did the trick.

Out in the hallway, Harv had a few framed rugby shirts hanging on the wall. Small plaques gave details of when and where they had been won. At the peak of his promise, Harv had played a few times for the Wales U18s. That was why, while Jack went to the local secondary school, Harv had been shipped off to a Catholic boarding school, St Patrick's, that offered rugby scholarships and high-quality coaching. St Patrick's had a string of alumni that had played international rugby around the world. Harv didn't quite make the grade, and Nick wondered whether when he had seen Harv drunk and angry in town, that was at the back of his mind. Harv was competitive to the point of arrogance, and not making the grade must have been difficult for him.

Nick passed another door, which he tried, but it was locked. He would ask Jack about that. Uniformed officers had taken some preliminary statements from neighbours in the apartment block and from colleagues at the internet support company where Harv worked. Nothing had cropped up yet that gave them a decent lead.

Entering the open-plan kitchen and dining area, Nick saw that Jack had made him a cup of tea, which he slid over the table as Nick sat down.

'Thanks, Jack,' Nick said as he drank the tea and wondered what Harv had done to provoke someone into murdering him. 'What's with the locked door?'

'Oh yeah, sorry. It's the single bedroom, but Harv turned it into a little study. I've got the key. He was a bit paranoid about break-ins.'

'Don't worry. I'll have a look in a minute.' Nick looked at Jack's face, which showed an expression of loss and disbelief. 'How's your mum doing?'

'Not sure it's really hit her yet, you know? And she's starting to get forgetful recently. I was the crazy, wayward son. If anything horrible was going to happen, then it was going to happen to me. Harv was the sensible one. Head screwed on properly,' Jack explained.

'Except when it came to women,' Nick said and then regretted saying something derogatory, however true it might.

'Yeah, he put it about.' Jack smiled. 'Man slag. I think he was proud of that.'

Nick wanted to broach the findings of the post-mortem but knew he needed to be delicate. 'When I saw Harv's body, he had marks all across his back. They looked like scars.' Nick left the statement hanging, seeing what Jack would say to this.

Jack shook his head and shrugged. 'No. I never saw them. But now I think of it, I never saw Harv with his top off. Even when we went to the beach a couple of times.'

'Your Dad wasn't around when you were kids, was he?'

'No. He did a runner just after Harv was born.'

'I'm just trying to work out how he got the scarring. Nothing at home that you can think of?' Nick asked.

'No. You know Mum. She's as soft as a brush. There wasn't anyone else around.'

'What about when Harv was boarding up at St Patrick's?' Nick asked, wondering if something had happened at the boarding school. His suspicions had been aroused when Jack mentioned that Harv had been looking up old school friends in his interview.

Jack thought for a moment. 'I don't know. He wasn't happy there. He would cry when he had to go back after coming home for the weekend. When we asked him, he just said he got homesick. Mum took him out of there when he turned fifteen.'

'And he didn't say anything more about it?'

'No. In fact, he never talked about it. It was as if he had never been there.'

Nick nodded. The immediate response could be to make assumptions given the terrible abuse that some children were victim to in a few of Britain's boarding schools. However, Nick knew it was a knee-jerk reaction with no evidence to back it up.

'Shall I show you the study?' Jack asked.

Nick nodded and got up to follow Jack, who unlocked the door and opened it. The office was as Nick had expected. Neat, ordered and tidy. There was a large desk over by the window with an expensive-looking computer monitor. There were more framed rugby shirts and other sporting memorabilia on the walls.

Nick went over to the desk and looked back at Jack. 'Don't touch anything, please, Jack.'

Shuffling through a neat pile of paperwork, Nick came across a school brochure for St Patrick's Catholic boarding school for 1995 to 1996. He quickly skimmed through it, looking to see if had been marked or written on. There was nothing. He then spotted a recent letter from the head-teacher of St Patrick's, Mr Owen Bates.

Dear Mr Pearson,

Thank you for your enquiry and I am so glad that you enjoyed your time here at St Patrick's. Thank you also for your kind comments about the staff.

Unfortunately, we do not have any information about the current employment or whereabouts of any previous members of staff for you to contact them and express your gratitude.

Kind regards,

Owen Bates

Nick thought that Harv's request was ominous, especially as Jack had told him that he wasn't happy at the school. Nick put down the letter and continued to search the desk. 'Would you or your mum remember any of the teachers that taught Harv?'

'I'm not sure. Mum might. Why?'

Nick found a business card propped up by the computer monitor and read it. *James Ferguson, Director, Vinci Printing Solutions.* 'Does the name *James Ferguson* mean anything to you?'

'No. Why all this interest in Harv's time at St Patrick's?'

'I dunno. At the moment, Harv's life seems to be pretty normal. No money worries. Good job. He's divorced but he gets to see his kids. Nothing on social media so far. The one thing that's out of the ordinary is his sudden interest in his time at St Patrick's.'

AS SOON AS RUTH ARRIVED, she was guided through the smart offices and laboratories of Abel UK Forensics. It was a private company that North Wales Police used for all of their forensic science services. Already covering everything from DNA, toxicology, ballistics, they had just moved into digital forensic investigation.

Before Ruth went any further into the laboratory, she was given a forensic suit, mask and blue latex gloves. Crime investigation had come a long way since when she joined in the early 1990s. It was no exaggeration to say that detectives would be smoking, drinking coffee and even eating as they stepped over bodies and stomped around crime scenes with no regard to forensics or DNA.

As Ruth entered, the temperature dropped significantly. The scientists were dealing with the remains from number four Abbey Terrace in Pentredwr and it needed to be cold to stop putrefaction. The laboratory was equipped with microscopes, test tubes and large machines that Ruth had no idea what they did but gave her, and her colleagues, incredible results.

Ruth spotted the wiry eyebrows of Professor Roy White, the senior forensic consultant, between his surgical hat and mask as he approached her. She had worked with him once before and found him to be a consummate professional but with the sense of humour of the cadavers that he spent his days with.

'DI Hunter, isn't it?' White enquired, clearing his throat.

'Yes. Have you got anything for us yet?' Ruth asked as she began to feel the chill of the laboratory. *Why aren't the lab coats padded?*

'We've got the SOCO swabs back from the pipes from the four houses that feed into that sewer. Only one of them has any human DNA in it, and that's from number four,' White explained.

'And that's the house where the blocked sewer was found,' Ruth said thinking out loud. It immediately made her wonder about Andy Gates, the owner.

White nodded. 'Three different DNA within these remains. And they seem to be the DNA of three adult men. They've been dead for one to two weeks, but it's hard to be more precise than that.'

Three? That was seriously disturbing. Three murders? Why were human remains in the sewage? Bodies were notoriously hard to dispose of but flushing away a corpse bit by bit seemed haphazard at best.

White continued with the tone of someone delivering a university lecture. 'As for any useful forensic evidence, that would have been washed away in the drains. Of course, nothing that we find will be any use to you given the amount of contamination. We're running the DNA against the National DNA Database but at the moment we've not found a match. But we do have one partial fingerprint from a fingertip which we're looking at right now.'

'I don't suppose there's any chance of finding cause of death?' Ruth asked.

'Not really. What we've got mainly is fibrous and soft tissue, and some muscle. A few fingers and toes. Internal organs. No bones of any magnitude. It's like some horrible human jigsaw.' White shook his head. 'I've never seen anything like it before.'

Ruth was surprised by Professor White expressing any form of emotion. 'So DNA will be the only way to identify who the victims are?'

'At the moment. Usually, we could use dental records, tattoos or scars if we didn't have DNA.'

A diminutive forensic scientist came over to White. 'Professor, I think we have a database match to the partial fingerprint.'

Ruth followed White over to a large computer monitor where White interpreted the data. 'The print belongs to a Stefan Olsen. According to the details on the PNC, he is aged thirty-six. He was arrested six months ago for assault but got a suspended sentence.'

Ruth knew exactly who Stefan Olsen was. And he was no longer a missing person. He was a murder victim.

CHAPTER 8

It was lunchtime when Nick pulled up outside Fiona Pearson's house, which lay at the end of a neat cul-de-sac of new builds. He had heard his phone buzzing with texts as he drove so took it out to have a look.

It was Amanda:

Hi Nick. Sorry to contact you like this. Feeling a bit wobbly. I haven't had a drink since I last saw you. I could do with a chat. Some advice from a friendly face who knows what I'm going through. I know you're busy, so no worries if not. Amanda xx

Nick took a moment. Was he meant to be meeting a very attractive, struggling alcoholic to give her advice? Shouldn't he pass this on to one of the women he knew in the fellowship? But then a voice from somewhere else told him that he was helping Amanda. The fact they knew each other meant that she felt comfortable enough to reach out to him and ask for help. That was a big step for an alcoholic. And if he simply passed her number on to a woman in AA she didn't know, she might feel abandoned and disappear.

What he should do is run the dilemma past Bill, his sponsor. He shouldn't trust his thinking or decision-making. He should get someone with good sobriety, wisdom and perspective to help him make decisions. But he knew that Bill would tell him what he didn't want to hear.

Bollocks to that! Nick ignored what his conscious was telling him and began to text:

Hi Amanda. Sorry to hear that you're struggling. It's brilliant that you've not had a drink. Let's meet after work. There's a café in town – Marmalade. About 7 p.m. any good? Nick xx

He sent it. It was done now. And if he could help Amanda stop drinking then where was the harm in that?

Striding up the neat stone path, Nick reached the door and rang the bell. He didn't think that he had seen Fiona since she married Harv, and that must have been ten years ago. Or was there a christening? Nick's memory of events during less sober times in life was hazy, to say the least.

The door opened and Fiona looked at Nick. Her face was dusted with freckles and her red hair fell in ringlets onto her shoulders. She was attractive but she had that look that Nick had seen so many times in his line of work. The fatigue and emotion of tragedy took its toll on everyone.

'Nick ...' Fiona blinked and Nick wasn't sure if she was going to cry.

She ushered him in and they went into the immaculate kitchen full of touches of shabby chic – there were homemade Christmas decorations across the window made from holly. That was Fiona. Too cool for school. Fiona made him coffee, and they made some awkward small talk before Nick asked her how she was.

'Doesn't feel real. You know what I mean?' Fiona said sadly and looking for Nick to confirm that was how he felt.

Nick felt conflicted. He was there in both a personal and professional capacity. They were two very different mindsets.

'Yeah. Harv was larger than life. Even with all that I've seen, I can't see why anyone would want to ... harm him.'

Fiona sipped her coffee. 'You've not found anything?'

'No. Nothing yet.' Nick took a moment. 'That's why I wanted to talk to you.'

'Me?' Fiona bristled a little.

'I know you're not together. But from what Jack said, you see each other a lot, even if it's just to sort out stuff with the kids,' Nick explained.

'Yeah. We do. But there's nothing I can think of.'

'As far as I can see, Harv's life was all right. Good job, nice place to live, no financial worries. From what I know, he saw a lot of the kids and he was a good dad,' Nick said, thinking out loud.

'Yeah, he might have been a total prick to me but he was a good dad.' Fiona realised what she had said, 'Oh God. I didn't mean to say that.'

Nick looked at her. 'We all know what Harv was like. We can't pretend he was a saint. But he didn't deserve what happened to him, so I need to find the person who attacked him. You're sure there was nothing out of the ordinary? Anything, no matter how small?'

Fiona nodded and then something occurred to her. 'A couple of drunken phone calls in recent weeks. He hadn't done that for quite a long time.'

'What did he say?' Nick asked. Perhaps Harv wasn't quite as happy at it might appear.

'In the first one, he just kept babbling what a horrible person he was. His words were "Why am I so fucked up?"' Fiona said as she pushed her hair away from her face.

'Do you know what he meant by that?'

'Not really. He apologised for cheating on me. He said he hated himself, but he was hammered so I just thought he was babbling.'

'You said there were a couple of phone calls?' Nick's instinct was that if there had been something troubling Harv, it might give them a clue as to who had attacked him.

'The last one he was banging on about his school days.'

Nick's ear pricked up. 'School days? What was he saying?'

'Yeah. You know what people are like when they're drunk. He kept repeating himself.'

'Any details? The smallest thing could help us.'

'Something about St Patrick's. He wasn't making any sense. Sorry,' Fiona said.

'Okay. Thanks,' Nick said as he put away his notebook.

Ten minutes later, Nick thanked Fiona for the coffee and left. Something about Harv's quest to go back into his past niggled at him.

THE TECH COMPANY THAT built and hosted *U've-GotMale.com* was based in a unit in an industrial estate off the A465 bypass. Sian had spent ten minutes talking to the company's owner, Jonathan Cheung, establishing that it was a one-man band that created websites, addresses, and hosted them for various companies based in North Wales. However, U'veGotMale was actually Cheung's own creation. He built and ran the website, allowing him access to all the data stored on it. Sian wasn't sure if that was ethical, let alone legal.

The room, with its large glass windows and new carpets, was a mess of monitors, computers and wires. It also smelt of stale coffee and body odour.

Sian's phone rang. It was Ruth. Social call or work, she didn't know.

'Sian? Are you at that internet company yet?'

'Yes, boss.' It was business and Sian slipped back into old habits.

'Stefan Olsen's DNA was in the remains we found at Pentredwr, which means someone murdered him. And the last person he was seen with was a man we think used U've-GotMale to meet Stefan on a blind date.'

'And that person could be our killer?' Sian thought out loud. It was a solid lead.

'Yeah. There's the DNA of three men in that sewer,' Ruth told her.

Even though Sian knew that SOCO suspected multiple bodies, it was still alarming to hear that three victims had been confirmed. 'Christ! Maybe there's a link with the website?'

'You read my mind. Get a list of clients for the website and crosscheck it with any missing men in the area aged eighteen to fifty. Check Stefan Olsen's chatroom and see who he had arranged to meet that night and if we can get an IP address.'

'Boss,' Sian said, then hung up and turned to Cheung who was shoving jelly babies into his mouth. He offered her the packet. 'No thanks. Mr Cheung, how many members do you have at U'veGotMale?'

'Dunno. Two hundred and fifty maybe,' Cheung said, blinking behind John Lennon glasses. He was slight, with the remnants of acne and a mole the size of a chocolate button to the left of his nose.

'I'm going to need all their details. Names, billing addresses, phone numbers, please,' Sian said.

Cheung looked horrified. 'I can't do that. What about data protection?'

Sian was having none of it. 'We're dealing with a murder enquiry. So I can get a search warrant. Then police officers will arrive, seize all of your equipment and take it to the technical forensic lab. They will go through everything and keep all your equipment for the next few weeks or even months as evidence.' Sian knew that she was embellishing the truth a bit but she wanted the information now. 'Or you can give me the information now.'

Cheung didn't hesitate as he went over, sat down and tapped away at the computer. 'Of course. No problem. I didn't realise how serious it was, you see?'

Well, that got him bloody moving, she thought.

'I need to see who Stefan Olsen has talked to in the past two weeks to start with.' Sian was pleased how quickly she had managed to get leverage over Cheung. Sometimes people stood their ground, insisted on warrants and brought in lawyers. She assumed that Cheung had calculated that being without any of his equipment for days or weeks would bankrupt him and destroy his business.

'Okay,' Cheung gestured to the chatroom on the screen. 'In the last ten days, Stefan, who is Stefan81, has been talking to this person, NightPorter.'

Sian scanned her eyes over the conversation and then came to something that caught her attention.

Stefan81: So Bar Lounge in Bala. 8 o'clock?

NightPorter: Sounds perfect.

Stefan81: Can't wait to meet you. We've really clicked, haven't we?

NightPorter: Completely. How will I recognise you?

Stefan81: Dark handsome man. Corner table.

NightPorter: See you then xx

Stefan81: xx ;)

Sian smiled. *Bingo.*

'I need all the information you've got for this "Night-Porter,"' Sian said, feeling energised. She wondered that if NightPorter was their killer, why had he made it so easy for them to track him down?

Cheung tapped away and then looked agitated. 'He's still on the site's thirty-day free trial.'

'What does that mean?' Sian asked, perturbed by Cheung's anxious tone of voice.

'He wouldn't have to add a billing address or credit card details until he joined the site,' Cheung explained.

'So you allow people to use your site to meet each other, but you have no way of identifying them until they actually join your site?' Sian asked in disbelief.

'It's not illegal,' Cheung responded defensively.

'It's not safe or ethical,' Sian snapped back. 'What about an IP address?'

'Yeah, I should be able to track them through that,' Cheung said, returning to the computer. The IP address was a numerical number that could pinpoint the exact geographical location of the device being used. Sian knew if they had that, they could pinpoint where NightPorter was located.

As Cheung tapped away, Sian gazed around the untidy office. Coffee cups, takeaways and other rubbish were strewn across one side of the room. It was like an overgrown boy's bedroom. She guessed that Cheung didn't have many visitors.

'He's using a VPN,' Cheung explained to Sian, who had no idea what he was talking about.

'A what?' Sian asked in a withering voice. Cheung was starting to irritate her, and she had never been good at hiding her feelings.

'Virtual Private Network. It encrypts the connection to make it safe. And that makes it untraceable.'

'Jesus. So we have no way of finding out where the NightPorter is located?' Sian muttered in frustration. There had to be a way of tracing the person who had set up the account.

'Not that I know of. But you could send him an email?' Cheung suggested.

Sian was about to explain in blunt terms that an email from the North Wales Police Force wouldn't be the best tactic if this man was, in fact, their killer. However, Cheung's suggestion gave her an idea.

'I need you to set up a profile for me,' Sian said.

'I don't think this is the right website for you,' Cheung frowned.

'Don't be a prick. I want you to set me up a profile that is almost identical to Stefan Olsen's. Hobbies, likes, preferences, everything,' Sian said as she worked out the logistics of how they could set a cyber-trap.

NICK WAS RUNNING LATE by the time he arrived at the offices where James Ferguson worked. A phone call earlier that day to the number on the business card that Nick had found in Harv's study determined that Ferguson was an old school friend. The reception area was decorated with a large real Christmas tree, tinsel and lights. It put the meagre decorations at Llancastell CID to shame.

As he navigated his way through the open-plan office, Nick caught snippets of conversations about 'sales forecasts' and 'quotas,' thinking that he was glad he didn't have to suffer the drabness of office life. However dark his demons, and despite the chaos and devastation he had sometimes witnessed, Nick knew that he was making a difference to people's lives. He didn't care if that sounded trite. It meant that in recent months, he could lay his sober head on a pillow secure in the knowledge that he contributed to the improvement of society every single day.

In the far corner, Nick spotted a glass-fronted office with the inscription *James Ferguson – Director of Sales* etched into the door. Through the glass, Nick could see that, with his slick, coiffed hairstyle, Ferguson was in good shape and smartly dressed. Nick bristled for a moment. Uber-confident men like Ferguson made him feel inadequate, something that seemed to contradict his thoughts only seconds before. *That's the beauty of the human psyche for you*, he thought sardonically.

'Mr Ferguson?' Nick asked, tapping the door and showing his warrant card. 'I'm DS Evans. We spoke earlier.'

Ferguson got out of his seat, came over, shook his hand firmly and gestured. 'Of course, of course. Please, take a seat.' His voice was one moulded by expensive boarding schools and an elite university.

'I'm investigating the death of Harvey Pearson,' Nick explained.

'Yes, I was so sorry to hear about that. He was a good bloke. It's a tragedy,' Ferguson said without an ounce of feeling.

'He had your business card by his computer. Do you know why?' Nick asked.

'Harv came to see me a few weeks ago. I gave him my card,' Ferguson clarified with a shrug.

'Can you tell me why Harvey Pearson came to see you? Were you friends?' Nick asked.

'Not really. We were friends at school. We were in the same dorm. But I had only seen him a few times since we left. He told me he was trying to organise a St Patrick's reunion, you know, class of '93,' Ferguson said and then paused. 'I found it ... surprising.'

'Why was that?' Nick asked.

'Harv didn't seem to like school that much. Eventually, his mother took him out before sixth form started. I was amazed that he wanted any type of reunion,' Ferguson explained.

This was the picture that Nick was getting from everyone. So why would Harv want to track down students and teachers from St Patrick's?

'Do you know why he didn't like school?' Nick asked.

'Not really. We didn't talk about stuff like that. There was a teacher there, Mr Chivers. He seemed to pick on Harv – a lot. It was bullying. Some of us thought that's why he left St Patrick's.'

Nick reflected on Ferguson's answer for a moment. Was there a darker purpose to Harv's search into his past at St Patrick's?

'Did he ever mention this teacher again?' Nick asked.

'Actually, he told me he had seen Mr Chivers in a supermarket car park a couple of months ago. He said he had followed him to his car, which I thought was a little weird. But it also worried me.'

'Why did it worry you?' Nick said.

'I bumped into Harv at a wedding a few years ago. We were both drunk. And we were talking about school days. And Harv said that if he ever saw Mr Chivers again, he would kill him.'

CHAPTER 9

It was ten minutes after Ruth had first knocked on the door before Gates finally opened it. Having forgotten her gloves, her knuckles were red from the cold air and she was about to leave when the key eventually turned.

'I'm so sorry. Kerry has been calling me, but I've been in the annexe doing a few odd jobs. I was miles away.' Gates smiled as he opened the door, and Ruth watched as he gestured for her to come in. Her copper's instinct still thought there was something 'off' about him. It wasn't just the tinted glasses, camp mannerisms and the anachronistic clothing. 'It's Detective Inspector Hunter, isn't it? Come in, come in.'

'Thank you, Mr Gates. I've just got a few things I need to clarify,' Ruth said, noticing how warm the house was now she was inside. Too warm. The hallway was small and simply decorated in creams and soft browns. A row of Christmas cards lined the windowsill beside a wedding photograph – a close-up headshot of Gates and Kerry kissing, shoulders covered in confetti.

'Of course. Not a problem,' Gates said, closing the front door behind her.

'Who is it, Andy?' a female voice called out.

'It's Detective Inspector Hunter, love. Don't worry, we won't be long,' Gates called back and then turned to Ruth and said in a low voice, 'My wife Kerry. She has MS and she finds it hard to get around these days.'

'I'm sorry to hear that,' Ruth said, but in truth, she was watching Gates's every move. Even though Gates had found the remains and phoned the police, that didn't make him innocent. She knew plenty of cases where the killer had put themselves right in the middle of an investigation, often to get some kind of sick thrill.

Ruth remembered the infamous 'Babes In The Wood' murders in Brighton in 1986. Two nine-year-old girls, Nicola Fellows and Karen Hadaway, were strangled, sexually assaulted and left in a park. The murderer, Russell Bishop, ingratiated himself in the middle of the search for the two girls after they had disappeared. He spoke to police officers as he, and his dog Misty, helped search the woodland. He even went on a march and handed out leaflets in 1989 asking for more information on the two girls' murders. But that was psychopaths for you. Complete and utter narcissists with no empathy for the emotions of other human beings.

'Make sure you ask her if she wants a cup of tea,' Kerry called from the living room, breaking Ruth's train of thought.

Ruth looked at Gates and said quietly, 'I'm fine, thank you.'

Gates gestured to a door which led to the small dining room. 'We can go in here.'

Ruth went in and sat down at the polished wooden table. The winter sun gleamed off the surface and made her squint. There were neatly arranged placemats that showed painted scenes of Snowdonia. The wallpaper was dark and patterned, giving the room a small, slightly claustrophobic feel. On top of a low table on the other side of the room, Ruth noticed a glass cabinet that featured a tableau of three stuffed animals – a rabbit, a stoat and a red squirrel. She hoped it was some Victorian artefact rather than Gates's own handiwork.

'Our forensic team have narrowed down where the remains came from. I'm afraid they originate from your house,' Ruth informed him.

'Oh dear. How awful,' Gates said calmly. His fingers moved rhythmically on the table, almost as if he was tapping away at a silent piano. When he noticed Ruth watching him, he stopped and smiled at her.

'Yes. We will need a DNA sample from you today so we can eliminate you from our enquiries,' Ruth explained. What she meant was so that the forensic scientists could look for Gates's DNA within the remains and create a forensic link.

'Of course. No problem.'

'And there is no reason we would make any forensic link between you and the remains we found in the sewer?'

'No, of course not. I wouldn't have called you if I had anything to do with this,' Gates said.

Nice try. Ruth knew that wasn't true. 'And you have given us the details of everyone who had access to your property in recent months?'

'Yes. I've given you the details for Dai Morris Builders. That's the only company that I use. No one else has been in there,' Gates said. 'You're sure about that tea, Inspector?'

'Yes, thank you.' Ruth took a moment as she scribbled notes in her pad. 'Mr Gates ...'

'Andy, please.'

'Andy. Can you tell me your whereabouts on the evening of Saturday the eighth of December?' Ruth asked.

'I would have been here, I think. I don't go out much.' Gates thought for a moment. 'Yes. I cooked us some food. We watched the television. Something on BBC Four, I think. I went and finished off some decorating in the annexe. That was about it.'

'And your wife will confirm that?' Ruth asked as she wrote in her notepad.

'Yes. Of course. Why wouldn't she?' Gates said, sounding a little annoyed.

'And you didn't go out anywhere? You didn't pop out to the shop or anything like that?' Ruth asked.

'No. I was here all night.' Gates smiled directly at her as if he didn't have a care in the world, let alone several bodies in his waste pipes.

Ruth waited again, taking her time as she wrote notes. She wanted the pressure to build with a prolonged and awkward silence before her next question. 'Does the name *Stefan Olsen* mean anything to you?' She looked for any reaction from Gates. A sign of recognition or anxiety.

There was nothing.

'No. Sorry. I've never heard that name before, I'm afraid.'

'You're sure about that?'

'Positive. It's not a name you would forget, is it?' Gates chuckled slightly.

Ruth paused again. It was stuff like Gates's little laugh that was creeping her out. As if he continually misjudged the appropriate tone or response.

'Okay. Do you own a computer, Andy?' Ruth asked.

'Yes, I've got a laptop. Not a very good one,' Gates said with a self-effacing smile.

Ruth nodded. At this stage, it wasn't worth revealing any suspicions about the dating website by asking him about it. If Gates had been using U'veGotMale to contact men, she didn't want him knowing that they knew anything about it. She couldn't make her mind up about him. Eccentric oddball? Yes. Multiple killer? She didn't know.

'Thank you, Andy.'

Gates sat upright and said a little too loudly, 'I know where I recognise you from, Inspector.'

Ruth was a little startled. 'I didn't realise that you did recognise me.'

'Yes, of course,' Gates said half to himself. 'That's right ...'

'Have we met before?' Ruth asked. Surely she would have remembered a crank like Gates ...

'No, no. From the newspapers. Those terrible murders over in Dinas Padog. Last year ...' Gates explained. 'The teachers.'

'Right. I did work on that case ...'

'Jonathan Noakes. I guess you got that one wrong?' Gates was smiling.

How did Gates know all about that? Had it been in the press? Was he messing with her head?

'I guess I did.' Ruth closed her pad and got up.

'Oh, don't worry, Inspector. We all make mistakes, don't we?' Gates said in an overly familiar way that was distinctly strange.

'Thank you for your help, Andy. We'll be in touch as the case develops.'

'Thank you. It's Ruth, isn't it?' Gates said as he closed the door behind her.

'Yes ...' Ruth said as she made her way to the door and Gates let her out.

As she got to her car, Ruth released a sigh and frowned. She didn't know why but talking to Gates had unnerved her. How did he know her first name? She rarely went by her first name in official capacities and she hadn't told him it at any point when meeting him. And the stuff about Dinas Padog and Jonathan Noakes was creepy.

CHAPTER 10

For the next hour, Gates sat and listened to Fleetwood Mac's *Rumours* album through a set of headphones. Listening to music like this allowed him a clarity of thought that he often lacked during the day.

He sat back and closed his eyes. He still wasn't sure why he had identified the human heart and offered to call the police the day before. He could have made excuses. He could have pacified the young man next door, promising to get a company to fix the problem right away. He had even planned on buying chicken breasts from the supermarket and removing the human remains from the sewer by the cover of night. He could then refill the sewer with chunks of chicken. But he didn't. Why not? On the surface, Gates knew that acting horrified at the remains and being the one that called the police would deflect suspicion. At least for a while. Yet Gates suspected a deeper desire. His longing to survive and not get caught was being overwhelmed by a different want. He craved to find some peace from the unbearable anxiety that he was living in. Holding onto these horrible secrets was utterly exhausting.

At first, he thought of suicide. Hanging or poison? But that would leave Kerry on her own and the thought of killing her as a release terrified him. He could run away, but he would still be left with himself. After all, that's what the killings were for. A temporary fix to ease the discomfort of being Andy Gates.

But like any addict, he wanted just one more fix. One more soul to fix that aching emptiness inside him. Then he'd stop. Actually, he was resigned to the inevitability of being arrested. Whether it was days or weeks, he didn't know. And to be honest, he didn't care.

Gates took off the headphones and wandered into the kitchen. He poured himself a large rum and coke and swigged at it thirstily. Going outside, he lit a menthol cigarette. *Bliss*. He checked that Kerry was now asleep under her favourite blanket in front of *The Chase*. She looked like an angel. As the light from the screen flickered on her motionless face, he marvelled at her beauty. He might be a psychopath, but what he felt for her was pure love. It was overwhelming.

Finishing his drink, Gates took his laptop, opened it and turned on the power. A website appeared on the screen and he started to type.

Time for one last fishing trip.

NICK GOT TO THE MARMALADE Café half an hour early. It was somewhere to unwind outside of his house and somewhere that didn't serve alcohol. The café was a bit of a find, he thought. It was cosy and modern with its painted wooden tables, blackboards with menus and its olive-and-brown colour scheme. Hipster chic, they called it. Fiona

Pearson would like it here. It was definitely more Chester than Llancastell.

Nick checked his phone but there was nothing to suggest that Amanda wasn't going to meet him there. He had decided anyway. He would listen and support her in her early recovery. Even though he was only a few months sober, Nick had been around enough to know what to suggest to remain sober. His problem in the past had always been not doing what he was told to do or not asking for help. That Amanda had texted him when she needed support was a good sign that she didn't have an ego like his, which had told him that he could get sober on his own. It never worked. It was the basics of Steps One, Two and Three.

As he waited, Nick ran through what he had learnt about Harvey Pearson's murder so far. The scars and the troubled times at boarding school. His recent interest in looking back at those days and contacting an old schoolmate. The chance sighting of an old teacher whom he had said he would gladly kill. How did that fit in with his murder on Snowdon? It was the only thing in Harvey's life that seemed out of the ordinary. His murder had been deliberate and targeted, but who had a motive to kill him? Unless it was a random act of violence? But they were rare and the strangulation after the fall suggested it was personal.

Just as Nick finished his black Americano, the door opened and Amanda walked in. She wore a camel-coloured overcoat, her hair was tied into a ponytail and as Nick looked her up and down, he could see she was wearing smart high heels.

She looked around for a moment, spotted him and then smiled. Her eyes twinkled in the soft lights. *Oh God, this is never going to work.* She was stunning and his pulse was quickening. How was he meant to keep this platonic?

'Nick. Thanks for this,' she said as she unwrapped her long scarf and took off her coat.

Nick got up and gave her a quick kiss on the cheek. 'No problem. Come and sit down. What do you want?'

'Oh, if they do a herbal tea, I'll have camomile,' she said.

'Living the rock 'n' roll lifestyle, eh?' Nick said sardonically as he went over to the counter. 'Cake?' he asked. Amanda didn't look like she ate cake.

She just smiled and shook her head as she settled herself at the table.

For the next half an hour, Amanda told Nick her history of drinking. Binge drinking at university like everyone else. It was when the stress of being on the Child Protection team got too much that she started to drink every day. A bottle of wine a night turned into two. The hangovers got worse and the goalposts continually moved. She would engineer her work so she could legitimately drink at lunchtime. And she wasn't sure when she crossed the line, but soon she was having a glass of wine before work. And that turned into vodka in her handbag and nipping to the toilet at work. She loved her job and didn't want to get sacked. But she wasn't sure how to stop drinking and stay stopped.

Nick reassured her that he had heard this progression many times in AA meetings. It was a progressive illness and there was no way back to safe drinking. It never got better.

She needed to come to meetings and listen, to start with. Talk to other alkies and get advice. He could help her.

They got another drink and Amanda went outside for a cigarette.

When she returned, she sat and put her hand on Nick's arm. 'It's such a relief to get all that off my chest.'

Despite the clanging of alarm bells in his head, Nick put his hand on hers for a moment. 'Talking about how you feel and what you're thinking makes all the difference. And this is from me, a rugby-loving Welshman.'

She laughed. 'That's what I like about you. You're easy to talk to and you're really open about yourself. It's a breath of fresh air as most blokes I know are dishonest, arrogant wankers.'

Nick smiled. 'Hey, get off that fence and say what you really feel.'

Amanda laughed again, leaned in a little and whispered. 'It's weird, isn't it?'

'What's that?' Nick asked quietly. Even her whisper was sexy, for God's sake!

'No, doesn't matter.' Amanda moved back a little.

'Go on.' Unless his imagination was playing tricks on him, there was growing sexual tension in the air.

'Well ... when I normally sit chatting to someone like this, I've had a drink. Well, more than one drink. It feels different because I'm sober.'

'Good different, or bad different?' Nick felt his willpower being pulled back and forth in his head like a frantic game of baseline tennis.

'I don't know. When you've had a drink, you say stuff because you feel disinhibited. You care less. You know what I mean?' Amanda looked directly into Nick's eyes and his whole body fizzled for a second.

'I think so. I suppose it depends on what you want to say?' Nick smirked. He knew that they were playing a little game of poker. And rather than folding, he was now in the game and raising the stakes.

'It's embarrassing.' Amanda continued to look at him. 'Come on, Nick, you know what I mean?'

Nick sat back for a moment and took a breath. The air was crackling with it.

Amanda picked up her phone and looked over at him. 'Pick up your phone.'

Nick picked up the phone and frowned. What was she doing now? 'Why?'

'I think I can replicate the effect of booze.' Amanda smiled and tapped at her phone.

'Are you texting me?' Nick laughed.

'No.' Amanda giggled, looking at her phone and continuing to tap.

Nick's screen flashed with a text message:

I know what you said the other day. But I think we really connect. And I've fancied you for the last three years. There. I've said it. Now I feel very stupid!! xx

Nick read it. It was out in the open now. This was *not* good.

'I think I'll go outside for a cigarette. Then I can go home and feel embarrassed for the rest of the evening.'

As Amanda got up and started to wrap the scarf around her neck, Nick stood up beside her and took her hand. He put his arm around her waist, pulled her close and looked at her.

Amanda smiled. 'Maybe the cigarette can wait?'

Nick kissed her, soft at first, and then building as they pulled each other close. He could feel the contours of her body pushed against his.

After a minute, they stopped and looked at each other. Nick had played his hand and now all bets were off.

'You know, I only live five minutes' walk from here,' Amanda sighed. 'I'm just saying, in case you want to walk me home, like a gentleman.'

They held hands as they walked along the high street. Christmas decorations and lights hung across the street in a magical criss-cross. Even though there were doubts in his mind, Nick couldn't remember the last time he felt this happy.

Ten minutes later, Amanda had led Nick into her flat and then into her bedroom. They kissed and giggled.

They made love with an intensity that Nick forgot he had. He hadn't been with a woman sober for many years. It felt electric and alive. His skin tingled all over. They both climaxed within minutes and then lay breathing deeply in the darkness.

'MISTLETOE AND HOLLY' by Frank Sinatra was playing from somewhere inside Ruth's home. It was dark and cold outside, but the fire was glowing orange with coal. Ruth and Sian were cuddling in the kitchen as Ella walked in.

'Oh God, get a room!' Ella exclaimed, hiding her eyes in feigned horror.

'We've got a room, thank you.' Ruth smiled as she went and switched on the dishwasher.

Sian moved over to the fridge to get some wine and pour them drinks.

Ruth put her arm around Ella's shoulder and escorted her towards the living room.

'Come on, mush, I need to show you these flats I found for you online,' Ruth said.

The living room was in virtual darkness. The Christmas tree twinkled in the corner but didn't have any presents under it. Ruth could smell the waft of pine from the tree. It was a long way from the small artificial Woolworth's tree they'd had in their flat in Battersea when she was a child.

'Very subtle, Mum,' Ella said.

Ruth could tell she was annoyed as they sat down but Ruth grabbed her laptop anyway.

'You know I love having you here ...' Ruth began. Maybe it wasn't the most sensitive way to have approached the topic, but Ella couldn't stay there for ever.

'But you're just going to show me some flats that I can rent before you pack my bags and shove me out of the door,' Ella said.

For a moment, Ruth thought Ella was joking. Then she saw the look on her face.

'It's fine. Sorry. We'll do it another time, darling,' Ruth said as she closed the laptop and put it down.

'No, no. Show me. If I get my skates on, I could be out before Christmas,' Ella snapped. Ruth had definitely touched a nerve.

'I thought you wanted your own place and to be independent?' Ruth asked.

'I'm pretty sure you said, "Stay as long as you want," when I moved in. But that's fine,' Ella growled.

'Come on. Do you really want to live with two boring old lesbians?' Ruth said, trying to lighten the mood.

'Oi, I heard that,' Sian said coming into the room with glasses of wine. She put them down and retrieved her phone from her pocket.

Ella stood up and said, 'I'm getting used to you being emotionally unavailable to me. It's what I expect.'

'Ella ...' Ruth said. *Ow. That hurt.* Mainly because it had been true for the past few years. Ruth felt overwhelmed with guilt.

Ella left the room and went upstairs. Ruth decided to leave her for a few minutes to calm down before going to apologise.

Sian was still staring at her phone and typing away.

'Kids are great,' Ruth said sardonically.

'Eh?' Sian wasn't listening. She was completely absorbed by whatever she was doing on her phone.

Ruth gave her a quizzical look. 'What are you doing?'

'Work stuff.' Sian was preoccupied looking at the screen.

'Are you going to elaborate?' Ruth asked, annoyed that she was being cryptic.

'Fishing. I'm doing some online fishing,' Sian explained. Then the penny dropped.

'Your U'veGotMale account?' Ruth asked. Sian had filled her in earlier on the online profile and trap that had been set.

'Exactly. And I think I'm about to get a bite.' Sian sat up and pulled a surprised face. 'Shit!'

'Be careful. We don't know who this person is,' Ruth said in a worried tone. She immediately felt protective towards Sian.

'Bingo!' Sian said, ignoring her.

'Are you listening to me?' Ruth asked.

'No.'

Ruth was now darkly fascinated. 'What's going on?'

'We're on.' Sian tapped her screen excitedly. 'I'm talking to NightPorter and he wants to meet me for a drink tomorrow lunchtime.'

CHAPTER 11

The morning briefing had started late because Drake was late. Ruth noticed that he seemed preoccupied as he came in and put his folders down next to her. It wasn't like him. Drake was always calm and focussed.

'Everything all right, boss?' Ruth asked in a hushed voice.

'Yeah, yeah,' Drake replied, but she wasn't convinced. 'Do you want to start us off, Ruth?'

Pointing to the scene boards, Ruth said, 'Morning, everyone. If we can get started, please ... We know that Stefan Olsen met an unknown man in Bar Lounge in Bala. He disappeared that night. His DNA has now been found along with that of two other males in the blocked sewer in Pentredwr. So we know he was murdered. And we think it is likely that the man he met that night murdered him and disposed of his remains at the Gateses' house in Pentredwr.'

'What about access to the house?' Drake asked.

'We don't know if or how the killer had access to number four Abbey Terrace. We don't know if the owner, Andy Gates' – Ruth pointed to a photo of Gates on the board – 'had any involvement in Stefan's or anyone else's murder. Stefan Olsen used a dating site, U'veGotMale, to meet the man, whom we only know as NightPorter ... Sian?'

Sian looked at her notes for a moment. 'We set up a fake account on U'veGotMale, replicating a lot of the details of Stefan Olsen's dating profile. Last night, at 9 p.m., someone contacted my fake account calling himself NightPorter. After an initial conversation, NightPorter agreed to meet me for a lunchtime drink at Bar One Hundred in Llancastell.'

'Why have we chosen Bar One Hundred?' Drake asked.

'It's well positioned for this type of undercover operation. The bar has only one way out. It is open plan with no back or side rooms,' Ruth explained.

'Nick will act as our date for the operation,' Drake explained.

Sian smirked for a moment and Nick gave her a withering look. 'Sian, if you say anything, I will swing for you.'

Sian held up her hands in an innocent gesture. 'This is serious, Nick. I wouldn't make a joke.'

'Nick has had nothing to do with the Stefan Olsen case nor the remains at Abbey Terrace. There's nothing to suggest that NightPorter will be able to identify Nick as a police officer,' Ruth explained.

'Plus, Nick has a certain quality that makes him the perfect choice for a gay blind date,' Sian joked.

Ruth wasn't sure what she made of the casual homophobia that passed for acceptable 'banter' in CID. She was a gay woman in a gay relationship. However, any preachy political correctness would be greeted negatively. It wasn't her style anyway.

There was laughter and Nick gave Sian the finger.

'Struck a nerve, have I, Nick?' Sian quipped.

Nick gestured to Merringer who was sitting close by. 'It's not like we're spoilt for choice in here. If Luke turned up, the suspect would take one look and run away.'

Merringer gave Nick the wanker hand gesture and there was more laughter.

'All right, everyone,' Drake said, trying to get them to focus.

Ruth smiled. Black humour really was the only way to get through the day sometimes.

'Nick will wear a wire, and as soon as the man identifies himself as NightPorter, we'll move in and arrest him,' Ruth explained.

Ruth knew that the use of any evidence gained in these types of 'sting' operations had been rendered untrustworthy ever since the Met tried to entrap Colin Stagg into admitting to the stabbing of Rachel Nickell on Wimbledon Common in 1992. The evidence obtained by an undercover female police officer was thrown out of Stagg's trial at the Old Bailey in 1994 as the judge deemed that it had been gained by complete deception and coercion and therefore had no place in any criminal trial.

So, Nick could ask the man they knew to be NightPorter if he had murdered three men. NightPorter could admit that he had. However, because of the nature of the undercover operation and how the confession had been acquired, it would be regarded as unsafe and not admissible in a criminal trial. It was easier to get the suspect into custody and question him so that everything was above board.

'Thank you, everyone. I want you all to be very careful today.' Drake called a halt to that morning's briefing and his tone was serious. 'And Nick. First sign of anything you're not comfortable with, you call for back-up. This man, whoever he is, has killed at least three people. I don't want anyone to take any risks. Clear?'

Ruth could see that everyone was starting to get nervous and the tension was growing in the room.

Nick nodded. 'Yes, boss. Let's get the bastard.'

BEFORE GATES GOT TO Bar One Hundred, he had stopped at another pub along the way for some Dutch courage. The Red Lion was so old that his grandfather used to drink there. It was old-fashioned, basic and full of regulars and drunks. Some office workers in red Santa hats were playing darts noisily and shouting.

Gates stood at the bar, drinking whisky and hoping that no one would recognise him. He knew that was silly. He hadn't been in the pub for nearly twenty years. It was just his paranoia. Even so, he was convinced the couple in the corner were talking and laughing about him. He turned his back and faced the bar. That would show them that he wasn't scared. That's what he did at school when he was bullied.

Then his thoughts turned to his grandfather, or Taid Lane as he called him. Alfie Lane, once a chief petty officer in the Royal Navy. He had been proud of his taid. He was the only person in his family he could ever talk to and also the only male influence in his life. His father had left the family home when Gates was only three so he couldn't remember him. No one ever saw Gates's father again. It was as if he had vanished from the face of the earth. And so Gates tried not to remember the father who had abandoned him.

What Gates liked to remember was sitting and bouncing on his taid's big, broad shoulders as they went down country lanes. Often, they went off in their own little world, playing on beaches and skimming stones. His taid used to find lost golf balls when they cut across the fairways of the local golf course. Then, to his delight, his taid would cut them open with a knife, unwind the rubber into a long strand and fish out the bag of liquid rubber at its centre. It felt like magic.

And then one sunny, peaceful Sunday morning, Taid Lane had dropped dead in front of Gates in the living room of his cottage. Gates was only eight. He sat with his taid's body on the floor, holding his hand and stroking his hair, listening to the birds chirping, until his mother came to pick him up in the evening. There was no phone and he was miles from home, and he didn't want to leave his taid's side.

His mother wailed and screamed for what seemed like hours when she found her father. Once the family had been called from a neighbour's house, she had to drag Gates away from his taid's body. He didn't want to leave him. He held onto his taid's icy fingers with all his might. And when he eventually let go, it scarred his very soul. From then on, life was very different and the magic never returned. No one ever explained to him what had happened to his taid. His mother and aunts muttered about him being in 'a better place.' Why did Taid want to go to a better place without him? Was death a nice thing then? Could he go to this better place too? His mother left him at home to look after the dog when his taid was buried. She told him that he was too young to understand. He watched from the window as the coffin arrived outside. And then watched as his entire family left for the church, returning drunk many hours later, singing and arguing.

After that, Gates began to wonder about this place where his father and taid had disappeared to. Was it heaven? And why had they left him surrounded by the misery and growing criticism of his mother and aunts? They called him 'fairy boy.' He would catch them whispering about him 'being a bit strange' and asking his mother if she thought he was 'a queer?'

There were never any men in their house as he grew up. He ached for male company and felt the fury of having been left by his father and taid. So he would wander away by himself. And he would watch boats from the beach where he and Taid had skimmed stones, making up stories in his head until darkness came.

It was nearly one o'clock when Gates drove down the high street, turned onto a side road that backed onto Bar One Hundred and parked. He was well over the limit but he didn't care. The police were too busy to breathalyse him. He had no respect for the police anyway. They were stupid. Why else would you do a job like that?

Walking out onto the festive high street, the anticipation of the next few hours excited him. The seduction, the deception and then the kill. Hunter and prey. 'Away in a Manger' played from some speakers as people collected for a children's charity.

Gates wasn't interested. He was lost in thought. The initial excitement after a murder was overwhelming, and Gates found himself jigging and smiling at the very thought. He couldn't contain himself. He felt like dancing. In the moments after the five murders that he had committed in the previous months, he had found the erotic excitement too much to bear and had to stop the car to masturbate while gazing at his victims.

The 'high' Gates would get from the memory of those moments would last for days. He would replay his previous murders over and over in his mind. It gave him a surge of excitement and pleasure that coursed through his whole body and gave him an immediate erection. He wondered if he should start making videos so that the memories would never fade.

Gates got out of the car. He was drunk, happy and content with the world. He began to sing to himself, a song his taid had taught him. 'I love counting, you can hide, one, two, three, four, five. I will find you, wait and see. There's no place to hide from me. Six, seven, eight, nine, ten. Should I start to count again? Maybe yes, maybe no. Am I coming, you don't know.'

Walking into the bar, he sniffed in the smell of booze and warmth. It was comforting. Now, where was his new love? A man in his thirties, handsome, with a beard, sat in the corner as arranged. *Lovely. How lovely*, he thought. And younger and prettier than he was expecting.

Gates walked over with a huge smile. 'Hi. I'm meant to be meeting someone here. Are you Nick?'

Nick smiled up at him 'Andrew?' *Wow. Deep velvety voice. Nick is sexy.*

'That would be telling,' Gates replied, trying his best to flirt. He found it awkward but he knew he had to play a role today. Wear a mask.

'Erm, I've arranged to meet Andrew here?' Nick said.

'Well aren't I the lucky one?' Gates said. He could already feel the energy and excitement. He needed to keep calm. Keep a lid on it. Stay focussed. Don't blow it. He could feel his breathing getting shallower.

'Would you like a drink?' Nick asked, getting up from his chair. He already had a drink on the table. He must have arrived early, Gates thought.

'No, no. I'll be back in a second.' Gates smiled. 'You just make yourself comfortable.'

Gates went to the bar. He needed more booze to take the edge off his excitement. He ordered a treble whisky in a glass and swallowed it in one. The burning sensation at the back of his throat brought him some relief. What was that old expression? His blood was up. That was it.

Gates patted the pockets of his jacket. On the left side, he had a new packet of menthol cigarettes. On the right, he had two-milligram dissolvable tablets of flunitrazepam, better known as Rohypnol, in his pocket. He just needed to find the right opportunity.

Gates returned to the table with his pint of beer and sat down. Nick had lovely brown eyes and good bone structure.

'Cheers,' Gates said, and they chinked glasses. 'You're very handsome, aren't you?'

'Thank you.' Nick seemed embarrassed by the compliment.

'So you're NightPorter?'

He was very direct, Gates thought.

'Am I? Why do you say that?' Gates said with a beaming smile. He liked to tease.

'That's why we're here, isn't it?' Nick asked.

'Oh. I thought it was because our eyes met across the bar and we decided to have a drink because we liked what we saw?' Gates smirked. He hoped he was being charming and flirtatious. It was certainly easier now he had a few drinks inside him.

'Night Porter ... It's a good film, isn't it? Dirk Bogarde and Charlotte Rampling. Very sexy. All that SS uniform stuff,' Nick said.

'You don't look old enough to know anything about *The Night Porter*,' Gates said and laughed, but he wasn't listening. He was waiting to set his trap. Then he glanced quickly out of the window as though he had seen something strange – it was a well-rehearsed act.

For a split-second, Nick glanced over his shoulder at the street outside. In that moment, Gates dropped one of the Rohypnol tablets into Nick's drink. *That should do it.* The momentary diversion had worked like clockwork, like it had done five times before.

Got you! Soon Nick would be his.

'You were saying about *The Night Porter*, Nick. I'm fascinated because it's my favourite film,' Gates said. He knew that in around ten minutes Nick would feel like he had been hit on the head with a claw hammer. He couldn't wait.

'Hence your name on the website?' Nick asked.

Gates nodded but didn't answer, and Nick didn't pursue it any further. They made small talk for a few minutes. Plans for Christmas, family. Gates was getting annoyed as Nick was giving little away. He wanted to get to know Nick before he killed him. That was part of the deal. He needed a glimpse into this man's very soul to know that he needed saving from the pain of his existence.

Nick needed to relax a little. The funny thing was, Gates thought to himself, that in a minute or two, Nick was going to be so very relaxed. He heard a little ironic laugh in his head.

'I'm ... er... I'm just ... going to nip to the toilet. I'm not feeling ... sorry,' Nick said. Gates was glad to see that Nick was now unsteady on his feet and his speech was slurred. The drug was really starting to kick in.

'Oh, gosh. Are you okay?' Gates asked. How he enjoyed playing the part of the concerned date.

'I'm ... fine. Really,' Nick mumbled as he seemed to lose his balance. He stumbled and knocked over a chair. He looked like a man who had been drinking all day.

Gates jumped up, putting his arms out to catch him and prevent him from falling.

'Whoops, don't worry, love. My car's outside. I can drop you home if you're feeling unwell. There are lots of nasty bugs going around this time of year,' Gates said. 'Come on, sweetie.'

One of the bar staff came over and frowned. 'Is he all right?'

Gates smiled and mimed drinking. 'One too many, I'm afraid. Don't worry, I'll get him home safely.'

'Okay, thanks,' the young man said as he picked up the chair.

Gates supported Nick as they headed for the door. However, Gates spotted a man and a woman running down the pavement. They were heading for the door with radios in their hands. They looked like police officers. *Shit!* He didn't know if they had anything to do with him but he was taking no chances. He needed another way out.

Gates turned and headed for the swing door that led to the kitchen, dragging Nick with him. Some of the kitchen staff, dressed in white, looked up and frowned.

'You can't be in here, mate!' a kitchen porter shouted.

'Yeah, sorry. Someone's collapsed by the door ... We can't get out.' Gates gestured to Nick, who could barely focus. 'And I think he's going to be sick. Can I take him out the back?'

Gates pulse was thudding with excitement. He threw a glimpse back through the kitchen window and the running couple were now in the bar. Why were police officers here? Maybe they were looking for him? Had he been set up? Or was he being paranoid?

The kitchen porter looked annoyed. 'Yeah, go on then. Through there.' He rolled his eyes and pointed to a door that led to the outside.

Gates pulled Nick with him. 'Come on, lovely. Let's get you some fresh air, eh?' He smiled at a teenage girl washing up. 'Office party. Sorry.'

As soon as they got outside, the cold air hit Gates in the face and stung his skin. *Now where?* There were bolted double doors that clearly led out onto a side road. He hoped it was where he had parked.

Gates ran through what had happened since he arrived at Bar One Hundred. Why was Nick so keen for him to admit to being NightPorter? Why had he been so reluctant to reveal anything of himself? Had the police linked him to the U'veGotMale website? Had Nick been undercover?

Gates stopped for a moment and pulled Nick's shirt open at the chest. There, clear as day, was a wire that had been taped to his chest.

'Oh dear, Nick. You have been a naughty boy, haven't you?' Gates said, shaking his head. 'Come on. I think it's best that you come home with me.'

'CONTROL FROM THREE-six. We're in position,' Ruth said into her police radio.

'Three-six received...'

As she looked out at the high street, she could see that the sky was colourless. Christmas shoppers wrapped in scarves and hats ambled along, their breath freezing as they exhaled.

Two minutes earlier, Nick had gone into Bar One Hundred to pose as the blind date for whoever NightPorter turned out to be. There were two CID officers with earpieces close by on the high street. The male and female detectives had shopping bags and were looping up and down, pretending to be a couple window-shopping. Meanwhile, two uniformed patrol cars were discreetly parked two hundred yards either side of Bar One Hundred.

Merringer sat at the wheel of their unmarked car and looked at his watch.

'He should be here any time now, boss.'

Ruth nodded. Even though they had checked there was one exit, she didn't like putting any officer in the vulnerable position of being undercover with a possible multiple murderer. The high street was busier than normal and it was office-party season so things felt a little out of her control.

And then she saw him walking along. It was Gates. Even though it wasn't a huge surprise, her stomach still flipped. Of course, it made perfect sense. They had found the remains at his property. He had used the website to lure gay men on dates, then murdered them, disposing of some of the body parts at the house he was renovating. How did he think he would get away with it?

Gates wasn't wearing his trademark tinted spectacles. *Maybe it was a sign of vanity*, Ruth thought. Walking confidently into the bar, Gates disappeared out of sight. Now they had to rely solely on the audio from the wire that Nick was wearing.

Ruth turned up the volume on the receiver. The noise of the chatter of the bar increased.

Gates: 'Hi. I'm meant to be meeting someone here? Are you Nick?'

Nick: 'Andrew?'

Gates: 'That would be telling.'

Nick: 'Erm, I've arranged to meet Andrew here?'

Gates: 'Well aren't I the lucky one?'

Merringer turned to Ruth. 'Just give him a straight answer, you prick!'

Ruth motioned with her hand for him to be quiet. She didn't want Nick to be in there any longer than he needed to be.

Nick: 'Would you like a drink?'

Gates: 'No, no. I'll be back in a second. You just make yourself comfortable.'

Ruth was frustrated. She knew that until Gates verified that he was the NightPorter, they couldn't make their move. That meant Nick had the delicate job of getting Gates to admit to his dating site nickname while keeping the conversation as natural as possible.

Ruth clicked her radio. 'All units from three-six. Target has made contact. Stand by.'

'Received.'

Gates: 'Cheers. You're very handsome, aren't you?'

Nick: 'Thank you. So you're NightPorter?'

Gates: 'Am I? Why do you say that?'

Nick: 'That's why we're here, isn't it?'

Gates: 'Oh. I thought it was because our eyes met across the bar and we decided to have a drink because we liked what we saw?'

Ruth and Merringer exchanged a frustrated look. Ruth shook her head. 'For God's sake!' she muttered.

Nick: 'Night Porter ... It's a good film, isn't it? Dirk Bogarde and Charlotte Rampling. Very sexy. All that SS uniform stuff.'

Nick's question concerned Ruth. He was trying too hard to get Gates to admit to the nickname, although she couldn't blame him.

> Gates: *'You don't look old enough to know anything about* The Night Porter. *You were saying about* The Night Porter, *Nick. I'm fascinated because it's my favourite film.'*

> Nick: *'Hence your name on the website?'*

There was a gap in the conversation as Ruth strained to listen. Still no admission from Gates. The tension was mounting. Was Gates on to them? Was that why he wasn't being drawn into the conversation? Or was he just being very careful?

Ruth and Merringer continued to eavesdrop as Gates and Nick's conversation drifted into small talk. However, Ruth thought she could hear a change in Nick's voice. At first, it was imperceptible. But then she was convinced that his words were slurring as though he had had a drink. She had noticed it when she first worked with Nick and he was still drinking. There was no way that Nick would decide to have an alcoholic relapse while working undercover with a wire.

Ruth was convinced that something had changed. She looked over at Merringer. 'Does Nick sound like he's had a drink? Like he's drunk.'

Merringer listened intently and then frowned at her. 'Yeah, boss. He does.'

Ruth started to panic when she heard Nick move his chair.

Nick: 'I'm ... er ... I'm just ... going to nip to the toilet. I'm not feeling ... sorry'

Gates: 'Oh, gosh. Are you okay?'
Nick: 'I'm ... fine. Really ...'

Merringer shook his head. 'He sounds hammered, boss.'

There was the sound of a chair falling over. It was at that moment that Ruth suddenly realised there was another explanation for Nick's rapid change.

'Shit! He's drugged him.' Ruth exclaimed. She clicked her radio frantically. 'All units from three-six. Something's wrong. Move in on target now. I repeat, move in on target *now*!'

Ruth leapt from the car, watching the two undercover officers running into Bar One Hundred ahead of her. She knew that nothing that Gates had said on the tape was incriminating but Nick's safety was at risk. At least there was only one way out of the bar and they could now arrest Gates and build a case against him.

Dashing into the bar, Ruth scoured tables and chairs. No sign of them. She pulled out her warrant card and flashed it at the barman. 'Police. I'm looking for two men that were drinking together. One had a beard.'

Where had they gone? She was feeling sick with fear.

The barman nodded. 'I saw them earlier.'

A female member of staff came over when she saw the warrant card. 'They went out the back through the kitchen.

The guy with the beard was drunk and was gonna be sick.' Ruth was now gripped with panic.

Gates had Nick.

The two plainclothes detectives jogged over to her from scouring the far reaches of the bar. 'Nothing, boss. They're not in here.'

Ruth sprinted for the door marked *Kitchen*. 'Quick! This way.'

Darting through the kitchen, Ruth glanced left and right trying to spot them. Nothing. She showed her warrant card as she shouted, 'I'm looking for two men who came through here a couple of minutes ago.'

'They went out the back to the delivery doors,' the kitchen porter yelled over at her.

Ruth threw open the back door. An area of concrete and then double doors that appeared to open out onto a side road. How could this have happened? Nick was in real danger now.

'Shit!' Ruth yelled in frustration as the two detectives caught up. She turned urgently to the kitchen porter. 'They definitely came out here?'

He nodded. 'Yeah. The guy with the beard was so drunk he could hardly walk.'

'What's that road?'

'Chapel Street.'

Ruth clicked her radio. 'All units. Suspect has escaped with DS Evans. Last seen entering Chapel Street. I need a PNC and DVLA check on an Andrew Gates and I need his car registration, make and model, now!'

CHAPTER 12

'Three-six to all units. No sight of target vehicle,' Ruth said as they hit sixty miles per hour.

The PNC and DVLA check on Gates had come back in a matter of minutes so they now knew what car they were looking for.

Ruth gripped the door handle in sheer frustration. How had this happened?

Merringer sat forwards over the steering wheel, staring through the windscreen.

'Where are you, you bastard?' he growled.

'Three-six to Control. Request air support to look for target vehicle. Foxtrot-whisky-five-nine, yankee-alpha-alpha. A navy-blue Renault Clio, over.'

'Three-six. Request received. Will advise.'

Ruth's anxiety was through the roof. She knew that if Gates got away with Nick, he would almost certainly kill him. As the SIO, it was her responsibility to have known that there was a way of getting out of Bar One Hundred through the delivery entrance on the side road. Why hadn't they checked that?

Ruth looked up, but the road ahead was empty. Her heart sank. Jesus, where were they? They were running out of time. The other patrols had taken the minor routes out of the town but had seen nothing. Ruth was hoping to get air support from the North Wales Police helicopter, but some-times that could take a long time to scramble. She was find-ing it hard to think clearly.

Suddenly, Gates's Renault came into view, speeding up a hill about a mile ahead.

Ruth's heart leapt. 'There they are!' She clicked her radio. 'Three-six to all units. Target vehicle spotted two miles north on the A-four-nine-four. Speed eight-zero. Over.'

'Received, three-six. Alpha-five rerouting.'

The car's back tyres were losing their grip and slipping as they cornered another bend. But at least they could see them. Now her concern was how to stop Gates and make sure Nick was safe in the process. They couldn't just ram him off the road.

They flew over a hump and Ruth's stomach lurched. Hammering up a hill, over the crest they could see Gates's Renault was now about half a mile ahead. They were gaining fast. A small set of stone cottages whooshed past in a sicken-ing blur.

Merringer pulled out to overtake a three-car queue. The drivers looked at them with startled expressions as they flew past.

Ruth's radio crackled again. 'Three-six from Control. Unit-tango-one is now one mile north of you on A-four-nine-four. Gold Command commencing stinger operation on target vehicle at intersection with B-three-zero-two. Over.'

'Three-six. Received,' Ruth said, but she wasn't sure this was the best way of stopping Gates. A stinger operation in-volved deploying a spiked strip across a road and puncturing the tyres of any vehicle that drove over it. Ruth had seen several cars tip and roll when a stinger had been used, and Nick was inside the car. At this speed, Gates and Nick would be killed.

Suddenly a tractor pulled out of a field in front of them. Merringer swung the car onto the opposite side of the road, missing the tractor by a few feet.

'Jesus!' Ruth yelled, her hands instinctively going to protect her head.

'For fuck's sake!' Merringer said.

Gates's Renault was now only five hundred yards away. Gates pulled out to overtake two cars narrowly missing a lorry. It was reckless driving. Ruth knew Gates was desperate and would take risks in his attempt to get away. At this stage, Gates might not care if he lived or died.

Ruth looked at the digital map on the car's satnav. The junction with the B302 was now a mile away. She hoped the stinger was in place but she also prayed that the car didn't go out of control and roll. Ruth took a deep breath, but she was so tense her stomach was cramping.

How was this going to end? She had a horrible feeling it would be badly.

Merringer looked over at her. 'Boss?'

Ruth glanced up as the road bent to the left.

In the distance, two Armed Response vehicles were parked with a stinger across the road. Gates's brake lights flashed bright red as he tried to slow the car. The screech of rubber. Ruth watched as the back of the Renault skidded from side to side.

Gates had nowhere to go and hit the stinger hard with black tyre smoke pluming into the air. Suddenly she saw the tyres on left-hand-side lift off the ground.

No! Please, God, don't let the car flip, Ruth prayed.

Ruth held her breath. The car dropped onto four wheels again as the Renault kept in a straight line. *Thank you, God!*

The shredded tyres rolled either side of the road as the Renault came to a shuddering halt.

What now? What was Gates's next move? He had nothing to lose, and that made him incredibly dangerous.

A few painful seconds passed as Ruth watched the stationary Renault for signs of movement. Nothing.

The Armed Response officers, Glock 9mms in hand, walked towards the vehicle, 'Armed police! Get out of the vehicle!'

Merringer stopped just behind. Ruth jumped out and saw the driver's door open as Gates appeared. She couldn't work out if he was in shock or if he was grinning. He held his hands up as one of the AROs cuffed him roughly.

Ruth sprinted to the passenger door and cranked it open. Nick looked at her but he was still very groggy. 'Paramedic. We need a paramedic!' Ruth yelled.

'I'm all right, boss,' Nick murmured.

'No, you're not. And you nearly gave me a bloody heart attack.'

'This is a quiet night out for me ...' Nick slurred with a smile.

'It's not bloody funny, Nick,' Ruth snapped.

She checked around the car as the ARO brought Gates towards Merringer's car.

Ruth watched as Gates was moved away from his car, but for a split second his eyes went to the boot. He couldn't help himself. Ruth spotted it and went to the boot. What the hell was she going to find inside? She clicked it open.

Laying inside was the body of a young man with blonde hair. From the colour of his skin and the smell, she estimated he must have been dead for at least a week.

Gates shrugged. 'I promise you, Ruth. I have never seen that person before in my life. I have no idea how he got in there.'

'Andrew Gates, I am arresting you on suspicion of murder. You do not have to say anything. But it may harm your defence if you do not mention when questioned something which you later rely on in court. Anything you do say may be given in evidence.'

CHAPTER 13

A Dean Martin Christmas song was playing on the radio as Nick drew up outside Amanda's house. The Rohypnol had worn off within a couple of hours of getting back to Llancastell nick, and the police doctor had given him the all-clear. The thundering headache the drug had given him was finally starting to wear off. Even though he felt tired, he had ignored the advice to go to bed and get a good night's sleep.

Looking up at the houses on the road, Nick could see the twinkling colours of outside lights and indoor Christmas trees. The festive holidays were looming ominously on the horizon. It would be his first sober Christmas and he knew that most alcoholics found it difficult. It was the festive season where everything was accompanied by booze. He used to love Christmas Day at Uncle Mike and Auntie Pat's. It was the only day of the year where he could openly drink mid-morning and then for the rest of the day. That was until they discovered that he had a drink problem and he had to go back to hiding his addiction. He consoled himself that he was sticking to the twelve-step programme and his sponsor would be there if he needed. There were meetings all over Christmas – even on Christmas Day. Support was there if he needed it.

Nick turned off the engine and took a breath. He hadn't seen Amanda since they had slept together forty-eight hours

earlier. He knew the experience had made him feel danger-
ously high. There was a part of him that worried that he was
risking both of their sobrieties by not doing the right thing.
The theory was that people in early recovery were emotionally vulnerable. They could launch themselves into a relationship because it was exciting and would make them feel better
about themselves. The dopamine and serotonin highs of alcohol would be replaced by similar chemical highs of a honeymoon period.

However, early recovery was also a time of emotional in-
stability and rawness, which weren't the best foundations for
a new relationship. And if that relationship failed, the alcoholic often couldn't cope and relapsed to dampen the emotional pain.

Nick had therefore decided, for the first time in his life,
to do the sensible thing. He would tell Amanda that seeing
her was too risky for both of them. There was a strong part of
his reckless side that was telling him to press the fuck-it button and have a relationship with her. But his determination
to stay sober was stronger.

The sound of a door shutting broke his concentration.
He looked up and saw Amanda locking her front door. She
gave him a little wave as she came towards the car. Nick's
stomach was already tense.

Amanda got into the car, leant over and kissed Nick
quickly on the lips. 'Hi there. You okay?'

She looked beautiful in the orange hue of the streetlights. And she smelt amazing.

'Yeah. I'm all right. But there is something I need to talk
to you about.' Nick said, avoiding full eye contact.

'No problem. It was one night. But I get the whole AA thing. And I need to keep sober. So that's the most important thing for both of us, isn't it?' Amanda said calmly.

Nick felt an immense sense of relief. 'Yeah. That's pretty much what I was going to say.'

'Good.' Amanda smiled, reached over and touched his arm. 'So ... we're okay?'

Nick smiled and nodded. 'Yes, of course. That sounds like the right thing to do.'

'I think I can just about resist you,' Amanda teased.

They drove to the AA meeting and sat separately. Nick watched Amanda as she stood by the hatch where coffee was being served and spoke to the women who had been around the rooms for years. He knew what they had decided was for the best, but when he watched her, he still couldn't help but wonder, *What if...?*

Wandering outside, Nick pulled out his mobile phone to check some work emails.

'Nick?' a voice said. It was his dad standing with a few of the smokers. Since coming out of rehab, Nick had seen his dad at an AA meeting most weeks. They always chatted and caught up, and even though conversations never went past that, Nick was glad that they had some kind of relationship. He wasn't sure they would ever talk openly, but Nick would take what they had now compared to recent years.

'How you doin', lad?' Rhys Evans asked, tapping out another cigarette from a pack.

'Work's busy. You know. Otherwise, plodding along nicely.' Nick replied.

'Plodding's good. You coming to the Blackpool conference?' Rhys asked.

Nick remembered that there was a huge AA conference up in Blackpool the following month. He wondered if his dad was asking because he wanted him to go. Maybe it would be good to go together, even if the thought made him feel anxious.

'Work dependent, you know? I'd like to go,' Nick replied.

'You on that murder up on Snowdon?' Rhys asked.

'Yeah. Harv Pearson was an old friend of mine.'

'Aye, I recognised the name. I knew his old man. I'm sorry to hear that, son.'

They continued to chat until it was time to go in for the meeting. The room was basic, with two rows of chairs. There was chatter, laughter and smiles. The atmosphere used to baffle Nick because, in his head, he only ever laughed and smiled in social situations when he was drunk. When sober, he used to find any gatherings excruciating. That was changing now, and he was starting to feel a little more comfortable in his skin.

Nick settled and, as always, the meeting gave him perspective and a calmness. Amanda shared briefly, saying that she was grateful to be there and that she had got a lot from the meeting. He was proud of her.

As the meeting packed away, Nick's sponsor 'Aberdeen Bill' wandered over and shook his hand with a smile. 'Nicholas?'

'William.' Nick smiled back. 'How are you, Bill?'

'Upright and sober, so I'll take that.' Bill gestured over to Amanda who was helping to wash up in the tiny kitchen, 'You're friends with Amanda, aren't you?'

'Yeah. I know her from work. She's in social services.' Nick explained but feared that Bill would probe a little more.

'How's she doing?' Bill asked.

'She's doing okay. Three to four meetings a week. Listening. She understands it's a day at a time.'

Bill nodded. 'Early days. She's a very pretty girl.'

Nick cringed for a moment. 'Yeah, I suppose she is.'

'Nothing funny going on, is there?' Bill asked.

'God no. She's a newcomer. And I'm only just starting to get it,' Nick replied. Lying to your sponsor was a mortal sin in AA.

'Good. Glad to hear it.' Bill nodded. 'Give me a ring and we'll go out for coffee. You might need to think about Step Four at the beginning of next year.'

'Yeah. Thanks. Will do.' Nick was squirming inside.

Feeling guilty for his deception, Nick wandered outside. Amanda was waiting on the path, smoking a cigarette.

'Come on, chauffeur. Chop, chop.' She chuckled as they turned to go.

'I really liked your share,' Nick said. He wanted to be as encouraging as he could.

'Did you? I thought I was waffling on about a load of old nonsense.'

'Far from it. I'm proud of how you're doing,' Nick said, and then regretted saying it. It was too intimate, wasn't it?

'Really? No one's ever said that to me before.' Amanda beamed. She stopped to look at him.

'What do you mean?' Nick asked. Surely someone in her life had told her they were proud of her?

'Pretty dysfunctional family. So no one's ever said that they're proud of me before. Never.' Amanda looked directly at him.

Oh God, Nick thought as he dropped his gaze to the floor, struggling to fight his feelings.

'Really. Right.' Nick knew they needed to keep walking.

As they rounded the corner to where the car was parked, he felt Amanda reach gently for his hand. He didn't resist. He linked his fingers in between hers and they walked hand in hand to the car. It was such a nice feeling, but Nick could feel his pulse quickening.

They got into the car and there was a moment of silence. Nick looked over at Amanda. The light inside the car highlighted her face softly. She looked stunning, there was no doubt about it.

Amanda frowned and pulled a quizzical face. The tension between them was mounting. 'What are we doing?' she whispered.

Nick sighed. 'I don't know. But I have an overwhelming desire to kiss you.' His stomach turned again in excitement. He was going against everything he had thought in the last two days. *Time to hit the fuck-it button,* he thought.

'You don't need to ask permission to kiss me.' Amanda whispered again as she leaned over and pressed her lips to his. Not breaking contact, she slid across and sat astride Nick in the driver's seat.

CHAPTER 14

'A ndy, can you explain why we found a body in the boot of your car yesterday?' Ruth asked.

Gates was unshaven and had his tinted glasses on. He was wearing a grey tracksuit as his clothes had been taken to be forensically checked the night before. Sitting back with his legs apart, Ruth could see Gates was trying to show that he wasn't fazed by being interviewed. They had been going at it for ten minutes and it frustrated Ruth that they were getting nowhere.

'Ruth, we've been through all this. I don't understand how it got there. Someone must have put it there. That's the only explanation I can offer.' Gates shrugged innocently. He was acting like it was a ridiculous question, and it was getting right up her nose.

Gates glanced over at the duty solicitor and shook his head as if to say that he couldn't believe he was being asked to go through this again.

'Andy, we found a rope in the boot that has blood on it. It matches marks that we found on the man's neck. When we check that for DNA, you're sure that we're not going to find anything to link you to that rope?' Ruth asked.

'No, of course not. Can't you see? Whoever is trying to set me up put the rope in the boot with the body,' Gates sighed in exasperation.

'And you have no idea who the man in the boot of your car is?' Ruth asked.

'No, of course not. How could I?'

Either Gates was enjoying playing with her, or he was so utterly deluded that he truly believed what he was saying. Both options were unsettling.

Ruth looked back at her notes. 'Okay, Andy. Does the name *Stefan Olsen* mean anything to you?'

'Ruth, you asked me that when you came to my house. And I told you quite clearly then, I have never heard that name before,' Gates said, sounding like he was reprimanding a child.

'You've never met Stefan Olsen?' Ruth asked, trying to remain calm.

'No ...' Gates gave a chuckle of disbelief.

'Have you ever been on a male dating site, U'veGot-Male?'

'What? Oh my God! That sounds like a gay dating site.' Gates looked at her in utter disgust. 'Is it?'

'Just answer the question, please.'

'Dear God! I'm sorry but I don't understand any of this. You know I'm married, Ruth. You met Kerry when you came to my house.'

Ruth had to give it to Gates. He was convincing in his protests of innocence. She was also aware, however, that only a madman would not realise that the remains at his house, meeting Nick at Bar One Hundred and the body and rope in his car were incontestable proof that he had carried out multiple murders of homosexual men.

'Andy, you know as well as I do that there are men who are seemingly happily married but are homosexual and live a double life.'

'I'm not naïve. But that's not me.' Gates shifted in his seat. 'Is this going to take long? I've got to get back to Kerry. There's no one else to look after her except our neighbour. I've got some roofers arriving tomorrow to give me an estimate on the roof. All this nonsense is completely ruining my life.'

Gates sounded like he had been caught up in a minor traffic accident rather than arrested for multiple murders.

'Can we turn to the property that you own, number four, Abbey Terrace.' Ruth looked through her notes again. 'As you know, we have found the remains of Stefan Olsen and two unidentified males in the sewer at the property. A DNA sample shows that the remains originated from your property. Can you explain that to me?'

'And once again, we've been through that. I have employed a building company to work on that house. I have no control over who comes and goes at that house. Anyone could have brought those remains to flush away.'

'You have no idea how those remains ended up being disposed of at your property.'

'No. No idea.' Gates was starting to get agitated. 'Is that all? I really need to get back.'

'No. Can you tell me why you were in Bar One Hundred yesterday?'

'Yes. I was going to do some Christmas shopping. I went into the bar to have a quick drink before I started. I don't think that's breaking any laws?'

'Can you tell me why you started a conversation with Detective Sergeant Evans in Bar One Hundred?'

'It was very busy. There was a spare seat opposite him, so I sat down. I was being friendly.'

'You told DS Evans that you were meeting someone.'

'Well, I had made a very loose arrangement to meet an old friend. That's all.'

'And who is that?'

'Brian Dawson.'

'And he'll confirm that, will he?'

'Yes, of course,' Gates said, shaking his head at his solicitor in disbelief again.

'You said that DS Evans was very handsome and that your eyes had met across the bar. That doesn't really fit with your story, Andy?'

'I was joking, messing around. I have a strange sense of humour,' Gates explained with a smile.

Before Ruth could comment on his ludicrous story, there was a knock at the door. Merringer looked at her as he opened the door.

'Boss, you need to see this,' Merringer said quietly but with a sense of urgency.

'For the purposes of the tape, DI Hunter is leaving the room,' Ruth said and followed Merringer outside. She wondered what the development could be.

Merringer clicked open a photograph on his phone. A man's face: it was a white-blue colour and clearly dead. It was Stefan Olsen. 'SOCO found a naked body sitting on the sofa in the annexe at Gates's home address.'

Ruth had mixed feelings. Gates had murdered Stefan Olsen for no reason except his sexuality. It was chilling, especially with how Gates was behaving during the interview.

However, the discovery of Stefan Olsen's body at Gates's home address now meant that the evidence against Gates was overwhelming. She just hoped that Gates would now do the right thing and put the families of the murdered men out of their misery by revealing their identities and the locations of their bodies – or, as Ruth grimly remembered, what was left of them – to bring some closure for everyone.

Ruth pushed open the door and sat down again. 'For the purposes of the tape, DI Hunter has now re-entered the interview room.'

'Everything all right?' Gates asked in an overfamiliar tone. It gave Ruth the creeps, but she knew she had him bang to rights now. *Fuck him,* she thought.

Ruth looked directly across at Gates. He looked straight back at her defiantly. 'Andrew Gates, further to the charges yesterday, I am now arresting you for the murder of Stefan Olsen. You do not have to say anything. But it may harm your defence if you do not mention when questioned something which you later rely on in court. Anything you do say may be given in evidence.'

There was a moment as Gates composed himself and then he smiled. 'Go on then, surprise me, Ruth.'

'The body of Stefan Olsen was found at your home address this morning. Can you explain that to me?'

Gates sighed as if to show that this was all boring him. He mimed zipping his lips and then raised his eyebrows arrogantly. 'No comment.'

NICK SLOWED THE CAR as he entered Betws-y-Coed, a small town at the heart of Snowdonia National Park. In Welsh, it means 'prayer house in the wood.' Lying in the valley, the River Llugwy joined the River Conwy, and the town was picturesque and popular with tourists keen to explore Snowdonia. There were many outdoor activity shops catering for everything from caving to abseiling down waterfalls. It was also the gateway to Mount Snowdon.

Nick hadn't been there for over a decade. He had trekked up to Swallow Falls. Rising amongst the towering peaks of Carnedd Llewelyn, the River Llugwy ran east and became a spectacular waterfall, Swallow Falls, with its foaming water falling 150 feet.

That morning, Nick had received some intel on David Chivers, the teacher that James Ferguson had mentioned when he spoke to him. According to the PNC and a uniformed officer, David Chivers had received anonymous phone calls and even thought he had seen someone at his home on several occasions. Nick didn't know if there was anything to it.

Parking outside one of the many climbing equipment shops, Snowdonia GO!, Nick turned off the ignition. The town was quiet at this time of year. It was too cold and too dangerous to explore Snowdonia in any depth. Nick's thoughts were drawn to Amanda. He couldn't stop thinking about her and that worried him. He'd been in obsessive and co-dependent relationships and they had always ended badly. He knew he wouldn't have the emotional strength to cope if what he and Amanda were doing were to finish like that. His priority had to be his sobriety.

Nick got out of the car. Today he was on police business and he needed to focus on that. The owners of Snowdonia GO!, Paddy and Christine Brennan, had been walking on Snowdon the day of Harvey Pearson's murder. However, they had been out of the country for a few days and had only just seen the news and police appeals for witnesses.

Nick approached the shop, which looked squashed in a row of old, grey stone buildings. The windows were dressed with mannequins in brightly coloured climbing and walking clothing. There were posters of the snowy peak of Snowdon and other stunning parts of Snowdonia.

As Nick walked in, he could see the shop was empty. It was still early and there was a smell of fresh coffee. Paddy Brennan was over by the till putting out some stock on a nearby shelf. He was well into his fifties, with thick grey hair and a beard, but looked fit and trim.

'Mr Brennan? DS Evans from North Wales Police. You spoke to our duty sergeant yesterday?' Nick confirmed, showing his warrant card.

Paddy nodded and put down the box that he was carrying. 'Oh yes. That's right.'

'Okay if I take a few details from you?' Nick asked as he got out his notebook and pen.

'Of course. Come and sit down. Can I get you a coffee or anything?' Paddy said, gesturing for them to sit down on two stools either side of the till.

Nick was tempted but needed to get back to the station. 'I'm fine, but thanks. I've got a note that you and your wife were walking on Snowdon on the afternoon of Sunday the ninth of December? Is that right?'

'Yes. I think we set off about midday. We weren't going to the summit, but my wife's a keen photographer and there had been snow. She wanted to get some shots up there.'

'Is your wife here?' Nick asked.

'No. She's with our accountant today? Do you need to speak to her?'

'We may do in the future. Can you remember if you saw anyone on Snowdon that afternoon?'

'Yes, well, that's why we rang. We didn't know that some-one had been killed up there that afternoon. It's terrible. We've been in France for a few days so it wasn't until we saw the local news last night that we realised we had been there. And we recognised the man in the photo,' Paddy explained quietly.

'You saw Harvey Pearson on Snowdon that afternoon?' Nick fished a photograph from his inside pocket and showed it to Paddy. It was one of the photos of Harvey on Snowdon that Jack had taken on the day of his murder.

'Yes. That's him. He was walking with another chap.'

Nick showed Paddy another photograph. This time it was Jack Pearson. 'Was this the man?'

Paddy nodded. 'Yes. I think so. He was wrapped up and I think he had a hat on, but it looks like him.'

'Did you speak to them?' Nick asked.

'Not really. I think we said hello. Nothing more than that.'

'Was there anyone else on Snowdon that afternoon?'

'I seem to remember a man walking his dog, but that was at the beginning of the path.'

'Could you describe him?' Nick asked. It was the first lead they had got about someone else being on the mountain.

'Sorry. He was in the distance. A red coat of some sort but that's about it.'

'Anything else?' Nick asked. It wasn't much to go on.

Paddy thought for a moment. 'He was quite young, from what I could see. But he had a limp and walked with a stick. Like he had been injured.'

Nick scribbled this down in his pad. 'Thank you. Did you see anyone else?'

'We passed four girls going up there too,' Paddy said, thinking back.

'Girls?' Nick asked.

'Well, I say girls. I guess they were your age,' Paddy said with a wry smile. 'They were walking together and they were all wearing a lot of pink. I don't know why.'

Nick frowned. It was a strange image. 'Pink?'

'Yes, pink. Pink scarves, hats and gloves. Maybe some other stuff. Anyway, they were laughing and seemed to be very jolly.'

Nick was thinking out loud. 'Maybe it was a charity thing? Could that have been it?'

He was thinking of the runs for Cancer Research UK that he had seen where participants all wore something pink.

'I'm sorry. I just saw the colour. But yes, it could well have been a charity thing.'

'Did you speak to these women?' Nick asked.

'Again, it was no more than a hello. They just seemed to be in high spirits.'

'And you were on Miners' Track, is that right?'

'Yes.'

'And can you show me where you saw Harvey and Jack Pearson, and then where you saw the women?'

Paddy nodded and gestured to the wall where there was a detailed map of Snowdon and all the different paths to its summit. 'We saw the women just here. That's the causeway over Llyn Llydaw. We saw the two men up here. You see that's where Miners' Track meets Pyg Track. It's a bit loose underfoot from there on.'

'And you are sure that it was Harvey Pearson that you saw?'

'Oh yes. My wife and I recognised him as soon as we saw the photograph on the news.'

Nick thanked Paddy for his time and began to make his way back to Llancastell. He ran the hypotheses around in his head as he drove. Harv had been deliberately attacked and murdered on Snowdon. The strangulation showed that the attack was personal and targeted, not random. Harv was walking with his brother Jack. They had had a row and Jack had left to go home. At the moment, there was no reason to suspect Jack. He had no motive and Nick knew him well enough to know that he would not have killed his brother.

Also on the mountain that day were Paddy and Christine Brennan. There was no evidence to suggest they were anything other than witnesses. They had seen a group of four women, who had not been identified and had not come forwards to confirm they were on Snowdon that day. Nick felt it was unlikely that none of the women had seen the news of the murder. So what were they hiding? There was also the man in the red jacket walking a dog near the foot of the mountain. Where was he?

There seemed to be little in Harv's life that provided an obvious motive for murder. Good job, divorced but a good relationship with his ex-wife and kids, no money problems and nothing on social media. The only thing that Nick could find was Harv's sudden interest in his time at St Patrick's boarding school. He had mentioned a reunion, but Harv had been very unhappy at St Patrick's. He had identified an ex-teacher, David Chivers, as someone he wished to kill. Did the historical scars on Harv's back and his miserable time at St Patrick's have anything to do with Chivers? Why was Harv trying to track down Chivers and others from his time at St Patrick's?

Someone had targeted Chivers in recent weeks. Could it be a coincidence that Harv was tracking Chivers down at the same time? Had Harv found him and been waging a hate campaign against him?

CHAPTER 15

Even though Gates was on remand, he was being housed on the Vulnerable Prisoners – or VP – wing, at HMP Rhoswen, close to the North Wales coast, alongside sex offenders, grasses, police officers, paedophiles, and any other high-risk inmates.

Gates was told he shouldn't start in the induction wing as there were already fears for his safety. The VP area was known as the 'fours' as it ran across the whole fourth floor. Old-time prisoners, 'old lags,' called it 'Fraggle Rock' because 'it was where the nonces, animals, fraggles, freaks and grasses' were housed. Outside, in the main prison population, the VPs could fall victim to extreme violence such as 'wetting up,' also known as 'jugging.' A bucket or jug would be filled with boiling water and a pound of sugar mixed in to make a blistering syrup that stuck to the skin. The liquid was then thrown in the victim's face and burnt the flesh away down to the bone.

Gates was worried since his case was breaking in the media. It wouldn't be long before everyone in the prison knew who he was. Serial killers were big news. Serial killers were also fair game for attacks. Even though Gates knew that his crimes had been against men, there would be many violent prisoners who would love the notoriety of having attacked or even killed him. He was a freak.

Before Gates had even sat down in his cell, he had found a razor blade carefully positioned on his pillow. It was a welcome gift from a guard or a fellow inmate. An invitation for him to commit suicide. He already knew that there might be faeces, urine or ground glass in his food, especially if the prison's general population had access to it.

During his trial, Gates would have to explain why he had killed his victims. He was looking forward to sitting down with true-crime writers and giving them a detailed account of his life and his crimes. However, in moments of self-awareness and self-analysis, Gates wondered quite how he had ever descended into such destructive psychopathy. He thought that somehow it came from the anxiety and fury of being left alone and a desperate search for sexual identity. Once he had killed for the first time, there was no going back. The high and the ecstasy was too overwhelming not to become addicted. Now he knew what the phrase *blood lust* meant – it was the perfect description. *Perhaps they could use that for the title of my biography ...*

Gates would have to explain his marriage to Kerry. He had always felt that he treated it like a game where he wore the mask of a doting husband. He had gone through the motions, said the right things, but it was true that he did care for her. At least he thought he did. He had no benchmark. Sometimes he doubted he could truly care for anything. Poor Heidi had been born just days after they got married. His mother had disapproved of Kerry being pregnant at the wedding, but Gates didn't care about what she thought. She was a cold bitch.

After the wedding, Gates, Kerry and Heidi had gone on their honeymoon to a local holiday resort. On the second night, poor little Heidi had left them for ever. And, for a couple of years, their grief brought them closer and their love seemed to be real. It did to Gates.

Once Kerry became ill, she served the function of Gates's childish need to please and look after someone. He felt like he was looking after a sick, innocent child. And that felt like love too.

However, if Gates was honest, he knew deep down what and who he really was. Maybe he had been born that way? Born with an innate evil nature.

As for why he killed, he knew that the men he had stalked and killed were all in great pain. He could tell from the time he spent with them. They were lost, confused and directionless. They were full of jealousy, rage and uncertainty. By killing them, he was releasing them from the pain of life. He could shed no tears for them or their families. He knew that wasn't normal. Even now, he couldn't see a time when he would feel any remorse. The ghosts of his victims never visited him when he was awake or when he was asleep, so he assumed that proved that they were now in a more peaceful place. It was a message from God.

Gates had spent the morning using a laptop in the IT area. Their use was highly restricted and there was no access to social media, gambling, pornography or anything sensitive or provocative. Any prisoners trying to access such sites would lose their computer privileges immediately.

Gates knew what he was looking for. He typed in *Detective Inspector Ruth Hunter* and a list of old newspaper articles came up on the search engine. Some of the articles were about Ruth's career and the cases she had worked. However, Gates could see that the majority were about Sarah's disappearance. The initial search to find her plus articles on the anniversary of her disappearance. *Vanished – The Strange case of Sarah Goddard.*

Gates smiled. He had hit the jackpot with DI Ruth Hunter.

An hour later, Gates sat in his single cell and clicked on the small colour television. For a while, the BBC national news reported dull political and foreign stories. Gates was eager to see if his crimes had made it onto the news agenda, but they hadn't yet. He felt a bit disappointed but told himself that it wouldn't be long before he had his day in the sun. There would be books about him. He could go on the shelves with Nilsen, Sutcliffe, Bundy and the Krays.

The BBC Wales news report then switched to shots of Snowdon and police officers in high-vis jackets scouring the paths and crags.

'*The search for clues continued on Snowdon today as police widened their search of the mountain. It was last Sunday afternoon that thirty-six-year-old Harvey Pearson's body was discovered at the bottom of this ridge along Miners' Track. The North Wales Police Force have said that they are now treating his death as a murder.'*

Gates watched the news story with growing interest. On the television screen, the news ticker tape introduced a Detective Chief Inspector Drake as he was being interviewed outside Llancastell Police Station. '*Mr Pearson's murder is a tragedy for his friends and family. We are keen to talk to any-*

one who was on Mount Snowdon, or in or around the area of the mountain, last Sunday afternoon.'

Gates began to hatch a plan.

NICK MET AMANDA AT the Pen y Pass car park. He thought she looked cute in her sky-blue woollen hat and gloves. Miners' Track was a longer route than the alternative Pyg Track, but Nick wanted to retrace Harvey Pearson's steps. He wanted to take a more focussed look at the site of his murder again, especially now that the search was being scaled down.

Amanda had the day off and said there was something she wanted to talk to Nick about. Nick had joked that walking to the site of a murder wasn't exactly romantic, but the scenery was spectacular. He was also wondering what she wanted to talk about and feared that she was having second thoughts about their relationship. He couldn't blame her. He had the same fears and doubts. The uncertainty wasn't about Amanda. Everything about her felt right. It was the emotional vulnerability that could destabilise their sobriety.

They had been walking for the first twenty minutes, chatting casually, when Amanda reached for Nick's gloved hand. He felt the same electricity spark through his fingers as he had felt when they held hands in the car park outside the AA meeting. He couldn't remember the last time he had felt that. His love life had been a dark, sordid and drunken blur in recent years, devoid of warmth, love or romance.

They reached Llyn Teyrn, a small lake that sparkled in the winter sun. The icy wind had picked up and numbed Nick's face. It wasn't long before they came to the much larger Llyn Llydaw. A narrow path crossed the lake and then ran right along its northern edge.

Nick stopped for a moment to look out over the spectacular view and pulled Amanda close. He had to raise his voice a little because of the noise of the wind. 'Have you been up Snowdon before?'

'No, never,' Amanda replied, tucking stray wisps of hair into her hat.

'A Snowdon virgin, eh?' Nick said with a grin, and Amanda gave him a playful shove. 'You know the story of this lake?'

Amanda frowned. 'No. I was never good at history.'

'You've heard of Excalibur, King Arthur's sword?'

Amanda smiled. 'Yes. I'm not a moron.'

Nick grinned. 'We'll see about that.' He then gestured. 'Sir Bedivere took Excalibur after King Arthur's death and threw it into this lake. And that is when the hand of the Lady of the Lake caught it and disappeared under the water.'

Amanda smiled at him. 'I didn't know that. Why didn't I know that?'

'Ignorance? Stupidity?' Nick shrugged.

She hit him on the arm as they turned to carry on walking. The winter sun was warming them, but they had to squint from its low glare.

Nick continued, 'This was the lake Arthur sailed across to reach the magical isle of Avalon. And that's where he died and was buried.'

'A romantic walk and a guided tour. I'm being spoilt,' Amanda said with a slightly sardonic edge.

They continued on, passing the ruins of the old Britannia Mine crushing mill.

After another ten minutes, Nick knew that he would have to broach what Amanda wanted to talk to him about. It was making him feel anxious and if she was going to suggest that they no longer see each other, he wanted to have that conversation sooner rather than later.

Nick looked over at Amanda and could see she was out of the breath. He gestured to a large rock to one side. 'Five-minute rest?'

'Yeah, good idea,' Amanda said, breathing hard.

'See those fags have helped your lung capacity,' Nick said sarcastically.

Amanda smiled and gave him the finger. 'Do one.'

'Probably going to struggle to light one up here.'

'No shit, Sherlock.' Amanda looked away for a moment, then turned back and took his hand. 'There's something I wanted to tell you, that you need to know.'

Nick started to feel anxious. 'Okay.'

Amanda's face changed and she looked troubled. She pursed her lips and for a moment she looked like she might cry. 'I'm ... sorry ...'

Nick put his arm around her. 'Hey, don't worry. Whatever it is, just tell me. When you're sober, everything gets a bit raw because you don't have anything to numb it anymore.' He pulled her closer and realised that whatever she was going to say, he really cared for her.

'I was raped, Nick.' She bit her lip, a tear ran down her face and she took a deep breath. 'I ... was raped last year ...'

Nick looked at her and held her closer. 'I'm so sorry.'

For a moment, they just held each other closely as the wind swirled around them and the sun lit their faces.

'It was a work night out. In town. I was hammered ... I was always fucking hammered.' Amanda stopped for a moment as more tears came.

'It's all right. You don't have to tell me what happened.'

'No. No ... I want to,' Amanda said, nodding her head. 'This guy was chatting to me. You know, buying me drinks. We were dancing. I went into a blackout and the next thing, we were in my flat. He was on top of me and he was really strong. And he had this look on his face like he hated me. It was terrifying. And he just pinned me down on the floor and raped me. I was struggling and saying no but I just couldn't ...'

'I'm sorry. That's just ... horrendous.'

Amanda nodded and wiped the tears from her face.

Nick nodded. 'Did you report it?'

'Yeah. I went to the sexual assault referral centre. You know, what I do as a job, I know all about it, don't I?'

'Any idea who did it?'

Amanda shook her head. 'No. I've been through CCTV with the police. Talked to my friends. Nothing. No traceable DNA. And the worst thing is ... if I can close my eyes, I can still see his face. And that's when my drinking took off twenty-four seven.'

'Of course.' Nick looked at her. 'You're doing well, you know that?'

'Thanks. I just wanted you to know. I felt I was hiding it from you and ... I really like you.' Amanda buried her face into his chest.

Nick put his hand comfortingly on her cold face and pulled her closer.

CHAPTER 16

By the time Ruth arrived at Llancastell Magistrates' Court, they had brought Gates up from the holding cells. He was freshly shaved, dressed in smart clothes and handcuffed to a prison officer. Looking around the courtroom, Gates had an expression of bemusement. Ruth found this incredibly annoying. She knew the devastation that he had caused the families of those he had murdered, many of whom still thought their loved ones were missing. And she knew all about the pain of that. Yet Gates's demeanour was obviously to show everyone that he didn't care and wasn't remotely fazed by what he had done. He was undeniably a psychopath, so she knew that was true. She also knew that he would get off on causing anger and misery at every stage of the investigation. His casual indifference and lack of remorse were all designed for this purpose.

The courtroom was newly built with light-coloured wooden-panelled walls, a blue carpet and blue padded chairs at a row of tables. It looked like a smart conference room rather than a court. Especially when she compared it to the dusty, old courtrooms of London.

Earlier that morning, Ruth had put in a phone call to Interpol to chase up information about Jurgen Kessler. How had he managed to avoid any detection in over seven months? Ruth wasn't naïve. She knew Sarah's case wasn't the top priority. However, Ruth was one of them, a fellow officer of the law, and that usually meant things got done more thoroughly and faster, even if that wasn't strictly ethical. She had to console herself that it would be several days before anyone got back to her.

As Ruth sat down in the public gallery, Gates spun around and immediately caught her eye, nodding in recognition with a smirk. Ruth couldn't help but feel unnerved by the fact that Gates seemed to feel that there was some kind of connection between them. It was as if he had known instinctively that she had just arrived at that precise moment. It made her physically shudder.

Even though this was just a preliminary hearing to establish Gates's name, address and the not-guilty plea he would be putting in, Ruth felt that as SIO she needed to be present.

Given the magnitude of the crimes that Gates had been charged with, the magistrate would categorise this as an indictable-only case that needed to go to trial at a crown court up at Mold. And Gates would be held on remand for many months as she, and the rest of Llancastell CID, gathered evidence and worked with the Crown Prosecution Service to mount a case against him.

The court clerk looked over at Gates. 'Could the defendant please stand?'

The prison officer and Gates stood.

'Could you please confirm for the court that you are Andrew Raymond Gates and that you live at Gabriel House, Hall Way, Llantysilio?'

Gates nodded. 'Yes.'

The magistrate looked over at Gates and frowned. 'Mr Gates, is it correct that you have declined legal counsel today?'

'Yes, sir.' Gates nodded. 'I intend to act as my own legal counsel so I don't require one.'

Ruth didn't know what the hell Gates was doing, but surely he wasn't going to try to defend himself in a criminal trial?

'In that case, Mr Gates, you have been charged with the murder of Stefan Olsen, along with the murders of other victims whose identities are yet to be confirmed. Can you enter your plea for the court today?'

Gates glanced up at Ruth. 'Guilty, sir.'

Ruth took a moment to process his change of plea. What the hell was he doing? Throughout their interviews, he had maintained his innocence. Ruth had assumed that he would enter a not-guilty plea and they would go to trial. It was a complete U-turn.

Gates cleared his throat for a second. 'For the record, I would like to establish that I am also guilty of the murder of Harvey Pearson on Mount Snowdon last week. The police haven't asked me about the murder, but I would like his family to know that it was me. I hope that will help give them a little peace and also save the North Wales Police a lengthy investigation.'

NICK LOOKED AROUND at the cold, grey crevices and the uneven landscape that loomed all around them. He and

Amanda had said little since her revelation, but he felt connected to her as they walked. The carved rocks and peaks were now dusted with snow that shimmered in the winter sunlight. Up to the right, a flock of white-fronted geese, who had migrated over from Greenland, flew in a circle. Their call was an unsettling, rhythmic screech like that of a gull.

Nick and Amanda arrived at the steep edge of the murder scene. As Nick looked down the ravine, he could see the blue-and-white police tape flapping noisily in the wind. It marked off the area where Harv's body had been found. The nearby ridge was decorated with various floral tributes, many of which had been scattered.

'How well did you know him?' Amanda asked after a minute, her voice raised a little against the noise of the gale.

'Pretty well. Went to school together. Spent a lot of time going out drinking in our twenties. We sort of lost contact recently,' Nick explained.

Amanda nodded as she gazed down at the large rock behind which the body had been found.

Nick's phone vibrated against his leg. It was Ruth. 'Boss?' He tried to move out of the direct blast of the wind so he could hear what she was saying.

'Gates has pleaded guilty at the magistrates' court.' Ruth said.

'What?' Nick knew that CID were all prepared for a not-guilty plea and a trial. A guilty plea would make life a lot easier and would mean less time negotiating with the CPS. But what the hell was Gates doing? 'You did say guilty plea, boss?' Nick clarified. Maybe the wind had affected his hearing.

'Yes. He has also admitted to the murder of Harvey Pearson,' Ruth said.

'What?' Nick was taken aback. It didn't make any sense. He quickly ran this development through his head and then said, 'The MO's completely different, for starters, boss?'

'Both asphyxiation. But yes, completely different to Stefan Olsen and the body we found in Gates's car. The PMs show they were strangled with rope. In fact, it would be hard to find any similarities.'

'Do you believe him?' Nick asked.

'No. I think he's dicking us about. He just wants as much publicity as possible now he's decided to confess,' Ruth explained. 'That's psychopaths for you.'

'I'm at the murder scene now. Then I'll get back.'

'See you later, Nick.'

Nick nodded and hung up the phone, still taking in the idea of Gates murdering Harv. The MO was different and there was no hint in Harv's life that he was homosexual. It was bullshit. And it made Nick angry that Gates was manipulating the death of his friend for his own narcissistic ends.

'Everything okay?' Amanda asked.

'Just work stuff,' Nick replied.

As he looked at the path and then the ridge, something about the murder scene suddenly occurred to him. Something he hadn't thought of before.

Turning back, Nick walked over to the footpath. It was at least fifteen feet from the edge of the ravine where Harv fell or, more likely, was pushed.

Amanda joined him and gave him a quizzical look. 'Something up, Sherlock?'

'Try to push me towards the edge of that ravine,' Nick said to her.

'What? Don't be stupid, Nick.'

'Seriously. You won't be able to do it, but just try to push me that way as hard as you can.'

'If you go over, I'm not pushing you in a wheelchair for the rest of your life, you do know that?' Amanda said with a smile.

'I'm not going anywhere,' Nick said as he smiled at her. 'Come on.'

Amanda shrugged and started to push Nick. He resisted and walked back two steps. She tried again, and he just moved out of her way. It was impossible. It was too far, there was too much room to manoeuvre and she wasn't strong enough.

'And I'm making a tit of myself because ...?' Amanda asked wryly.

'Okay. How many extra people would you need to push me over that edge? From here?' Nick asked. He was starting to realise that it was almost impossible for Harv to have been attacked by one person.

'What are you talking about?'

'Humour me.'

'Three. No, four to be on the safe side. You're quite big,' Amanda said with a bemused smile.

'I'll explain in a minute.' Nick took out his phone and dialled Ruth.

'Nick?' Ruth said, answering the phone.

'Boss. I'm at the point from which Harvey Pearson was pushed down the ravine. How tall is Gates?'

'Five foot eight, I guess,' Ruth answered.

'Ten or eleven stone?'

'Thereabouts. Why?'

'Harvey Pearson was sixteen stone and six foot four. There is no way Gates pushed him off the footpath and down the ravine. And I think you're right. There was definitely more than one killer up here. I think it would have taken three or four people to get him over the edge. And that explains how the body was moved after he was dead.'

'Do we have any leads in that direction?' Ruth asked.

'Two walkers who saw Harvey and Jack Pearson on Snowdon that day also saw a group of four women climbing the mountain. They were dressed in pink.'

'Maybe they were climbing Snowdon for charity?' Ruth suggested.

Nick nodded. 'That was my thought, boss. My other thought was that, given all the publicity, why hasn't one of them contacted us to say they were on the mountain that day? Unless they have a good reason why they don't want anyone to know they were here.'

IN THE STARK LIGHT of Interview Room One, Gates sat next to the duty solicitor rubbing his eyes. Ruth noticed a scar across his left eyelid that was normally well disguised by the frame and tint of his glasses. Gates replaced them again. Drake had taken the seat beside her. Given the growing magnitude of the case, Drake wanted to be in on Ruth's interview of Gates to get a handle on him. Ruth knew that there would be increasing pressure from higher up the police food chain and from the media for the case to be settled in an efficient and dignified manner with no mistakes.

Ruth had already reminded Gates that he continued to be under caution. The room was painted a cold pale-blue with simple chairs around a central wooden table.

Ruth shuffled her papers and looked over at Gates, who was now sitting back as if he was on holiday. 'Why did you change your mind about pleading guilty, Andy?'

'Look, Ruth, I have judged and punished myself more harshly than any court ever could. I just need to address what I have done morally,' Gates said, but Ruth thought his words sounded rehearsed and hollow.

'We are going to need the details and identities of every murder,' Drake said.

Gates nodded but continued to talk directly to Ruth. 'Of course. Ruth, I know that I can trust you implicitly. And I think that you trust me too. I think of myself as two characters and I want to explain both to you. So you understand. In one, I played an angel. I was a caring husband, friend and son who would have done anything to help those I loved. The other, an evil, primitive creature who revelled in causing and playing with death. There was no mid-ground for me. No balance.'

Ruth gave Drake a withering look that she was happy for Gates to see. She wasn't interested in his pseudo-psychological philosophies on life. She wanted to move the interview on. For her, the most important thing was finding out how many murders Gates had committed and getting the identities for the families. 'How many were there, Andy?'

'Seven.' He nodded. 'Yes, there were seven, I'm afraid.'

Gates was again trying to make direct eye contact with Ruth. She wouldn't be intimidated by him. She had interviewed her fair share of killers.

'You have the names of all of them?' Drake asked.

'Yes, of course. They were my friends, my lovers, to me. I know that's hard to understand.' Gates continued to stare directly at Ruth.

Looking up, Ruth met his gaze and said, 'The most important thing for us to do at the moment is to get the identities of those men and retrieve their remains. That's what we need to do for their families.'

Gates nodded. 'Of course. I will do everything I can to assist you.'

Ruth feared that this was all an act and he had no intention of helping them. She had worked with killers before who had got a kick out of not revealing where the bodies were.

'Did you find all of these men through internet dating sites?' Ruth asked.

'Oh, no. That was a development. It started last year with me going to pubs where I thought I could pick men up. It wasn't until recently that I realised what a wonderful thing the internet is. A marvel. So I could do all that from the comfort of my home. I can let you have all their names.'

'And their remains?' Drake asked.

'Well, this is where it gets a little complicated. I dissected five of the seven bodies. I didn't get around to the other two. I did that in the bath in the annexe at my home. Drained away the blood after the rigor mortis had been and gone. But

I always took their hands and hearts with me to the house at Abbey Terrace. Then I flushed them away.'

Gates's matter-of-fact tone seemed no different from someone explaining how they had built an extension. It struck Ruth how completely devoid of any emotion or empathy Gates was. It wasn't a surprise, but nonetheless, it was still disturbing to see it manifested in a human being directly in front of her.

'Why did you do that?' Ruth asked him.

'A man without hands or heart causes and feels no pain. Pain is delivered by his hands. Pain is felt in his heart. Without either, he is pain-free. I saved them from the torment of life, you see?' Gates smiled and nodded, seemingly pleased with his explanation.

'We need you to take us to the locations where you disposed of the bodies,' Drake said.

'Of course. They're relatively close to each other.'

Ruth looked over at Gates with a frown. 'You stated in court that you murdered Harvey Pearson?'

'Correct,' Gates replied.

'Can you tell me how you murdered Harvey Pearson?' Ruth asked, thinking that this would trip him up for starters.

Gates sat back, looking confident. 'Let me see. I was pretty drunk that day.' He pushed his chair back and then crossed his legs.

'I'm sure you would remember how you killed somebody,' Ruth said, trying to hide her growing revulsion for Gates.

'Yes, of course. I remember now. It's coming back to me. I pushed him down the mountain.'

'You killed Harvey Pearson by pushing him down a ravine?' Drake clarified.

'No. no. The fall didn't kill him. So I had to make my way down to where he was lying and finish the job.'

'And how did you do that?'

'How did I do that? Well, I must have strangled him. That's it. I hit him on the head with a rock and then I strangled him.'

'This is bullshit,' Drake said, shaking his head.

Ruth wasn't sure. She had been convinced that Gates was lying, but how did he know that Harvey Pearson had been pushed down a ravine and then strangled at the bottom? Had that information been released to the public?

'Not bullshit, I'm afraid. In fact, it's now very clear in my mind. Before I strangled him, I unzipped his jacket so I could get at his throat properly. I noticed that he had a tattoo that appeared just at the top of his sternum. It was dark blue. It might have been oriental, like a dragon or something.' Gates looked smug as he gave them information.

Ruth shot Drake a look. *How the hell does he know that?*

CHAPTER 17

Early the next morning, Nick arrived in the tiny village of St George, which was just a few miles away from the A55. He had never heard of it and discovered it was hidden away close to the town of Abergele.

As Nick slowed, he scoured the rustic buildings for the address he was looking for. He had used the PNC and council tax records to track down David Chivers, Harvey Pearson's old teacher from St Patrick's boarding school.

Even though Gates had admitted to killing Harv, Nick still wanted to pursue all lines of enquiry. And he suspected that Gates was somehow lying. The MO was completely different, which was unheard of for a mass killer.

Nick had also now established that it would be very difficult to overpower Harv and get him over the ridge. Nick's instinct was that there must be more than one killer. Despite learning of the group of women walking that day, it felt unlikely that four women dressed in pink for a charity walk would have attacked Harv that afternoon. What would be the motive? However, he was keen to eliminate them from the enquiry so he had tried to contact the relevant charity to see if a sponsored walk up Snowdon had been registered. Unfortunately, there seemed to be various charities that used pink – The Pink Ribbon Foundation, Breast Cancer Care,

Breast Cancer Now, Cancer Research and many more. It was going to take a while to get that information.

Cancer was also something that struck a chord for Nick. His own mother had died from it when he was only eight. Once it got hold of her, it was a hideous disease and she had died in a matter of months. From then on, Nick had been brought up by his Auntie Pat and Uncle Mike. His father, Rhys, had been stationed abroad with the Welsh Fusiliers.

Thornbank Cottage was a charming, detached cottage just down from St Steven's church. Nick could see that it had been recently painted white and had neat flowerbeds and lawns around its perimeter. Retirement was a wonderful thing.

David Chivers, now in his seventies, answered the door, and Nick explained vaguely why he wanted to ask some routine questions. Chivers was everything Nick had expected from an old boarding-school master. Cut-glass accent, verbose with a calm air of superiority. Chivers showed Nick to the tasteful living room where the walls were lined with books and records.

Nick wondered what had happened at St Patrick's. Were Harv's scars and unhappiness due to violence, bullying or abuse while he was there? Harv had made it clear that he wished David Chivers harm and even death. Why? And why was he trying to organise a reunion for a school where he went for only a few years and was deeply unhappy?

'Could you tell me when you left St Patrick's, Mr Chivers?' Nick asked, opening his notebook.

'Let me see. 2001, just after the millennium,' Chivers said.

'And how long had you been a teacher there?'

'Just short of thirty years by the time I took early retirement. It was a wonderful school. Do you know it?' Chivers's tone was a little pompous.

Nick wasn't interested in the education of the privileged. 'No ... And you were a history teacher and a housemaster?'

'Yes, that's right.'

'Do you remember a pupil, Harvey Pearson? He was at St Patrick's from 1994 to around 1998?' Nick asked.

Chivers gave a bemused smile. 'I'm sorry, Sergeant. The name doesn't ring a bell. I've taught thousands of pupils over the years.'

Nick nodded. Maybe it was a long shot, but if there had been anything sinister between Chivers and Harv, he might have seen a reaction.

'He was a very good rugby player,' Nick said to see if it jogged his memory.

'Not my sport, I'm afraid. Cricket man, myself.' Chivers frowned and sat forwards on the sofa. 'I'm a little confused, Sergeant. I was under the impression that you were here regarding the incidents from last week? I did speak to one of your colleagues.'

Nick only had very vague intel on the incidents. It was only natural for Chivers to think that's why he was there.

'Of course. It's part of the same investigation. I do need to get the exact details of what you talked to my colleague about first,' Nick explained.

'There were the phone calls to start with, about two weeks ago.'

'And what was said in these phone calls?' Nick asked.

'"I'm going to kill you. You're going to die. You know what you've done." The man was disguising his voice.'

'So it was definitely a man?' Nick asked.

'Oh yes. There wasn't a distinct accent though. I'm normally pretty good at identifying an accent.'

'How many phone calls were made?'

'Three.'

'And what time of day were they made?' Nick asked.

'During the evening. I gave all this information to the other officer who came,' Chivers grumbled.

'Sorry. It's just that as we run through it, you might remember something that you didn't last time.'

'Yes, I suppose that is a possibility,' Chivers said as he crossed his legs. Nick noticed he was wearing mustard-coloured corduroy trousers. He made a mental note to get someone to shoot him if he reached the stage of life where he thought that was okay.

'You said there were phone calls to start with?' Nick asked.

'Yes, then there was the peeping tom, or stalker, or whatever you want to call him. That was during the evening, about ten days ago. It happened twice.'

'So you saw someone?' Nick asked.

'Yes. The first time, I saw someone running away through my back garden and over the fence. They were dressed in black so I couldn't see anything. The second time, I heard a noise at the side of the house. When I looked out, a man walked past and he was wearing one of those balaclavas.'

Nick didn't like the sound of the incidents. Someone had clearly been trying to put the frighteners on Chivers. He wondered if Harv had anything to do with it? It didn't sound like it was local kids messing around.

'But nothing recently?' Nick asked. What he really meant was whether there had been anything since Harv's death?

'No. Nothing since the weekend. I refuse to be driven out of my home, but I'm getting on a bit so it's rather frightening,' Chivers said. Nick could see that the events had got to him and he was spooked.

'Yes, it sounds very scary, Mr Chivers. Is there anyone that you can think of who would want to scare or even harm you?'

Chivers thought for a moment. 'No, no. Of course not. I've never harmed a fly.'

Nick knew that this wasn't true. Harvey Pearson had told his old schoolfriend that if he ever saw Chivers again, he would kill him, which can't have been unprovoked.

Gazing around the room, Nick spotted lots of family photos on the mantelpiece. They seemed to feature a lot of women, who Nick assumed were Chivers's daughters. One photo caught his eye. Four women, all in their thirties or early forties, standing with Chivers at some kind of celebration.

'Mr Chivers, do you have any daughters?' Nick asked.

'Yes, four,' Chivers said, glancing over at the photo.

'That must be nice,' Nick said, trying to disarm him a little.

'Yes. They're wonderful, as are my grandchildren.'

'They all live around here?' Nick asked.

'Yes. All in North Wales. I'm very lucky to have them. And I have seven grandchildren, so Christmas is an utter joy for me,' Chivers said with a beaming smile.

'What do they do, if you don't mind me asking?'

'Two of them have just had babies so they're pretty busy. My eldest two daughters live in Llanberis,' Chivers explained.

And Llanberis was at the foot of Mount Snowdon.

IT WAS MID-MORNING, and Ruth stood beside the unmarked black Volvo V70 in the visitor's car park at HMP Rhoswen. Behind her, a patrol car with blue-and-yellow markings and *POLICE – HEDDLU* in black lettering on the bonnet. Ruth gave the two uniformed officers, who would be with her for the duration of the day, a static wave of acknowledgement. Her attention was drawn to the arrival of the Dog Search team van with their specially trained cadaver dogs. A small white SOCO van followed and parked up alongside them.

The wind had dropped, but there was still frost and a scattering of snow on the grass verges and the prison's AstroTurf football pitches. Towering wire fences encircled the whole area, but the newly built cell blocks wouldn't have looked out of place in a business park. On the other side, a prison officer, in a black woolly hat pulled low over his ears, patrolled with an enormous German shepherd dog.

Ruth could see that the sign for HMP Rhoswen had been given a modern twist. It featured primary colours and a backdrop of triangular grey shapes that were there to symbolise the mountains of Snowdonia. It was a change from the ageing signs of the London nicks that seemed so ominous and sombre. Prisoners going to Wormwood Scrubs, known just as 'the Scrubs,' in West London were greeted by a huge black sign that simply said *HMP WORMWOOD SCRUBS* in white lettering. Combined with the Grade-II-listed late-Victorian architecture of the impressive gatehouse, she remembered thinking that the Scrubs didn't look like it had modernised since the days of Dickens and Sherlock Holmes.

Merringer was still sitting inside the car at the steering wheel, keeping out of the cold. In the back of the unmarked Volvo sat a burly male uniformed police officer, PC Harris. Harris had the unenviable job of being handcuffed to Gates for the day.

Ten minutes later, Ruth got the call that they had escorted Gates down from his cell and were getting ready for their little 'day trip.' The paperwork for a temporary release had to be approved by the Welsh secretary of state's office in Cardiff such was the magnitude of the offences that Gates was facing. The chief constable of North Wales Police and HMP Rhoswen's governor, Gordon Holmes, had also signed the release forms.

Ruth was feeling nervous. She could feel it in her stomach. Taking a killer out to locate their victims' remains was a big operation, and it wouldn't be long before the media caught on to what they were doing. That could mean everything from high-powered telephoto lenses to TV helicopters scrutinising their every move. She needed the day to go well.

Gates had agreed to take them to all the sites where he had buried the bodies along the Dee Valley. At first, he was reluctant to tell Ruth anything until he was in the car. She explained that he would be going nowhere until she had the rough locations of where they were going so they could carry out a risk assessment. She appealed to Gates's ego, saying that it was very rare for prisoners to be allowed to visit the scenes of their crimes. He was a 'special case' by being allowed to help them.

Ruth put her phone away and indicated to Merringer and PC Harris that it was time to go get their prisoner.

Merringer got out of the car and pulled on leather gloves. 'Glad I put on my thermal vest, boss,' he said with a smile.

'And thank you for sharing that with me,' Ruth said sarcastically, looking at his ample stomach that stretched over the waistband of his trousers.

They reached a large red steel door marked *Reception – Derbynfa*. Mounted to the brick wall was a modern video entry phone, which Ruth buzzed and showed her warrant card to.

A minute later, an enormous prison officer clunked open the door and escorted them down to a holding cell where Gates was being held. The booking area was clean and white, with plenty of light from the frosted skylights above. There were Christmas cards and a small white Christmas tree on the reception desk.

As Ruth signed the paperwork in triplicate, Gates was brought over and gave her his usual creepy, overfamiliar smile as he was handcuffed to PC Harris. He was dressed in the standard uniform of a grey sweater and grey tracksuit bottoms. He seemed fidgety, like an excited schoolboy before a day trip.

They took Gates, went back outside into the cold and headed for the car.

Gates took a deep breath and looked up to the sky. 'Ruth, I was researching something last night that I thought might help you. In fact, I thought specifically of you when I was reading it.'

Ruth tried to ignore Gates. She did not want him getting inside her head.

'Just be quiet, Gates,' Merringer barked.

As they got to the car, Merringer and PC Harris pushed Gates down into the back of the car, while Ruth got into the front.

Gates wanted to continue with his story. 'You see there was a homeless man on the streets. He had been homeless for many years. Decades.'

The sound of Gates's voice was grating on Ruth. 'No one's interested. Please, just be quiet until we get to where we're going. It's going to be a long day.'

Gates wasn't remotely fazed. 'Oh dear, Ruth. I had you down as somebody who was enlightened. Let me continue. So a stranger walked by. "Spare any change, mate?" the homeless man said, holding out an old coffee cup.

'The stranger looked at him. "Sorry. I haven't got anything." But then the stranger said, "What's that you're sitting on?"

'"Nothing. It's just an old box. I've had it for years."

'"Ever looked inside?" asked the stranger.

'"No. Why? It's just an old box. There's nothing in there."

'"Have a look inside." The stranger said.

'So the homeless man ripped the box open. And to his astonishment, disbelief and excitement, he saw that the box was filled with money and gold.' Gates stopped for a good few seconds. 'You are that homeless man, Ruth. And I am the stranger. I'm telling you to look inside. Deep inside yourself.'

Ruth gazed out of the window. God, she couldn't wait for the day to be over.

CHAPTER 18

It was mid-morning by the time Nick sat down opposite Drake to report back to him on the Harvey Pearson murder case. He had drunk too much coffee and felt jittery. Compared to swigging half a bottle of vodka or alcohol withdrawal, Nick would take too much coffee any day.

Nick knew that Drake had the same reservations about Gates's confession as he did. He liked Drake as a boss. There were no hidden agendas, game playing or internal politics. He was upfront and clear about everything. That didn't make him a soft touch. Far from it. When you were out of line or not performing, he made that very clear. He was also aware that Nick was in recovery and had been incredibly supportive.

'Still doing the meetings?' Drake asked.

'Three times a week,' Nick replied. 'Keeps me sober.'

'Good for you. I know it's early days, but I'm impressed, Nick,' Drake said, looking directly at him.

'Thank you, boss.'

'It's not easy. I had to watch my brother-in-law drink himself to death because he just wouldn't admit he had a problem. He was only forty-three. Brilliant barrister, three kids. Horrible,' Drake said.

Drake rarely talked about his family, and Nick felt privileged that he had shared it with him.

'It doesn't discriminate,' Nick said.

'No ...' Drake said grimly.

Nick gulped down the rest of his coffee. He had felt tired all morning and hadn't been sleeping well. Whenever he went to bed, he couldn't get the image of Harv's body in the mortuary out of his mind. He had been to many PMs and he had seen more than his fair share of dead bodies. But Harv was a mate, and the more he discovered about him, the more it seemed like he had a troubled childhood. Nick knew he had to be cold and dispassionate to do the job properly. He had to 'cultivate a heart like a swinging brick' as one of his instructors had told him and the other trainees at the police training college.

'You think Gates has anything to do with Harvey Pearson's murder?' Drake asked, getting down to business.

'No, boss. Gates is grandstanding. Now he's in custody, he wants as much attention as he can get,' Nick said.

Drake nodded as he tilted back in his large office chair. 'I agree. I don't know how he knew some of the details of Harvey Pearson's death, but everything we know about Gates's MO is different. And killers like Gates don't just change their MO on a whim. They have a purpose and a method that they stick to. So I agree, he's lying to get media attention.'

'Isn't Gates going up Snowdon today?' Nick asked.

'DI Hunter is taking him up there this afternoon. I want you to meet them, and I want you to go through every detail with Gates. I want to rule him out of the Harvey Pearson case by the end of the day if we can,' Drake said.

'Yes, boss,' Nick said.

'What happened with David Chivers?' Drake asked.

'Someone was trying to freak him out in recent weeks. Abusive phone calls and he saw someone lurking outside the house,' Nick said.

'What do you think?' Drake asked.

'Chivers seemed genuinely scared. And looking at Harvey Pearson's computer, he had tracked down Chivers and got his address,' Nick explained.

'Harvey Pearson was targeting David Chivers? Why?' Drake asked, raising an eyebrow.

'Something happened at St Patrick's boarding school in the early nineties. Harvey got a rugby scholarship there. However, everyone knew he hated it. He changed overnight. You could see it when you spoke to him. He was just quiet and not himself.'

'And David Chivers taught at St Patrick's at that time?' Drake asked.

'Yeah. Do you remember from the PM, Harvey had historical scars all over his back?'

Drake nodded for a moment. 'So, we think David Chivers was beating and possibly abusing Harvey Pearson while he was at the school?'

'There's no evidence, but it certainly feels like that, boss. Harvey told a friend that he had seen Chivers in a supermarket car park and that if he ever saw him again, he would kill him. Next thing, Harvey is telling everyone that he's organising a St Patrick's reunion and is tracking down ex-pupils and old teachers.'

'Which seems very unlikely from what you've told me.'

'Exactly. Harvey tracked down Chivers for a reason.'

'How does this connect to Harvey Pearson being attacked on Snowdon? I assume that David Chivers is kicking on a bit?' Drake asked.

'Oh, yer. David Chivers wouldn't be able to get up Snowdon or attack anyone. I went up Snowdon yesterday to the murder scene. Harvey was six foot four, sixteen stone and physically fit. The walking track is some distance from the edge of that ravine I don't think there's any way one person got him and dragged him over.'

'Multiple attackers, which fits with DI Hunter's theory?'

Nick nodded. 'Yes, boss. And it's a bit of a stretch, but Chivers has four daughters in their thirties and forties.'

'And we're looking for four unknown females who were on the mountain that day and haven't come forwards,' Drake said, thinking out loud.

'It feels unlikely, but at the moment it's all we've got,' Nick said with a shrug. If he was honest, four middle-aged women going up Snowdon and murdering someone who was terrorising their father sounded like a weak theory.

'Right, find the daughters. Let's see if they have an alibi,' Drake said.

RUTH FINISHED HER CIGARETTE and tossed it out of the car window as it started to snow. Merringer flicked on the windscreen wipers as large flecks landed on the glass. Gates had told her that the first place he had buried remains was Llidiart-y-Parc, beside the River Dee and beneath the Berwyn Mountains.

'Perfect weather for Christmas time, wouldn't you say?' Gates said as he gazed out of the window.

No one said anything. There was a stony silence.

Gates wasn't perturbed. 'I grew up around here, Ruth. Having snow at Christmas isn't that unusual in Snowdonia. It really makes Christmas, especially for kids. But you're not from up here, are you?' Gates waited for a response, but Ruth wasn't interested in making any conversation. 'That's right. You're from South London if I remember correctly. Peckham. Actually, Peckham Rye, isn't it?'

Ruth felt uncomfortable. How did Gates know that? Was it one of his informed guesses? However he knew, she didn't want him to have any information about her.

'You see, Ruth, I've been reading up about you. That's the thing about being on the VP wing at Rhoswen. They give you access to laptops during the day. You can't use social media. And porn and gambling are out. But you can use Google to do some research.'

Merringer glanced at Gates in the rear-view mirror. 'Just shut up, Gates. No one's remotely interested in your bullshit.'

'You say bullshit, but the funny thing is that me and your Detective Inspector Ruth Hunter have far more in common than you would think.' Gates nodded and frowned as if he was trying to remember something. 'The fifth of November 2013, wasn't it?'

Ruth felt her stomach lurch. It was the date that Sarah had gone missing. She took a breath but tried not to show it. Gates would use what he had found to get into her head. Criminals had done it to her before, but no one had ever used Sarah's disappearance to get to her. She knew she couldn't let Gates see that she was reacting.

'That must be a date that is etched in your mind for ever, Ruth? And that's why we're the same, you see? We both know the pain of being left. The agony of not knowing why someone has gone. No answers. No resolution. That's what happened to me. My father left me and I can barely remember him. Then my taid. Dropped dead in front of my eyes. Just like that!' Gates clicked his fingers loudly and it made Ruth jump, though she managed not to show it.

'Where are we going?' Ruth asked in an as composed a voice as she could muster.

'All in good time, Ruth. Now, what were we talking about?' They slowed over some potholes and Gates looked outside. 'Just here. This right-hand turn.'

Merringer turned from the main road and they made their way down a narrow track towards the River Dee. On the left was Carrog Station Camp Site, which Ruth could see was deserted. On the other side were rusted, corrugated-iron sheep pens and a long steel gate that had been padlocked.

'But Sarah just disappearing that day and never seeing her again. I don't know how that must have made you feel. Something like that must eat you up inside. You must lie at night wondering what happened to poor Sarah. Is she dead or is she alive? Was she kidnapped by someone? Did she have an accident and lose her memory? Or did she just leave you and didn't have the courage to tell anyone? Who knows? Will you ever know? The same thing happened to me. My Dad left one day and just never came back. No-one said anything to me. It's impossible to live with. Isn't it, Ruth? In fact, there must have been times when you didn't want to carry on living. I know I didn't. When the pain was just too much to bear? Was it like that for you?'

Ruth felt the emotions twist inside her. She felt sick, but she also wanted to turn round and punch Gates in the face until he was unconscious.

PC Harris glared at him. 'Another word from you, Gates, and I'm going to really hurt you.'

'That's not very friendly. And I think that would count as police brutality.' Gates smiled at him.

'Not if this car has to stop suddenly and you face-plant straight into the metal on the back of that seat,' Harris growled.

'You're very good-looking, officer, did you know that?' Gates smirked and sat back for a moment.

Ruth didn't want the argument to develop or Gates to feel that he had had any impact on anyone in the car. 'It's fine, PC Harris. The sad thing is no one is listening.'

'Yes, it's fine, PC Harris,' Gates mimicked.

The car slowed as the dry-stone walls and stark hedgerows gave way to barren fields. To the right, the swollen waters of the River Dee drifted downstream. The far bank was about six or seven hundred yards away and as the engine quietened, the noise of the powerful river could be heard. The water was high and the bottoms of several large trees on the banks were now submerged.

'Andy, you said that you buried your first victim, Darren Parnell, down here?' It pained Ruth to use his name and be polite, but she knew that she needed him to know that his mind games had not affected her at all.

Gates had given information to Ruth about all of his victims. It had been chilling to see the names of seven young men whose lives had ended so horrifically all in Gates's meticulous handwriting.

Darren Parnell was a twenty-three-year-old barman from Llangollen who lived on his own. Gates had befriended him at the Mill pub. He was originally from Dunfermline in Scotland and police had informed his parents. They didn't hear from Darren from one month to the next so they had no clue that he had disappeared, let alone been murdered.

'Yes. That's right. We'll have to walk over to the bank for me to show you exactly,' Gates explained.

Ruth didn't want Gates pulling any tricks. Nor did she want Gates dragging himself and PC Harris into the icy depths of the Dee where they would surely die. 'How far from the bank?'

'Thirty, forty feet, I guess. It was very dark when I was down here.'

The four vehicles ground slowly to a halt and stopped.

Ruth clicked her police radio. 'Central from three-six. We are at target location one, over.'

'Received three-six,' Central replied.

Uniformed officers positioned their car across the road and one of them stayed to redirect traffic. Police dog handlers went to the back of the van, opened it and brought up two large German shepherd dogs who immediately began to strain at the leash. The SOCOs began dressing in white protective suits and unpacking the trays and forensic bags that they might need.

As they turned to walk towards where Gates thought he had buried Darren Parnell's remains, Gates shot Ruth a look that seemed to become an imperceptible smirk. Ruth didn't react. She wouldn't let herself.

Ruth watched for the next fifteen minutes as uniformed officers and SOCOs dug at the surface of the earth, which was covered with patches of light snow.

'You never forget your first, that's what they say,' Gates said out loud to no one in particular. 'Poor little Darren. I think I was a father figure to him. He was a long way from home, and I think he was lonely. Darren wasn't going to contribute much to mankind. Nothing of any significance. And I think Darren knew that, which is why he was so sad.'

The wind picked up a little, but the snow had stopped. Out of a nearby tree, a bird flapped its wings noisily and caught Ruth's attention. It was enormous – two feet in length with wide, brown wings. She thought it was an osprey but she might have been mistaken. For a moment, Ruth wondered if Sarah was buried somewhere like this. An unmarked grave that only one individual knew about.

The chief SOCO looked up and waved from where they were digging. 'Boss. Got something.'

'You're looking for bright-blue plastic bags,' Gates said.

The chief SOCO heard Gates's comment, looked at Ruth and nodded.

They had found Darren Parnell.

CHAPTER 19

Llancastell Police Station had received a call from Harvey Pearson's workplace, Halo Technology. They had accidentally opened Harvey's locker during a revamp of the changing rooms and there were personal items in there. They thought the police should know.

Nick was greeted at reception by the head of HR, Mandy, who was young and full of energy. *Too much bloody energy and cheerfulness*, Nick thought to himself. *Halo Technology* was blazoned in red across the wall as was the italic subtitle *Digital Business Solutions* and a slogan that promised, *We deliver what you need.*

Mandy showed Nick the men's changing room, showers and toilets and took him over to the row of lockers. Mandy explained that employees could keep possessions and clothing in them. There was a gym up on the third floor for employees.

'This is Harvey's locker,' Mandy pointed solemnly.

'Thank you.' Nick took purple forensic gloves from his pocket and squeezed his hands into the tight rubber. He had brought an evidence bag with him.

'Do you need me to wait with you?' Mandy asked awkwardly.

'No, no. I'll give you a shout when I'm done,' Nick replied with a kind smile.

The locker door was open, and it was about four feet high with space for hanging shirts and suits. There were shelves to one side.

Nick took a small torch and peered inside. A smart blue polo shirt hung from a hanger. There was deodorant and aftershave on one of the shelves. Beside that, some shampoo that promised to 'cover grey hair.' Nick smiled to himself. That was Harv. Vain until the end. He remembered being in the pub with him and Jack and putting on Carly Simon's 'You're So Vain' on the jukebox. Jack and Nick had sung the song to Harv as they swigged their pints and laughed.

Nick was struck by the sadness that had crept up on him. They were such carefree, innocent days. That's how he remembered them.

At the bottom of the locker was a navy Ralph Lauren gym bag. Nick took it out and unzipped it carefully. Inside were some clothes that were black and navy. There was a black hoodie.

As Nick fished around more he found something. He pulled out what he thought was a black ski hat. As he unfolded it, he saw that it was, in fact, a black balaclava.

CLENARTH QUARRY WAS the location of the Gates's next victim. It had begun as a terraced and open slate pit working from about 1868, with the arrival of the railway. Later, the slate mining moved underground. As Ruth looked up at the long twisting pathways, she could see the quarry was located on the south side of the Dee Valley above Carrog.

The police convoy had stopped in the gravel parking area at the foot of the mountain. Cupping her hands, Ruth lit a ciggie as she watched Nick pull up and park alongside them.

'That's it. Suck in all that fresh air,' Nick quipped as he got out.

'Drake send you to keep an eye on me?' Ruth asked with a smile. She was always glad to see him.

'Something like that. If we get to Snowdon, we need to grill Gates and rule him out as Harvey's killer,' Nick explained.

'Okay ... Gates claims the next victim is at the top of here,' Ruth said, gesturing up the steep track with a withering look.

'Great ... Finish off your cancer stick, and we can get going, eh?' Nick said with a grin.

Given the steep climb, Ruth had been advised that it was dangerous for Gates and PC Harris to climb the hillside handcuffed together. Gates had been uncuffed from Harris and now his hands were cuffed together in front of him. He had protested that if he fell, he would have no way of breaking his fall. No one was interested. Part of Ruth hoped that Gates did fall and break his neck. His relentless mind games had taken their toll, and she just wanted the day to be over. However, she also knew how important it was for the families to find out what had happened to their loved ones.

As the uniformed officers, SOCO and dog handlers assembled, Ruth gazed upwards. It looked like a steep walk and the wind was whining and blustering around her face and ears.

'Right. Let's go, everyone,' Ruth shouted loudly.

The pathways were covered in frost that crunched under their feet. The surrounding bracken was frozen and white. Sheep moved away as they passed by. The winter sun disappeared behind the dark clouds that loomed in from the west and the temperature seemed to drop almost instantly.

Ruth and Nick walked together as the track widened, but the noise of the wind made conversation almost impossible.

Ruth stopped for a moment to get her breath, gazing down at the Dee Valley below them. Thickets were dotted across the rolling countryside and brown paths and tracks dissected the snowy ground. The River Dee itself snaked smoothly through the middle of the valley floor, its bends and straights looking almost symmetrical. It was such a peaceful, tranquil place, Ruth thought. And yet their task was so hideous and full of pain and destruction.

The muscles in her calves were starting to ache a little as they continued their ascent. Up ahead of them, a line of derelict stone quarry buildings bordered the path. A rusted metal track marked where the loaded slate had been carried up and the then empty carts sent down to the quarry to be refilled. It was embedded in a slope of wooden slats that plummeted down the hillside, dropping hundreds of feet. Ruth thought that it looked like the slope of a ski jump she had seen on television for the Winter Olympics. It was covered with ice and snow and looked terrifying.

A pair of peregrine falcons hovered together on the air currents looking down on the group's progress. The birds turned, banked away to the east and disappeared out of sight.

Ruth approached Gates, who had been strangely quiet for an hour. She hoped that he had realised that his attempts at mind games were proving futile and that he had shut up. 'Where are we going from here?'

'Just up here, Ruth. About another two minutes and you'll see,' Gates said with excitement in his voice as if he was going to show them something spectacular.

Nick shot Ruth a dark look and shook his head.

Ruth saw that Gates was looking at the cigarette packet in her pocket.

'I don't suppose those are menthol?' Gates asked.

'No. They're not,' Ruth said, thinking that she wouldn't give him a cigarette anyway.

'Yeah, I only smoke menthol,' Gates muttered under his breath.

A moment later, they reached the summit of the quarry and the ground levelled out. Ruth could see in every direction for miles. She looked down at the other side and the endless stretch of lowlands towards the dark mountains. The drop was steep; it gave her vertigo just looking down.

They stopped close to the steep rail-track. Glancing around at the stone buildings that surrounded them, Ruth looked over at Gates. 'Here?' she asked.

Gates nodded and pointed over at a large stone hut that still had its roof intact. 'Over there. In there.'

Ruth turned to the SOCOs and gestured to the hut. They needed to go in first if it was a crime scene or there were remains. She stamped her feet, trying to get the circulation going in her frozen toes. It was a grisly wait as the SOCO team took out torches and disappeared into the darkness.

Ruth watched as Gates shuffled to keep warm. He began to whistle a Christmas tune with a smile.

Ruth and Nick shot each other a look. They both knew that they would gladly do Gates a lot of physical harm at the moment if they could get away with it.

A SOCO came out of the slate hut and waved. There was something in there for them to see.

Suddenly there was a commotion and Ruth spun to see Gates knocking PC Harris to the ground. Before anyone could react, Gates had sprinted away from them and towards the summit of the mountain and jumped. Gates disappeared out of view and vanished as if he had plummeted off the side of the mountain.

Ruth's heart sank. Gates had committed suicide before revealing all the locations of his victims. And it was her fault he had been out of the handcuffs. *For fuck's sake!* she yelled in her head.

Ruth, Nick and the other officers dashed to the precipice, assuming they would see Gates tumbling to his death down the mountainside.

Instead, they saw that Gates had hit the steep wooden slope and was now skidding downhill on his back on the thick ice and snow. *Oh my God! He's getting away!*

Gates manoeuvred himself into a sitting position, his legs outstretched. With his hands still cuffed together, it was as if he was tobogganing down the hill.

Ruth couldn't believe her eyes. That exit route had not been on the risk assessment. Gates was escaping. She felt paralysed, wondering what to do next.

Nick reacted first. He wouldn't let a monster like Gates get away. He ran, launched himself into the air and hit the icy, wooden slope, banging his left elbow and back hard. Feeling the wind knocked out of him, he gasped for a moment as he skidded down on his back completely out of control. Straightening himself, he tried to sit up as he slid down at increasing speed. The scraping noise of his body and boots skating against the wood got louder as he sped up. He could feel every tiny bump and divot in his back, legs and behind. The ice-cold wind blustered against his face as he drew in breath. Such was the velocity that it was hard to take in air.

Gates was about a hundred yards further down the slope and now close to where it levelled off at ground level.

Wondering what Gates's next move would be, Nick was buoyed by the thought that Gates's hands were cuffed together, which should slow him down. At least in theory.

Up ahead, Gates came off the end of the track, tumbled onto the snowy ground, picked himself up on his elbows and sprinted away, all in one seamless move.

Shit!

Thirty seconds later, Nick flew off the track at speed. He rolled over the uneven ground, clambered to his knees and then his feet, and gave chase. His back and elbows throbbed with pain.

There was an old wire fence in front of them, and beyond that, a stretch of frozen heathland leading across to the snow-capped mountains and deep caves. Gates threw himself over the short fence and dropped heavily down the other side.

'Stop! Police!' Nick shouted to make sure that Gates was fully aware that he was now being pursued.

Gates got up again and glanced back. He wasn't fazed. Nick could see Gates was now getting into his running stride. He had the build and gait of a natural runner as he settled into a rhythm. This wasn't good news.

Nick arrived at the fence, stepped onto the mesh and scaled it easily. A snowy pathway led right and down through the heathland. Gates was running flat out and was already two hundred yards ahead. A dark green sign read: *Public Footpath – Llwybr Cyhoeddus.*

Nick skidded in a shallow hole, twisting his ankle a little. No time to stop or slow. He would run it off. A fence with wooden poles and barbed wire to the left marked out a field where sheep ambled obliviously.

Breathing heavily, Nick was sprinting at full pelt but not making any headway. Gates wasn't slowing or tiring. He must be fitter than he looked.

Crunching through the deepening snow, Nick felt it seep into his boots and soak his socks. He wiped the sweat from his eyes, which were now stinging.

The rocky terrain at the foot of the mountains was only five hundred yards away, and Nick could already see Gates clambering up some rocks. His handcuffs didn't seem to be impeding him in any way.

A stretch of rusty steel fencing marked the end of the heathland. A weathered tractor was parked by stacks of hay bales and an enormous feed shed.

Gates was nowhere to be seen. *Where the hell is he?*

Nick sucked in air as his lungs burnt and his pulse thundered. His eyes scanned around looking for the smallest movement, but the icy wind and sleet hindered his vision. He blinked, trying to clear his eyes.

Then a slight movement from higher up the rocks. A figure emerged from behind a boulder and then disappeared. Gates.

Nick's legs felt heavy as they slipped and lost their footing on the loose rocks leading up to the lower reaches of the mountain. Pulling himself up, Nick got onto the steep, icy pathway.

The sudden noise of rocks falling two hundred yards above him brought his attention hard left. *There's the fucker.* Nick could see Gates moving up ahead of him. Nick zigzagged around the boulder and rocks as he ran up the pathway and picked up speed. Surely the handcuffs would slow Gates down now they were going uphill?

Nick's boots were rubbing painfully and he could feel the sweat running down his back. He reached a level piece of ground and glanced around. *Shit! Lost him again.*

Then he heard a metallic sound he didn't recognise.

Up ahead were steep, damp, moss-covered slopes that were partly hidden by the wild undergrowth. Along the wall was a dark opening, a rusted metal-mesh gate. It was the entrance to an abandoned slate mine. However, there was a small gap in the mesh at the far end. The metallic sound Nick had heard was Gates going through the fence.

Nick saw the sign attached to the mesh fence. *Keep Out! – Cadwch Allan!*

Following Gates through, Nick trod carefully down the rocky pathway that descended into darkness. He stared and squinted into the black. He clicked on his torch.

Stopping for a moment, he craned his neck trying to listen for the smallest sound. Nothing.

Flashing his torch ahead, he could see there were three possible routes down into the mine. There was also a rickety ladder that hung in the darkness. Which way had Gates gone?

Trying to catch his breath, Nick stopped, his hands on his knees. He had no idea of where to go next.

Gates had escaped.

CHAPTER 20

I t was four hours later when Drake entered the incident room and everyone went quiet. They knew he was livid. Ruth had already spent a few minutes debriefing him on how Gates had escaped. However much she dressed it up, it sounded bloody incompetent. Someone should have spotted that there was a possibility of escape down the track. It should have been covered. Drake had avoided eye contact with her, which made it clear that he wasn't happy. There also seemed to be something else troubling him. He just wasn't himself. But at that moment, that was the least of their worries.

'What a fucking shambles!' Drake boomed, his arms folded aggressively. 'The chief constable wants to know how we managed to lose a multiple murderer at the top of a mountain when he was handcuffed and surrounded by ten police officers. I had to tell him that I had no idea, because I don't. And that makes me sound like a twat!'

Ruth squirmed in her chair. Drake rarely lost his temper, and it made everyone uncomfortable. It was definitely out of character.

'The media are all over it. We've even had comments from cabinet ministers.'

'To be fair, boss, we didn't know he would turn into Eddie the Eagle to get away,' Nick said.

Ruth winced. It was an ill-judged comment and there were a few seconds as the tumble-weeds rolled past.

Drake gave him a withering look. 'This is not a time for jokes, DS Evans. No one cares how he got away. We've managed to create the biggest manhunt in North Wales in living memory. We're taking a complete hammering on social media. Frankly, I'm surprised that some of us, including me, have got jobs to come back to tomorrow morning.' There was yet another prolonged silence. 'By tomorrow, we will have Armed Response Units from Merseyside and Greater Manchester helping us. We also have two helicopters from South Wales with thermal imaging cameras to help search Snowdonia Park.'

Ruth knew that Drake would expect her to find Gates. She was the SIO, and she was responsible for taking Gates out to locate his victims' remains. She was in charge and she was therefore accountable. If there had been any chance of his escape, then she should have planned for that. She could not have foreseen the extraordinary way in which Gates had got away – it was like something out of a movie – but that didn't matter. Gates was her responsibility, and if she didn't get him back in custody, her career would be over.

Drake had calmed a little as he sat on a table. 'Right, Ruth, how do we get this bastard back?'

Ruth went over to the computer and Gates's face came up on the screen. 'Andrew Gates, aged forty-five. Suspected of the murder of seven men in the Dee Valley area. Married to Kerry Gates. She has advanced multiple sclerosis and is unable to walk more than a few steps unaided. Gates will be worried about how she is coping without him, so we need round-the-clock surveillance on their home. Gates isn't stupid, but his need to see his wife might mean that he tries to make some kind of contact. We will do that in shifts.' Ruth clicked the mouse and a photo of the house at Pentredwr appeared. 'Gates owns and has access to a property, number four Abbey Terrace, Pentredwr, which is where the remains of some of his victims were found. He'll know that we'll be watching that property. Gates has no money, so I need uniform to report any instances of shoplifting or theft in the area where he escaped, however insignificant they might be. Gates will have to steal if he's going to eat. Luke?'

Merringer looked through his paperwork. 'As far as we know, Gates doesn't have access to a phone or any other technology. If he has no money, he can't get a phone unless he steals one.'

'What about the threat to our wider community?' Drake asked sombrely.

'High. Gates has nothing to lose. He gets a thrill out of killing and he has no reason to stop. We have a criminal psychologist coming in from the university tomorrow morning, but I think she will tell us that Gates is a danger to the public, especially men.'

'Ruth, liaise with the press office. I want a press conference first thing,' Drake said. 'I need him back in custody in the next twenty-four hours. No fucking excuses.'

BY EIGHT O'CLOCK, RUTH and Sian were on the sofa together. They had had a couple of drinks and were sitting in comfortable silence after another taxing day.

Ruth lay back on Sian, put her feet up on the long sofa and gave a sigh.

'Better?' Sian asked.

'Much,' Ruth answered, sipping at her gin and tonic. Even though she was trying to clear her head – or anaesthetise it with gin – she couldn't shake off what Gates had said about Sarah. She was angry with herself for letting him get to her. It felt like a little worm that turned every few minutes, burrowing further into her head.

'Doesn't feel like Christmas yet, does it? Despite the decorations, the tree, the music,' Sian muttered.

'People don't stop doing horrible things to each other just because it's Christmas. If anything, it makes everything worse,' Ruth said. There was always a big spike in crimes like burglary, robbery, domestic violence and assault over the festive period. And that meant police officers were even more stretched.

'You haven't said much about what happened this afternoon,' Sian probed.

'No.' Ruth didn't know if she had the energy.

'You don't have to talk about it.'

'Silver Bells' by Tony Bennett played quietly. The tinkling tune was incongruous with Ruth's dark mood.

'This music is pissing me off,' Ruth admitted.

'Shall I turn it off?' Sian asked.

'No. Just something less cheerful and cheesy. I know it's bah-humbug, but I'm responsible for some bloody maniac being out there, so I'm finding being festive difficult.'

'Oh, well, if you had told me, I would have brought my Smiths and Radiohead compilations,' Sian said with an ironic smile.

'You know what I mean.' Ruth rolled her eyes in amusement.

Sian wandered over to the Bluetooth speaker and looked at her phone to find something else. Soon the laid-back sound of 'When The Morning Comes' began to play.

'Can't beat a bit of Hall and Oates,' Sian said as she dropped back onto the sofa.

They sat in more silence as Ruth's need to share what was whirring around her head got the better of her. A problem shared ...

'It's just ... Gates got to me,' Ruth explained. 'So now I'm angry at myself for letting him.'

'I thought you would be used to all that crap?' Sian said.

'Yeah, me too. I've had old lags threatening all sorts, especially when I was younger. They were going to come and rape me and my mum. Cut my kids' throats in their beds. Nasty pieces of work.'

'So what happened today?'

Ruth was uncomfortable talking about Sarah. Sian had been incredibly supportive and said Ruth should discuss how she felt whenever she needed to. However, Ruth knew it couldn't be easy for Sian to discuss her feelings about a person who Ruth had told others was 'the love of her life.'

'Gates knew all about Sarah. What had happened, and how it had made me feel.'

'How?'

'He'd been reading stuff online. Newspaper articles. If you google my name, that's what pops up.'

'I'm sorry. But remember, Gates knows nothing about you, the real you. He's a very sick, unhappy and disturbed excuse for a human being.'

Ruth nodded. She knew that was true, but it didn't help.

'I know. There's something about Gates that gets under my skin. I've met killers who have murdered out of anger or for revenge. I've met people who have killed for greed or because they have terrible mental health conditions. With Gates, it's the lack of emotion or motive that makes it so chilling. He just doesn't feel anything.'

NICK RUBBED HIS HAND through his beard as he settled back in an armchair and watched as Auntie Pat and his cousin Cerys chatted with Amanda, laughing and screeching. Even though he knew it was very early days, he wanted Auntie Pat and Cerys to be the first people to meet Amanda. They were his family, and it mattered what they thought.

The living room was small and a little cluttered. There were two adults and a baby in a two-bedroom miners' cottage, so it would never be spacious. A white Christmas tree stood behind the sofa, and they had decorated the walls with gold and red tinsel. In a corner, brightly coloured toys, cars and little stuffed animals were stacked neatly. Nick's baby nephew Alex was now fast asleep.

When he and Amanda had first arrived, they had been ushered in and, for a moment, had watched him sleep in his white-painted cot. A moment of peace and joy that felt a little overwhelming. As they tiptoed quietly out of the room, Nick couldn't help but wonder what Amanda would be like as a mother, and then told himself this was not rational thinking.

Nick worried that he was being sucked into a relationship that was out of his control. He hadn't dared tell his sponsor that he and Amanda were seeing each other. He had known sponsors to sack their sponsees for not doing as they were told or not doing the right thing.

He caught sight of a picture of Auntie Pat and Uncle Mike on their wedding day tucked out of sight at one end of the mantelpiece. He hadn't told Amanda about Uncle Mike or how he had died two years earlier. It was still a difficult subject for him to discuss.

'Here you go, love,' Pat said, handing Nick a cup of tea from a tray.

'Ta,' Nick said, taking the mug. It was hot.

'Now, are you sure you don't want anything, Amanda?' Pat said as she took two small glasses of white wine for her and Cerys.

'I'm fine. Honestly,' Amanda said.

'Go on ... We've got plenty of wine,' Cerys said.

'I don't drink on school nights,' Amanda said with a smile.

They laughed.

Nick raised his mug. 'And every night's a school night for me.'

Cerys shot him a look and indicated Amanda.

'Oh God, Amanda knows all about my drinking. We had to get that out of the way early on,' Nick explained.

'I don't really drink anyway. Doesn't bother me,' Amanda said, looking at Nick. He knew it might not be the time to explain that they were both alcoholics.

'He's doing so well, isn't he?' Pat said with a proud smile.

'God, I remember the first time Nick ever had a drink,' Cerys said with a grin.

'Oh, really ....' Nick rolled his eyes as Pat started to laugh.

'He had been drinking cider and eating peanuts with John next door. He came back hammered in just his skimpy white underpants, went into the bathroom and pebble dashed the whole wall! Disgusting!'

Amanda laughed with Pat and Cerys.

'Thanks, Cerys. That's an image that Amanda really needed in her head,' Nick said with a wry smile.

'You're welcome, cuz.'

An hour later, Nick and Amanda were sitting in his car outside her house. He turned off the radio and the wind whistled through the car.

'Alex is beautiful, isn't he?' Amanda said.

Nick grinned at her in the darkness. 'Yeah. It's genetic.'

Amanda laughed and shook her head. 'You really are a twat.'

'Charming,' Nick said smiling and then leaned over and kissed her.

'You do know that despite your twat-ishness, I'm falling for you,' Amanda said.

'Is "twat-ishness" even a word?' Nick said as a way of skirting what she had said.

Amanda looked directly at him with a frown. 'Is that it?'

'If I say "I've fallen for you too" then I sound like a prize nob.'

'I think that ship has sailed, Nick.'

'But just so you know, I fell for you the first time we ever kissed,' Nick said.

CHAPTER 21

Ruth looked out at the press conference with some trepidation. Journalists from around the country were clamouring over Gates's case and the hunt for his whereabouts. The room was bustling with local and national newspapers, radio and television. Ruth could feel the nerves in her stomach. Behind them was a banner on the wall: *Heddlu Gogledd Cymru – North Wales Police, Gogledd Cymru diogelach – A Safer North Wales.* The irony of the slogan wasn't lost on Ruth. In the last twenty-four hours, they had created a far more dangerous North Wales. There was also a large map of North Wales with various locations along the Dee Valley marked with red plastic pins.

On the table in front of Ruth was a jug of water, glasses and several small tape recorders and microphones that eager journalists had placed there.

'Good afternoon, I'm Detective Inspector Ruth Hunter and I am the senior investigating officer on the Andrew Gates case. I want to update you on developments in the last twenty-four hours. Our primary concern at the moment is the safety of the public in North Wales, in particular the Snowdonia Park area.' Ruth took a moment and sipped her water. Now she had started, her nerves were under control. 'Andrew Gates escaped from police custody while taking officers to the site where we believed that he had buried one of his victims. All measures and precautions had been taken with regards to Andrew Gates's security and it was an extraordinary set of circumstances that led to his escape. Our thoughts are with the families of the victims of these horrific crimes at what must be a very difficult time.'

Ruth looked up to see Drake enter at the back of the room. He gave her a supportive nod and his appearance settled her. She was glad that Superintendent Jones hadn't shown his face. He was a spineless politico, and she didn't have much time for him.

Clearing her throat, Ruth continued. 'We are absolutely committed to finding Andrew Gates and we are using every resource available to us to bring our search to a conclusion as quickly as possible. There are currently a number of operations underway in the Snowdonia area. For obvious reasons, I am unable to explain where or what those operations are.'

For the next five minutes, Ruth continued to update the press on the developments of Gates's case before opening up the conference to questions, which she was dreading.

A young male journalist at the front of the room indicated he wanted to ask a question and Ruth nodded in his direction. 'Jonathan Holmes, Daily Express. Can you explain to our readers how Andrew Gates, a dangerous, violent killer, was allowed to escape even though, from what I understand, there were ten officers from the North Wales Police with him? That seems extremely negligent and has put the general public in danger.'

'I'm not at liberty to give details of Andrew Gates's escape yesterday. However, the incident will be investigated thoroughly. We have also voluntarily referred this to the Independent Office for Police Conduct and we will fully cooperate with their independent investigation and any rulings.' Ruth knew this wasn't what the journalist was looking for, but no one was going to tell the press how Gates had got away.

Ruth pointed to a middle-aged television journalist who was standing towards the back of the room. 'Katie Lawton, BBC News. Can you tell us what resources you have available in the search for Andrew Gates and whether you believe they are adequate?'

Ruth nodded as she began. 'We have over a hundred police officers working on this case at the moment. We have received resources, in terms of officers, vehicles and expertise, from Merseyside, Greater Manchester, Cheshire and Shropshire Police Forces. I would like to thank my colleagues from across the country for their ongoing support.'

Ruth fielded a few more questions and then thanked the assembled media.

By the time she got back to CID, Ruth was exhausted. She needed a ciggie and coffee.

There was a note on her desk that Steven Flaherty had called and left a message to ring him. He was her liaison officer at the Met dealing with Sarah's disappearance. Flaherty was a kind man who had never given up hope that they would find out what had happened.

Each time there was a message or any kind of contact from him, Ruth's heart would leap. She wouldn't let herself believe that Sarah could ever be found alive, but she prayed for something concrete about the events that day.

Ruth dialled the number and tried to remain calm. Her hopes had been dashed too many times before. 'Steven, it's Ruth Hunter,' she said.

'Hi, Ruth. Thanks for getting back to me. It's nothing earth-shattering, but we've had a message from Dorset Police. Someone fitting Jurgen Kessler's description tried to get a job at Bournemouth University. He had fake certificates, but someone thought there was something wrong with the passport. When he was challenged, he disappeared,' Flaherty explained.

'Have they got the passport?' Ruth asked. It could be very useful.

'Yes. They've lifted a fingerprint from it and sent it to the police in Berlin to match against Kessler's.'

'What about CCTV?' Ruth asked.

'There's something from the car park and the corridor. I'll have a look and let you know as soon as I can,' Flaherty said.

'Thanks, Steven.'

'I'm sorry it's not more. And I'll call you in the next few days. Okay?'

Ruth felt a little deflated. She always did, but she had to console herself with some progress. The other question that now rattled around her head – why had Kessler decided to hide out in the UK?

GATES HAD SPENT THE night sleeping in a shed at the end of a large garden in the village of Carrog. It had been freezing, but he had managed to find an old sleeping bag. It smelt of damp earth and wood, but he didn't care.

The house was detached, modern and large. Gates could see the occupants were affluent. And for him, affluent was just what he needed. He had spent the last hour watching a well-dressed, middle-aged woman come and go from the double garage. She had swept away snow and replenished the bird table with seeds.

Overnight, Gates had conceded that he would not be able to stay on the run for ever. One day he would get caught or killed. It was just a matter of how long. In his head, he had imagined being interviewed on a television documentary. Something you might find on Netflix these days. It would be a male interviewer – intelligent, thoughtful and keen to understand. He had imagined and rehearsed the questions they would ask him as he drifted in and out of sleep on the wooden floor of the shed.

He could see the television cameras and lights that had been set up to record the interview in his prison. The camera crew and director watching him as they waited for the interview to begin.

> Interviewer: So, Andrew, the question that gets asked the most about the types of crimes that you committed is why? Why did you feel the need to murder seven innocent young men?

> Gates: I think as a child I felt very alone and abandoned. After my father left us, I was effectively brought up by my grandfather, my taid, for a time.

But he died in front of me when I was eight years old.

Interviewer: I've read that you felt that this was a pivotal moment in your life and the way you developed?

Gates: Yes. I stayed with my taid's body for the whole day. I was just looking after him. And even though he was dead, I didn't feel alone or scared because his spirit, his being, was still with me.

Interviewer: There are other things as you grew up that you believe had a profound influence on your character?

Gates: Yes. My mother was very cold and suffocating. It was just me and her, and she seemed to be scared for me to do anything by myself. So I felt that I had very little control as a child or as a teenager. Maybe those feelings became mixed with my confusion about my sexuality. Doing what I did gave me complete control for those moments and I found that sexually very exciting and liberating.

Interviewer: Were you, therefore, attracted to the men that you murdered?

Gates: Very much so. And my control over whether they lived or died was a very addictive feeling. And once they were dead, I just wanted to keep them with me for as long as possible. Sometimes that meant just keeping a part of them. But I believed that by doing this, I had part of their soul, their being, with me at all times.

Gates was familiar with Carrog. It was a village in Denbighshire, a few miles from where he had made his escape. It lay within the parish of Llansanffraid Glyndyfrdwy and took its modern name from the Great Western Railway station on the opposite bank of the River Dee.

He looked at the scratches and bruises on his forearms. He was covered with minor injuries but he didn't care. He was desperate to get the handcuffs off, for starters, and had identified the garage as a place he could do that. He just needed the right moment when he could slip out of the shed unnoticed, through the hedgerows and bushes, and into the double garage where he assumed there would be tools.

Ten minutes later, Gates saw his opportunity. The woman's mobile phone rang, and she answered it and went inside the house, talking loudly about a Christmas recipe she needed to find for the caller. Moving quickly on his toes, Gates was inside the garage thirty seconds later and rooting around for tools. Bolt cutters were too much to hope for. Then he spotted a metal hacksaw. It might take a few minutes, but it would cut through the link between the cuffs for starters.

Trying to avoid slipping and cutting himself, Gates cut the metal enough for him to break the link between the cuffs. He would keep the hacksaw and try to get the cuffs off later. It was such a relief to be able to move his arms properly.

He swung and bent them, trying to stretch out the muscles. *That's better,* he thought as the feeling returned to his shoulders.

Looking around the garage, a white Volvo C90 4x4 sat in the main part of the room. That would be perfect, Gates thought to himself.

A noise interrupted Gates's train of thought. He glanced over and saw the middle-aged woman coming into the garage. She was distracted and didn't see him at first. She had a black labrador beside her. The labrador sensed his presence and strained at the leash for a moment. Gates held his breath and froze. Opening the tailgate, the woman clicked her fingers, and the dog jumped in and sniffed in Gates's direction.

'Good girl,' the woman said as she closed the tailgate with a slam.

Grabbing a long screwdriver off the workbench, he moved towards her. She had a handbag over her shoulder and as she locked the garage door to the house behind her, Gates guessed that she was going out.

In a split second, Gates moved behind her, his arm locked around her throat as he pressed the screwdriver to her neck. The labrador began to bark in the car.

'I'm not going to hurt you if you do exactly as I say. If you don't, I will kill you right here. Do you understand?' Gates could feel the woman shaking with terror as she nodded her head.

Gates slowly released his grip, came around the front, grabbed her by the hair and pushed the screwdriver hard against the skin at the side of her neck again. The labrador scratched noisily at the glass at the back of the car and barked.

'What- what do you ... w-want?' the woman stammered.

'Car keys. Then your purse. And phone,' Gates said in a relaxed voice. 'Please ...' He was enjoying himself and he knew that with a car, money and a phone, he had a good chance of making his escape out of the area, even if it wasn't for long.

The woman fumbled in her handbag but she was shaking too much. Gates let her hair go in frustration, grabbed the bag and poured its contents onto the concrete garage floor.

'Please, I have ... six ... grandchildren.' The woman bent down, gathered up the keys, purse and phone, and handed them to Gates.

'PIN number for your phone and bank cards.'

'They're all the same number,' the woman said.

Gates pulled a face. 'Not very secure. You're not meant to do that. What is it?'

'One-nine, three-four,' she said.

'1934? As in the year? What happened in 1934,' Gates asked, intrigued.

The woman looked at him as though he was mad. 'My father was born.'

'Right. Makes sense. You do know that if your PIN number is not one-nine, three-four, I will be back and I will kill you and whoever lives here in your sleep,' Gates said nonchalantly.

The woman nodded. 'I'm not ... lying. I promise.'

Gates clicked the car key, the indicators blinked as it automatically unlocked. He then turned to face the woman.

'Okay. I want you to face that wall and count to a hundred as I drive away. Do not look up before you get to a hundred. Understood?' Gates said as though he was running a children's party.

The woman looked at him and turned towards the back wall of the garage, still shaking with fear. The labrador's barks had turned from angry growls to more anxious whimpers.

'Are your eyes closed?' Gates asked.

'Yes ...'

'You can start counting,' Gates said and waited a moment. 'Now!' he snapped.

'One, two, three, four ...' the woman whispered.

Gates grabbed a steel spade that he had spotted earlier, swung it and cracked the woman across the back of the skull, hard. She crumpled and fell in a heap. He wasn't sure whether he had knocked her unconscious, put her in a coma or killed her. And frankly, he didn't care.

Ten minutes later, Gates was driving along the A5 towards Llangollen with Christmas songs playing on the radio. The sense of total freedom he felt was overwhelming. No one knew where he was. The labrador had laid down in the boot and stopped making any noise.

And then his mind turned to what was next on the agenda. He needed to save one more young man, at least. Release his soul and his being from the pain of being alive. Like an addict craving his next fix, Gates could feel the excitement growing. The elation of the power, that feeling of total superiority and control combined with a sexual thrill, was overwhelming. It was better than any drug he could ever imagine.

I need to kill again.

CHAPTER 22

It was twelve o'clock when Nick saw the first signs to Bethesda, where Carol Chivers lived. Knowing that David Chivers had four daughters, Nick needed to see if they had alibis for the time of Harvey Pearson's murder. If they knew that Harv had been intimidating and threatening their ageing father, it would give them motive to attack him. Nick had also already established that the attack was likely to have been carried out by more than one person. Moving Harv's body behind the rock would also have been almost impossible for a lone killer. And witnesses had spotted a group of four middle-aged women on Snowdon on the afternoon of the murder. The hypothesis was that they had followed Harvey and Jack Pearson to the mountain. When Jack had left Harvey alone on Miners' Track, the daughters had made their move. Maybe they had just meant to warn Harv off? Things got out of hand and he ended up being pushed or falling down the ravine. They had strangled him to cover themselves and hidden his body.

Nick could see the sun trying to burn through the grey clouds that lay still across the sky. To his right, he looked over to see Llyn Ogwen, a spectacular ribbon lake that ran alongside the A5. It lay between the two mountain ranges of the Carneddau and the Glyderau and stood at the head of the Nant Ffrancon Pass, four miles from the village of Bethesda.

It was another lake that claimed to be the final resting place of the sword of Excalibur.

Ten minutes later, Nick walked along an uneven, stony track towards a small cottage off the main road through the village. An inquisitive ewe with a muddy coat looked up at him and scuttled away. *Charming*, Nick thought to himself. The path to the front door was potholed with ice. From somewhere, a dog barked aggressively, and it seemed to echo all around.

Carol Chivers answered the door and invited him inside. She was small, with a brunette bob, and a little frumpy. Nick followed her into the kitchen and sat at the long wooden table. He spotted half a dozen bottles of homemade gooseberry wine and a bottle of scotch with only an inch left. That was the thing with being an alcoholic, you were always hyperaware of booze; who was drinking what and where drink was kept. Nick would watch in amazement as people in restaurants left half a glass of wine at the end of the meal. It made little sense to him.

Sitting down on a hard wooden chair with arms, Nick tried to settle himself and took out his notebook. Carol stood by the cooker as the blue gas flame flickered under the kettle before bringing it to a boil.

'Miss Chivers ...' Nick clicked his pen.

'Carol,' she corrected him.

Nick didn't know if she had ever been married. There were no signs that anyone else lived in the cottage and no evidence of kids or grandchildren.

'Could you tell me your whereabouts on Sunday the ninth of December?' Nick said.

Carol came over and handed him a mug of tea. He noticed that the mug was chipped and stained. He might give the tea a miss.

Carol went over to a paper calendar and looked at the date. 'I was here. All day, by the looks of it.'

'Can anyone verify that?' Nick asked.

Carol shrugged. 'I don't think so. Why?'

'You have three sisters, is that right, Carol?' Nick asked.

'Yes. I'm the eldest,' she explained.

'And they all live in the area, is that right?'

Carol took her tea and sat down at the end of the table. 'Yes. Isn't this to do with all the stuff that's been happening with my father? That's why I thought you were here?'

'I am looking into the phone calls and the prowler that your father reported.'

'Good, good. He's been scared to death. He has high blood pressure, so it's been a nightmare for his health,' Carol said as she wrapped her fingers around her mug. Nick noticed that she didn't wear any jewellery, not even earrings.

'Do you have any idea why someone would target your father?' Nick asked.

Carol paused for a moment as she sipped her tea. There was a faint look of something that Nick couldn't pin down but also couldn't ignore. 'Please, Carol. You need to tell me anything that would help us in this investigation, whatever it is.'

'My father is not a popular man. And he certainly wasn't well-liked in the thirty or so years that he taught at St Patrick's,' Carol revealed reluctantly.

The comment seemed to hang in the air for a moment. Nick wasn't surprised but he had assumed that the Chivers family would close ranks regarding David's past behaviour.

'Why do you think that was?' Nick asked, although he had a good idea what type of man David Chivers had been.

'He was old-fashioned. And he was a disciplinarian. In his later years as a teacher, that approach was seen as outdated.'

'Would you have described him as a bully?' Nick asked.

'No, not really. He was just a man from a different generation. He was born during the Second World War. That was a long time ago,' Carol said defensively.

Nick looked at his notes for a moment. Reading between the lines, Nick thought that David Chivers had been a bully and even violent with the students. If he had been like that with Harvey Pearson, it might explain Harvey's scars, unhappiness and his confessed hatred of Chivers. It wouldn't be a leap for Harv to have targeted Chivers out of revenge. Whether that had escalated to murder on Mount Snowdon was another matter.

'We're also investigating a murder that took place on Mount Snowdon on Sunday the ninth of December,' Nick explained.

'Yes, I saw something about that on the news, but I wasn't paying attention. What does that have to do with my father?' Carol asked in a worried voice.

'The victim was a former pupil at St Patrick's. Your father was his teacher and his housemaster. Harvey Pearson. It was in the early nineties.'

Carol gave him a quizzical look. 'Harvey Pearson?'

'Did you know him?'

Carol nodded. 'Yes. That's terrible. How awful.' She was clearly shocked by the news.

'How did you know Harvey Pearson?' Nick asked.

'My sisters and I all went to St Patrick's. And we lived on-site too. It was one of the benefits of being a teacher there,' Carol explained.

'So did you know Harvey well?' Nick asked.

'Fairly well. He went out with my sister Claire for a year or two when they were teenagers.'

The manhunt for Gates was in full swing. Every national newspaper was covering the unfolding story, and Ruth could feel the growing scrutiny and pressure they were all under. Gazing down at her phone, she looked at the *Mirror*'s headline: *Killer On The Run – serial killer escapes in North Wales. How?* Gates's escape was a PR disaster for everyone.

Ruth had arrived in CID at dawn. After a mountain of paperwork, a pot of strong coffee and two cigarettes, she had wandered down to Drake's office. They were due to have an early meeting with Jones.

Spotting Drake at his desk, she saw that he was looking into space and lost in thought.

'Morning, boss,' Ruth said as she tapped lightly at his door.

'Oh, Ruth. Yes. Miles away,' Drake said, sitting up and rubbing his hand over his face. He looked tired.

'We've got a meeting with the super,' Ruth said.

'Yeah. Perfect start to the day,' Drake said sardonically. 'Give me five minutes, and I'll be with you.'

Ruth nodded. 'Boss.' She walked away, thought for a moment and then turned. 'Are you okay, boss? It's none of my business, and I'm not the world's greatest detective, but you don't seem yourself?'

Drake paused. Ruth wondered if she had crossed a line. Drake was usually a closed book when it came to anything personal.

'It's Cathy,' Drake said almost inaudibly. Cathy was his wife. 'She's had some tests and they think she might have breast cancer. Nothing definite yet.'

'I'm sorry to hear that, boss,' Ruth said. No wonder it had been affecting him.

'Could be nothing. But there's a family history of it,' Drake said.

'It's difficult not knowing,' Ruth said.

'Yeah, it is.'

'If you ever need a chat, boss ...' Ruth said with an empathetic smile. She meant it.

'Thanks, Ruth. Appreciate that. By the way – the cock-up with Gates aside – you're a bloody good detective,' Drake said and then looked at his watch. 'Better go see what Captain Marvel wants.' The irony of the nickname wasn't lost on either of them.

THE MEETING WITH JONES was thankfully brief. He informed them that they had drafted the North West Air Support Unit in from Greater Manchester to scour Snowdonia. Their helicopters had 'night sun' equipment that could light up an area the size of a football pitch from seven hundred metres. The terrain of Snowdonia was tough and difficult to search, and both dog units and mounted police units were being used because they could search areas where vehicles couldn't go. There was also talk of getting the SAS, who trained in the area, to help track Gates down. According to Jones, it was the biggest UK manhunt since the Raoul Moat case in 2010.

At eleven o'clock, Ruth made her way to Interview Room One. She was meeting Professor Jane Douglas, a criminal psychologist and profiler from Llancastell University. Professor Douglas had worked for many years at University College London's Centre for Criminal Psychology and profiled criminals for various UK police forces.

Ruth wanted to know if Gates's next move could be predicted. His mind didn't work in the same way as a rational person so she hoped Professor Douglas could provide an insight into where Gates would hide and what he would do next.

With greying hair tied up in a neat bun, Professor Douglas wore a long camel-coloured cardigan and brown skirt. Presumably to hide the fact she was overweight, but it wasn't really working.

Ruth gave her all the background information that they had on Gates and showed her some of the interview he had given at Llancastell Police Station. She also mentioned Gates's research and knowledge of Sarah's disappearance, mainly because it had unnerved her so much.

Douglas was a cold fish and keen to let Ruth know that she should be honoured to be benefitting from her considerable experience.

'Why does Gates murder?' Ruth asked. She needed to know, as she did for any criminal investigation, what the motive was. For Gates, it just wasn't obvious due to his psychological make-up. Most crimes were motivated by rage, jealousy, revenge or money. She had already concluded that Gates's motives were a complicated mix of psycho-sexual factors.

'I would suggest that Andrew Gates has some internalised feelings of hostility, low self-esteem and self-pity. Despite his heterosexual marriage, his chronic inability to form social relationships and his frustrated, latent homosexual desires manifest themselves in these murders.'

'So, Gates is homosexual?' Ruth asked.

'Yes. But somewhere along the line, he has formed the idea that homosexuality is shameful, disgusting and even immoral. It's likely that this stems from childhood. The murders resulted from a pent-up sexual aggression. He killed those men because he wanted to kill the source of his homosexual attraction to them. In killing them, he killed what he hated in himself,' Professor Douglas explained.

Even though Ruth had taken an instant dislike to Professor Douglas, her shrewd analysis of Gates, his psychology and motives was impressive.

'What about the body we found almost intact on the sofa at his home?' Ruth asked.

'That's about his desire and need to have power and control. Andrew Gates has had very little control or power throughout his life. The ultimate power is to kill, and the ultimate control is to possess the body, to do what you want with it. Mixed up somewhere in his psyche is a dangerous connection between sex and death. So he now gets huge sexual pleasure from controlling and then killing.'

Ruth nodded. 'He keeps the bodies so he can, for want of a better word, play with them?'

'Effectively, yes. But there's also a desire for companionship. Andrew Gates has kept his homosexuality a secret from the world for the whole of his life. That would have made him very lonely. In his head, having the company of a gay man, dead or alive, gave him some peace of mind, as well as the sexual thrill of the kill.'

'Does that mean it's likely that he will kill again?' Ruth asked, although she thought she knew the answer.

'Almost certainly. Andrew Gates is like any addict now. The compulsion to murder will be overwhelming,' Professor Douglas said in a detached tone. *That's intellectuals for you,* Ruth thought to herself.

'So he will be hunting for another victim?' Ruth asked. That would rule out Gates heading into the wilds of Snowdonia to hide. He would need to head for the centres of population and that was worrying.

'Yes. He won't be able to help himself. And he's arrogant enough to go into towns, cities or any populated areas, not caring if he is caught.'

'Anything else that might help us?' Ruth asked. She was under increasing time pressure to find Gates.

'His wife ...?' Professor Douglas said as though the thought had just occurred to her.

'Kerry,' prompted Ruth.

'Kerry. I suspect that he will try to make contact with her. She seems to be the only emotional bond he has ever made in his life. He probably doesn't see her as his wife, but more like his child to be looked after and protected. He will worry about how she is going to survive and he will need to see her.'

'We have round-the-clock surveillance on their home,' explained Ruth.

'That might not stop him. He thinks he is superior to everyone, especially the police. However, he seems to have made a connection with you.'

This was unsettling news for Ruth. 'Should I be worried?'

Professor Douglas thought before answering, which did little to allay Ruth's fears. 'I'm afraid to say, yes, possibly. I am worried about the conversation you had with him about your missing partner. He seems to have taken an unnatural interest in you and your life.'

'How might that manifest itself?' Ruth asked, feeling anxious.

'He might try to do something to get your attention.' Professor Douglas looked at Ruth. 'Or he might try to reach out to you directly.'

HAVING DEVOURED A SANDWICH in about thirty seconds flat, Nick realised that he was only a mile or so outside Llanberis. As he slowed for the speed-limit sign, he could feel the bread sticking in his chest and massaged it. He swigged on his Diet Coke, which seemed to do the trick. Not that long ago Nick would have been swigging wine or vodka on a trip like this.

However many times he came here, Nick loved this part of Snowdonia. The way the twin lakes of Llyn Padarn and Llyn Peris cut through the mountain range and then created the Llanberis Pass. The rolling, desolate landscape scarred with disused slate mines.

As Shakin' Stevens's 'Merry Christmas Everyone' played on the radio, Nick looked at his Google Maps app. He had tracked down Claire Sinclair, formerly Claire Chivers, daughter of David and sister of Carol. She worked in the Llanberis Outdoor Education Activity Centre. Knowing that many people used Llanberis as a base for climbing Snowdon, it wouldn't be a stretch for Claire to have extensive knowledge of the mountain.

Nick soon found the busy activity centre, which was a hive of noise. Claire Sinclair was guiding and supporting a group of noisy teenagers in harnesses and an assortment of coloured safety helmets on high ropes and poles between a series of tall trees. He couldn't believe that anyone would be up climbing trees and ropes in this weather.

'Mrs Sinclair?' Nick asked as he showed her his warrant card.

'Yes?' Claire replied with a smile. She was wearing a bright-blue safety helmet and had ropes around her waist and her gloved hands.

'Bit chilly?' Nick asked, gesturing to the teens who were shouting and laughing and generally having a great time.

'We're booked all year round,' Claire explained with a smile. She was pretty in a cute sort of way.

Nick asked her virtually the same questions as he asked her sister, Carol. And it was then that she threw a spanner into Nick's growing theory about Harv's murder.

'Oh yes. I know exactly where I was on that Sunday. It was the day after my husband's fortieth birthday bash. We were with all his friends and family in a pub in Wem, down in Shropshire.'

Nick immediately knew that there would be plenty of witnesses, so that effectively ruled Claire out of being on Snowdon that afternoon.

'But you do remember Harvey Pearson?' Nick asked.

'Yes, of course. Harvey and I went out for a bit when we were thirteen and fourteen. Nothing serious,' Claire explained.

'Had you seen him since then?' Nick asked.

'I bumped into him at a wedding a couple of years ago. He was very drunk and not making much sense. That's the last time I saw him ... It's so horrible that he's been killed.' Claire said as her brow furrowed at the thought.

Back in the CID office later, Nick looked at a report that uniformed officers had taken from the third sister, Emily Williams, formerly Emily Chivers. She was a little vague about her whereabouts but thought that she had been Christmas shopping in Llancastell until six that evening.

Feeling that the investigation into Harv's death had stalled a little, Nick knew he needed to confirm the whereabouts of the final sister that day. However, as a hypothesis, it was looking like a non-starter.

Nick was back to square one.

CHAPTER 23

By two o'clock, Ruth and the rest of CID had received the breaking news of Gates's assault on Gwenda Chadwick in Carrog. Gwenda had a suspected fractured skull but had been conscious long enough to describe her assailant to uniformed officers. As soon as the metal cuffs on his wrists were mentioned, the officers knew it had to be Gates.

Gates had got away with Ms Chadwick's new white Volvo C90, along with her bank cards and phone. Everything was now being checked with a huge sense of urgency. Ruth could feel the growing tension amongst the detectives as they waited to see if, where and when Gates had used the bank cards or phone.

Within half an hour, Ruth sat down with Superintendent Jones and Drake. Jones was portly and bald except for the silly wisps of hair around his ears. Since her arrival in North Wales Police, Ruth had seen Jones for what he was. An arse-covering, rank-climbing policeman who was often too frightened to make a decision until it was too late.

Drake shifted in his seat and picked up his coffee. 'At least Gates is out in the open and moving. He's far more likely to be spotted or make a mistake.'

Ruth nodded. 'Yeah, if Gates went to ground in Snowdonia, he would be bloody difficult to find.'

Jones nodded but Ruth knew he wasn't listening. 'I know you guys are doing everything you can. And I have complete faith in both your abilities.'

Drake shot Ruth a blank look but she knew what he was thinking. Jones would throw either of them or both under the bus if it would further his career.

'I'm getting pressure from the chief constable,' Jones continued. 'He's worried about the impact the escape is having on the public confidence in North Wales Police. The media office is being deluged.'

Ruth knew that wasn't the problem. Jones was ambitious and Gates's escape was a serious blot on his career. It was on Jones's watch, after all, and no one would care about the minutiae of how it had happened. That was the politics of modern policing.

Ruth returned to her office to find that the National Police Air Service had scrambled a black and yellow pursuit helicopter EC145 from Hawarden Airport. Another helicopter was on its way from Manchester. Drake would coordinate the manhunt from Llancastell CID.

Ruth looked at the map of North Wales on her screen and then sat back for a moment. She could feel the tension in her shoulders and her neck. She pushed back her shoulder blades to see if she could get rid of the stiffness. However, the spectre of Gates, his escape and his unhealthy interest in her life loomed ominously, as if physically weighing her down. Ruth widened the map on her computer screen and took a swig of cold coffee. She needed caffeine and didn't care. If Professor Douglas was correct, Gates could head east from Carrog towards his home and his wife, Kerry. He could also have been travelling towards the towns of North East Wales. Going South or West would have just taken him into the sparsely populated parts of Snowdonia Park and that didn't fit his MO. Ruth thought that Gates would avoid the A5 as it was a major route east. Therefore, Armed Response vehicles were trawling the other roads that came out of Snowdonia's eastern borders. ANPR cameras were also being manned as they scrutinised traffic with the aid of computer recognition.

Drake came over and looked into her office.

'We've got something!' he said excitedly. Drake was unusually energised. He was normally the epitome of calm but the national scale of the manhunt was getting even to him.

Ruth sat up and looked at him. 'What is it?'

'Gwenda Chadwick's car was fitted with a GPS tracker. We've got a location on the car. It's been stationary for twenty minutes. I'll show you where.' He gestured for her to follow him with urgency.

Ruth got up and she and Drake walked over to the main screen in the incident room that was now showing the 'active map' of North Wales. A small red digital pin showed where the Volvo was located.

Ruth nodded. It could be the break that they needed. 'Where is that?' Ruth asked as she studied the map.

'It's just out by Moel Siabod. Basically, it's the middle of nowhere.'

Moel Siabod was a solitary mountain, isolated from all the other enormous peaks of Snowdonia in its own space to the north of the park.

Merringer came into the incident room and pointed up to the digital map. 'Boss, there's a series of disused agricultural buildings here on the track where the car is located. And this here is an old smelting house.'

'Maybe Gates is trying to get shelter and hide out for the night?' Ruth suggested, thinking out loud.

'Is there a shop or a petrol station near there?' Drake asked.

Merringer shook his head. 'Not in walking distance, boss, no.'

'What about the bank cards?'

'Nothing yet,' Merringer shrugged. The bank had been told in no uncertain terms not to cancel Gwenda Chadwick's cards. They needed Gates to use them in shops or cash machines to track his movements. If he found it wasn't working, then that would shut down that possibility. But Ruth knew that Gates might be smart enough to know that.

Ruth pointed up to the map. 'We need an ARV to block off this track at the top, boss.'

Drake nodded. 'Take as many AROs with you as you need. And we need AROs either side of this track in case Gates makes a break cross-country. I want a dog unit on both sides to be safe.'

'We've got two helicopters out on Snowdonia,' Merringer said, thinking out loud.

'Luke, contact Air Support. Tell them to keep well away from the area but to be on standby if Gates makes a move. I don't want anything spooking him.' Drake thought for a moment and then pointed at the map. 'And we need marksmen here. If Gates tries to escape, we need someone to shoot and kill him. I don't want that psycho on the loose and taking any more lives.'

THE WINTER SUN WAS dropping low towards the horizon as Ruth and other officers from Llancastell CID moved into positions overlooking the disused farm buildings. She immediately spotted the white Volvo C90 parked to one side. The intel had been correct. It looked very likely that Gates was inside. Her stomach was tense and adrenaline pumped hard through her veins. This was a world away from the armed operations on the stinking stairwells of Peckham's violent and drug-infested estates. However, the feeling in the pit of her stomach was just the same.

The late-afternoon sky flared an incredible flamingo-pink and the wind off the nearby mountains was bitter on her face and ears. Behind the buildings, at 2,600 feet, loomed the grey and purple peaks of Moel Siabod, the highest point in the Moelwynion mountain range.

As Ruth moved forwards, she was accompanied by AROs dressed in their black Nomex boots, gloves, and Kevlar helmets over balaclavas. Carrying Glock 9mm pistols, the AROs moved purposefully behind some old, rusty farm machinery. Their movements were well-rehearsed. ARO training was repetitive, thorough and precise.

Ruth adjusted the thick stab vest that she and the other CID detectives were all wearing. It was too small, or maybe she was putting on weight. No one was taking any chances with Gates. He had committed multiple murders and had nothing to lose by killing someone else today. She motioned silently for the CID officers and the AROs to begin heading for the farm buildings, guns trained on the weather-worn doors and broken windows.

Ruth murmured into her radio, 'Three-six to Gold Command. Officers in position two at target location, over.'

The radio crackled back. 'Three-six received. Units to proceed to position one, over.'

Ruth gestured and the officers moved quietly over the final few yards of icy grass and gravel, which crunched under their feet. There were two large wooden doors at the front of the main building that had been padlocked closed. Ruth noticed that the padlock was rusty and looked like it had been there for years. If Gates was in the building, he hadn't come in this way.

Ruth motioned and four AROs moved away from them, heading for the sides and back of the building. Then two AROs stepped forwards with what they liked to call 'The Enforcer,' a steel battering ram that would knock the door open in one hit.

Ruth clicked her radio. 'Three-six to Gold Command. All units are at position one.'

There was an anxious moment as they waited and then, 'Three-six received. Gold Command order is go.'

Ruth nodded at the AROs and moved back against the grey stone wall. It was cold and hard, even with the vest on. Where was Gates? Was he lying in wait or was he oblivious to the operation?

Bang! Ruth flinched as the doors smashed open with an almighty crash and the AROs moved in, weapons trained in front of them.

'Armed police!' they bellowed as they stormed into the building. 'Armed police!'

Ruth followed, her heart pounding in her chest. She scanned left and right into the darkness of the building. Were they going to have to play a tense game of hide and seek to smoke Gates out?

The building smelt damp and musty, and the floor was covered with straw and dry mud. As the wind picked up outside, the roof timbers creaked with an eerie groan. Ruth continued moving, heart thumping, eyes searching left and right for any movement. CID officers and AROs had fanned out throughout the building, clearing the stalls.

'Armed Police!' the AROs bellowed as they moved on through.

Ruth's heart started to sink. There was nothing. Gates was nowhere to be found and there weren't any places left to hide.

Merringer appeared at her side and shook his head. 'Nothing here, boss.'

'Shit!' Ruth muttered to herself. She told herself that Gates could still be in an outbuilding on the other side of the yard, but the AROs would have swept through that in seconds. She would have heard something.

Ruth looked up as a senior ARO came through the main doors. 'You need to come and see this, ma'am,' he said with a serious tone.

With her mind racing, Ruth followed the ARO across the yard towards a small stone outbuilding with a flat iron roof. *What is it? What have they found?* There were a couple of AROs outside and she immediately felt uneasy.

'It's in here,' the ARO pointed. Ruth took a step inside the stone room and then stopped.

A dead black labrador was hanging from a central wooden beam with a rope noosed around its neck. It was Gwenda Chadwick's dog that she had reported being in her car when Gates stole it.

As the dog's corpse moved in the breeze, Ruth could see a handwritten note that had been nailed to the dog's back. *Look, Ruth. A dead bitch just like Sarah Goddard xx.*

Ruth felt as if she had been punched. She turned away, went outside and steadied herself.

The senior ARO came to her side. 'You okay, ma'am?'

'Yes. Let's just get that photographed and cut down, please,' Ruth said with the image of the dog and the note still burning in her mind.

CHAPTER 24

Nick had been trawling the shops in Llanberis for over an hour now. While interviewing shop and café owners, he was also searching for any CCTV footage from the afternoon of Sunday 9 December. He had spoken briefly to Drake to update him on the Harvey Pearson investigation, but he was too embroiled in Gates's escape to really focus on what Nick was saying.

That morning, Nick had picked up emails from two more cancer charities. They had no record of any charity events on Mount Snowdon at any time in December. It was frustrating as none of the major cancer charities had any record of anyone raising money by climbing Snowdon – it was another dead end.

Then he had made a quick phone call to Rosie Chivers, the fourth sister, who confirmed what he had feared. She too had a watertight alibi for the afternoon of Sunday 9 December. She had been at the cinema with a friend who would vouch for her. She even told him that they had seen a showing of Peter Jackson's World War I documentary *They Will Not Grow Old* at three o'clock. Rosie Chivers had only ever climbed Snowdon once and she snorted at the idea of going up the mountain in December. It seemed that the theory of the four Chivers sisters being on Mount Snowdon that afternoon, and having any involvement in Harv's death, was now looking less and less likely.

Nick still felt the key to Harv's murder was the four women seen on the mountain. As far as he could ascertain, they were the only ones at that location apart from Harvey and Jack Pearson.

Nick hoped that if they had been in Llanberis that day, someone would have seen them. Four middle-aged women, dressed in pink, all set to climb Snowdon on a very cold day. That must have registered with someone. He also came back to the fact that none of these women had come forward to the police. Someone somewhere, who knew about the charity climb, would have seen there had been a murder on the mountain that day. They would know that the police were looking for witnesses. The fact that they hadn't contacted the police was deeply suspicious.

Crossing the road to start heading back down the main street, Nick popped into a newsagent to pick up a drink.

The shop was old-fashioned, and Nick thought it smelt just like a new paperback novel. Reaching the open fridge full of drinks, his eyes went to the array of beers and cider. Thank God he no longer felt the compulsion to grab a couple. That was a miracle, he thought to himself. He took a Diet Coke and went to pay, smiling at the middle-aged woman behind the till.

Taking his change, Nick got out his warrant card, and she immediately looked concerned. He was used to it. Most people did.

'I'm from North Wales Police. I'm trying to find a group of four women who were in the area on Sunday the ninth of

December. They climbed Snowdon at some point and they were all dressed in pink. We think they might have been climbing the mountain for charity.' Nick explained.

The middle-aged woman looked serious and nodded. 'Oh yes. They came in here.'

'Right. Could you describe them for me?' Nick said as he took out his notebook and pen. He was finally getting somewhere.

'They were ... I suppose they were in their thirties or early forties. They were laughing a lot, I remember that,' she explained with a smile.

'Anything that might help identify them?' Nick asked, hoping she could narrow down her description.

The woman thought for a moment. 'They were wearing hats and scarves. They were nice-looking. One of them was half-caste.'

'Mixed race.' Nick corrected her without realising it.

'Sorry? Yes ... ' the woman frowned. She had no idea what he was talking about.

'Were they locals?' Nick asked.

The woman's eyes widened. 'That was it. Two of them bought some water and some energy bars. To me, they sounded American. But my husband said that one of them had the Canadian flag on their rucksack, so he thought they were from Canada. American or Canadian. Sound exactly the same to me. I can't tell the difference, can you?'

'No, not really,' Nick said as he stopped writing in his notebook. 'Anything else you can think of that might help?'

The woman shook her head, and Nick handed her a card so she could give him a call if she thought of anything.

The accents and the flag were useful details. However, he now feared the suspects he was looking for might not even be in the country.

Even though it was only late afternoon, the sky was pitch black by the time Ruth reached the Gateses' home. In the darkness, it felt far more remote and isolated than in daylight. If Gates was out there, watching and waiting for his chance to see Kerry, then he would be invisible in the impenetrable blackness.

Ruth could see the unmarked patrol car parked further up the track. She assumed that inside were the two CID officers who were keeping watch in case Gates tried to return home to see Kerry. Directly outside Gates's home was a small blue Clio that she didn't recognise, but she had learnt that Kerry had a variety of health visitors during the week. Now that Gates had gone, Kerry Gates had a few people to look after her.

Ruth turned off the ignition and sat in the comforting silence of the car for a moment. The wind buffeted outside noisily. Although her instinct was to reach for a cigarette, Ruth knew that she needed to breathe and calm herself. She had suffered from panic attacks before, and after the events at Moel Siabod, her nerves were frayed and jangly. Looking up at the winter sky, she watched the tiny red flashing dot of an aeroplane pass silently overhead. Behind that, an irregular scattering of stars. Perspective. She needed to remember the reassuring feeling that she was a tiny speck of dust in an infinite universe. Some people found that a scary prospect. Ruth found that it calmed her and things that seemed so overwhelming were given perspective. Tracking down a killer like

Gates wasn't to be taken lightly. However, gazing up at the night sky and recentring herself meant that she could start to take the heat and emotion out of how she was feeling.

Taking in a deep breath to the count of four, Ruth then held it for six, and then let it out slowly from her mouth for seven. As she did this, she counted her breaths, trying to clear her mind of the inordinate chatter that went on a repetitive loop. After about five minutes, she opened her eyes. A sense of calm and clarity had returned.

Now she could have a smoke. She wound down the window, lit the cigarette and blew the smoke out. Even though she was a smoker, she thought there was nothing worse than a car that smelt of stale cigarettes. From somewhere outside, she caught the unmistakable hoot of an owl. Its echo was distinctly eerie.

Clicking on the radio to change her mood, her mind turned to Christmas for a moment as 'Driving Home For Christmas' by Chris Rea played softly. Her benign thoughts about the coming festivities felt like a relief from the darkness and horror of recent days.

She flicked the cigarette away, wound up the window and got out of the car. Her hair flicked in the blustering wind and there was the smell of wet grass and coal from an open fire somewhere.

Reaching the unmarked patrol car, she gave the officers a wave. They smiled back.

'DI Ruth Hunter,' she said and showed her warrant card.

'Evening, ma'am,' said the two officers.

Ruth gestured to the Clio. 'Visitor?'

'Just the district nurse again. She's in daily at the moment, ma'am,' the officer in the driver's seat said.

'Anything out of the ordinary, Constable?' Ruth asked.

He shook his head. 'Nope. Not a peep. Her sister popped in this morning. That's it.'

'Thanks. I won't be long.' Ruth turned and headed back towards the house. She was keen to get as much information from Kerry Gates as she could. Kerry would have a good idea of where Gates might be heading, even if she would be reluctant to tell her. However, she assumed that Kerry wouldn't want any other innocent people being killed. Were there relatives or friends that Gates could hide out with? What places did he feel comfortable in? In Ruth's experience, criminals stuck to areas and places that they knew because they felt secure and safe. The irony was that it actually made them easier to catch and therefore more vulnerable.

Walking up the uneven path, Ruth continued to run questions through her head. The front door was only pushed to, which she had come to expect in the countryside. It creaked as it swung open and she went in. It was warm and there was the distinct smell of mulled wine spices.

'Hello, Mrs Gates?' Ruth called out. 'It's Detective Inspector Ruth Hunter. We met before.' Ruth carried on through the narrow hallway. The door to the living room was open and the glowing coals of an open fire cast a flickering orange light across the carpet. White Christmas lights that had been carefully placed around the room twinkled in the semi-darkness.

Kerry Gates was fast asleep under a blanket on the sofa. There was a glass of unfinished mulled wine beside her. That's why Ruth wasn't getting an answer.

Through the doorway to the kitchen, Ruth could see the district nurse, blonde and in her light-blue uniform, washing up at the sink. That was the amazing thing about nurses, Ruth thought. Their capacity for compassion and care was incredible.

Ruth called out. 'Hi there. I'm DI Ruth Hunter. I've come to talk to Mrs Gates.'

The nurse gave a quick wave as she finished off the washing up and put away the tea towel.

Ruth watched Kerry sleeping. She would have to wake her in a minute. How had she fallen in love with a man like Gates? She must have had her suspicions in recent months. She had seen co-dependent relationships before. Andrew and Kerry Gates had provided what the other needed in their relationship, however dysfunctional it looked from the outside. Kerry wanted something that Gates was able to give her, and that was a dark thought.

As Ruth gazed at Kerry's serene face, the district nurse came bustling in. Ruth needed to get the answers to her questions and get back to Llancastell nick to continue the search for Gates.

'I'm going to have to wake her up in a minute, I'm afraid. I've got some questions I need to ask her,' Ruth said quietly.

'You might find that quite difficult I'm afraid, Ruth,' a voice said.

It was a deep man's voice that she recognised instantly. Ruth froze.

She glanced up at the district nurse who was now smiling down at her. She knew the scarred eyelid and the face.

It was Gates.

For a moment, she looked at Gates's face, which was covered in make-up and a blonde wig.

It was a shocking, garish sight.

'Surprise, Ruth,' Gates whispered through his dark-red lips.

Every part of Ruth's being lurched in terror. Her pulse accelerated rapidly and her breath quickened.

'What ...' Ruth stammered, and then she looked at the enormous kitchen knife that Gates was holding. The blade glinted in the glow of the Christmas lights. Was this how she was going to die? A physical sickness swept through her.

'What am I doing here?' Gates wiped some of the make-up from his face and it smeared across his cheeks and then onto his hand. 'If you make a sound, I will slit your throat and watch you bleed out like a pig. So my advice is to keep very quiet and I won't hurt you.'

'What are you doing here?' Ruth was playing for time. Her eyes darted around the room looking for anything that could help her make an escape. There was nothing.

'I couldn't let my poor, sweet Kerry suffer in some home or hospital. There was no one to look after her except me. So I came to release her.'

Ruth looked at Gates and then down at Kerry. She wasn't sleeping, she was dead. 'You mean you killed her! You're not freeing or releasing anyone. You are killing innocent people. Let's not dress it up in any other way.' If she was going to die, then Ruth was going to have her say.

Gates shook his head in mock disappointment and tutted. 'That's disappointing, Ruth. I thought you, of all people, would understand.'

'If you're going to kill me, then you'd better get on with it.' Ruth had found a strength from somewhere and she certainly would not die crying, shaking and pleading with Gates for her life.

'Ruth. Ruthie. I'm not going to kill you. You know there's a connection between us. You can't deny it. You feel it too. I know you do. I could never kill you.'

Even though Ruth felt alarmed that Gates felt like that about her, it was a relief that he wasn't going to kill her. She composed herself. 'You need to hand yourself in.'

'Why? I've got nothing to lose, have I? And to be honest, Ruth, I'm having the time of my life making you lot look like fools.'

'Kerry wouldn't have wanted you to have hurt anyone else,' Ruth said, trying to appeal to Gates.

'Oh dear. I don't think you could ever understand what Kerry and I had together.' Gates sounded like he was scolding a child. He pulled out a plastic tie, approached Ruth and put the blade to her throat. The metal was cold and sharp against her skin.

'Do you plan to just keep running for the rest of your life?' she asked, trying to get Gates to see the bigger picture.

'God no. I have a few things I need to take care of and then I'll give you a ring and you can come and get me. Deal?' Gates smiled as he secured Ruth's hands behind her back. The plastic cut into her wrists and she twisted. She wouldn't be able to free her hands on her own.

Gates then put a screwed up dishcloth that tasted of washing-up liquid into her mouth. At first, she struggled to pull the air in through her nose and felt claustrophobic. She wondered how long she would be stuck like this? *This is a bloody nightmare!*

'I've got to go now. I'm sure the officers outside will come and free you when they wonder why you've been so long. Until then, you can keep my Kerry company,' Gates said with a smile.

Gates turned, went to the kitchen where he grabbed a coat and the nurse's bag and left through the back door.

CHAPTER 25

It was seven o'clock by the time Nick cut through central Llancastell. The traffic was still heavy because of late-night Christmas shoppers getting ready for the festive season. But that was the last thing on his mind. Amanda had texted him to say that she wasn't feeling well and wasn't able to go to the AA meeting with him that night. When he had tried to ring her, her phone had been switched off. For Nick, that rang alarm bells. She might have been genuinely ill, but he had personal experience, as well as the experience of others in the fellowship, that suggested when someone started changing plans, making excuses, turning off their phone and avoiding meetings, it normally meant one thing: a relapse. It was classic alky behaviour. Alcoholics had problems with honesty, pride and ego. To admit they had started drinking again was difficult. More worryingly, during 'a slip' alcoholics often didn't want to stop drinking. They had spent weeks, months or even years not drinking. If they were going to have a relapse, they were going to give it a fucking good go before they stopped.

Amanda was still early on in the programme and to have some kind of 'slip' was understandable, even expected. So as Nick parked, got out of the car and approached her front door, he hoped that she was ravaged with flu, but was anticipating that she might have 'picked up.'

The front door opened about three inches and Amanda's face appeared. Her eyes were glazed and her eyelids droopy. She was hammered. *For fuck's sake!* Nick thought to himself and then told himself to be calm and understanding.

'Can I come in?' Nick asked with a kind smile. Given his record in recovery, he couldn't judge anyone.

'I've got terrible flu and I don't want you to catch it.' Amanda's words were slurred. She wasn't fooling anyone.

'Yeah, but I think it's probably best if I come in anyway,' Nick said pushing the door open gently.

'Okay. Just as long as you're very quiet. I have a very, very bad headache. So shh.' Amanda stumbled back into the house and then put her hand onto the wall to steady herself.

Nick crossed the threshold and already he could smell the booze in the air. Recovered alkies were like bloodhounds when it came to sniffing out the faintest molecule of alcohol.

Now that the front door was closed and all pretence was over, Amanda let down her guard. Nick could see how drunk she really was.

She smiled, trying to focus a little, and then came at him with open arms. 'Nick, it's so lovely to see you. I've missed you.'

'Shall we sit down?' Nick said, hugging her back while trying to avoid her kisses and her breath.

'I've got an ad ... an admish ...' Amanda stumbled over her words. 'Ad ... mish ... admission to make. *Admission* – isn't that a funny word? Anyway, I'm vewwy, vewwy sowwy. But I had a little drink ... And then I had another drink.'

'Yeah, I know,' Nick said as he nodded.

Amanda pulled a face and slumped onto the sofa. 'Oh, do you hate me? Please don't hate me.'

'No, of course not. Hey, you're an alcoholic. It's not a huge surprise.' Nick smiled at her. It was an illness. And it was the only illness he knew of that told you that you didn't have it.

When Amanda saw him smile at her, she gave a sigh of relief. 'Oh, aren't you lovely? You're lovely. Oh, and you're fit. You know that, don't you? Fit. F ... I ... T ... Fit. I showed a friend of mine a photo of you on my phone and she agreed.'

Nick nodded with a smile. 'Thanks. You're not so bad yourself. How much have you had?'

'Well, that's the thing. I thought I would just have a bottle of wine. Just one. But when I finished that, I thought that I fancied some vodka and tonic. Just a couple though.' Amanda frowned as she tried to think, 'And then ...'

'Where's the vodka?'

'In the kitchen, babe.' Amanda giggled. At least she wasn't an aggressive drunk. 'Babe. I've never called you that before. Have I, *babe*?'

Nick smiled as he got up to get rid of the rest of the vodka. 'No.'

Striding quickly into the kitchen, he immediately spotted the litre-bottle that had about an inch of the spirit left. No wonder she was hammered. He poured it down the sink and the fumes went up his nose. It immediately took him back to his drinking.

Returning to the living room, Nick took her hand. 'We need to get you to bed.'

'Oh, are you trying to take advantage of me?'

'No. You just sleep it off and you'll be okay in the morning.'

Nick led her to the bedroom where she flopped onto the bed. He pulled the duvet over her and she closed her eyes. He then put her in the recovery position. She would probably be asleep in a few minutes.

Now he had to scour her house for more hidden booze and get any cash or cards off her so she couldn't go and replace it. He would return after the AA meeting and sleep on the sofa.

He spent the next twenty minutes checking all the likely hiding places for secret stashes of alcohol – drawers, wardrobe, washing machine, behind the sofa. He found nothing. Taking her purse from her bag, he took all her money and her credit and debit cards. He checked on her; she was fast asleep.

Twenty minutes later, Nick was in the AA meeting beside the detox centre at the hospital. He poured himself a cup of coffee and greeted various people he knew. A figure approached. It was his sponsor, Bill.

'Your phone broken, Nick?' he said dryly.

'No, sorry.' He was meant to ring his sponsor Bill at least once a week for a chat and a catch-up on his recovery.

'You caught up in this bloody awful thing with the fella that's escaped?' Bill asked.

'Sort of,' Nick said. He knew the reason that he hadn't called Bill was because he was seeing Amanda. He didn't want to lie to Bill, but he knew if he told him about their relationship, Bill would tell him to end it.

'I was following it on the news. Biggest manhunt for years, they said,' Bill continued.

'Yeah. We've got officers coming to us from all over,' Nick explained.

'No Amanda tonight?' Bill asked.

'No. Working late,' Nick lied and hated himself for doing so.

'Oh, right. How's she doing?'

'All right. Early days, isn't it?'

'Christ, early days. You've only been sober for five minutes, Nick. Don't you go taking anyone else's recovery on like some knight in shining fucking armour,' Bill warned him.

'No, no. We just go to meetings and then talk about them after. We text each other. That's all.' Nick could hear his own voice and what he was saying and wanted the world to open up and swallow him.

SITTING BACK ON HER sofa, it was such a relief to be home, Ruth thought.

'I thought he was going to kill me.' Her voice was calm, but she felt rocked by Gates's appearance, and being tied up by him had left her feeling vulnerable and powerless.

Ella handed her an enormous glass of red wine. Ruth still had the taste of washing-up liquid in her mouth and hoped the wine would take it away.

'I know this sounds horrible, but why didn't he kill you? Sorry ...' Ruth could see that Ella regretted asking, but Ruth knew it was a valid question.

'No, that's fine. Possibly because he only gets a kick out of killing men. I don't know. Maybe because he seems to think we have this strange connection.' Ruth was thinking out loud, but the thought had crossed her mind as she sat tied to the chair that Gates had nothing to lose if he had slit her throat. He was already facing eight life sentences now he had murdered Kerry.

It took the officers in the car outside nearly an hour before they decided to see if everything was all right. They cut her free and were incredibly apologetic at not having clocked that the blonde nurse that drove away in the Clio was Gates. She didn't blame them one bit. There were no streetlights outside, and in the darkness, all they would have seen was a figure in a uniform and coat with blonde hair. Gates wasn't tall or particularly muscular either, so that wouldn't have thrown up any red flags.

Karen Crane, the actual district nurse, had been attacked, stripped and tied up by Gates and left at her home for the whole afternoon. She had been suffering from cervical cancer and her chemotherapy had made her bald, so she wore a wig. Gates had even stolen her bra and make-up. However, he hadn't murdered Karen Crane either, so perhaps there was a gender element to his MO. Kerry was an anomaly as he saw that as a necessity and a mercy killing.

Ruth was keen to change the subject. 'Any more flats for you to look at?'

'Mum. You've just been kidnapped and attacked,' Ella said with a frown.

'So I need something to take my mind off it,' Ruth explained. 'Come on. Show me.'

'There's a couple, actually.' Ella grabbed her phone and brought up the details of the properties that she was interested in.

Ruth looked at them. It was nice to do something mundane for once.

'Are you going to look at any?' Ruth asked.

'Maybe a couple tomorrow,' Ella said.

'Want me to come with you?' Ruth suggested.

'Mum, I can cope with going to look at some flats on my own.' Ella laughed.

'I know. Sorry. It's just there are some very weird people out there, that's all.'

'Mum, you deal with the freaks, the murderers, the gangsters every day. It's your world, but it's not the real world,' Ella said.

Ruth nodded. How had she produced such a wise child? 'You're still my baby. And you always will be.'

THE RAIN WAS GETTING heavier as Gates sat in the van outside a small convenience shop. It was nearly six-thirty in the morning and the lights in the store had just burst into life. Someone was inside setting up for the day. *Or at least, so they think*, Gates thought to himself.

Gates had showered and changed at the drive-in McDonald's in the retail park. He had got a decent night's sleep in the van he was now driving. Changing vehicles would make it far harder for the police to catch him. It worried him that after all the death and mayhem he had caused, how well he did actually sleep. It couldn't be normal, could it?

The steady pitter-patter of rain seemed to create a protective shield around him. Gates loved that sound. The puddles were growing on the pavement and road; puddles that were peppered by drops that sent mini ripples scurrying across their surface. The sky was getting brighter but it was still grey. Gates thought it was every shade of grey that he could imagine. What colour do things become when it's raining? Or did colour just vanish and things become shades of black or white?

As he gazed around, he felt a sense of peace inside him. Kerry's spirit was in some blissful place that the human mind couldn't begin to imagine. The thought comforted him as he stared into the gloom.

He clicked the radio on inside the old white Ford van that he had stolen from a builder's yard in Capel Garmin. He had learnt how to hot-wire older cars and vans by watching tutorials online. He wasn't sure why he'd been researching it; maybe, deep down, he knew that one day he would be on the run and need that skill? He didn't know. What he did know was that he had felt a huge sense of satisfaction when he got the van to start. He had loosened the ring in the ignition switch with a hammer and screwdriver that he had found in a discarded toolbox. He then pulled the ignition switch out of the dashboard. He yanked out the wires and looked for a red or black wire with a yellow or green stripe. Touching the wires together in the plug. He had laughed out loud as the engine growled into life. *God bless YouTube,* he thought.

Tuning the radio, Gates heard something on the BBC News and turned up the volume. He was getting a big thrill from hearing and seeing his name everywhere he went. Fame was an intoxicating drug.

'The BBC understands that armed police officers failed to recapture Andrew Gates in an operation at a disused farm in the heart of North Wales's Snowdonia Park. Tactical firearms officers moved into the area of the farm at around five o'clock yesterday afternoon after a tip-off, but officers found that Andrew Gates had already left the area. Police have appealed for the man dubbed "Britain's Most Wanted" to give himself up. A police spokesperson said that the manhunt for Andrew Gates was the biggest in the UK for nearly a decade and over a hundred officers had been mobilised from four different counties for the search. Earlier this week, Andrew Gates pleaded guilty to the murder of seven men and had been helping police recover his victims' remains when he managed to escape.'

Gates turned off the radio. He smiled to himself. It really was such a rush to hear about himself on the news. In fact, he didn't want it to stop.

Noticing that the shop was now displaying an *Open* sign, Gates climbed out the driver's door, holding some rope and a crowbar that had been left in the back of the van. Glancing around the empty street momentarily, Gates entered the shop door and a little bell rang. *How quaint*, he thought. What was that programme that he and Kerry used to love? *Open all Hours* with Ronnie Barker. That was it.

A man in his thirties, small and wearing glasses, looked at him with a friendly smile. 'Early bird, eh?'

'That's right,' Gates said. 'Gets the worm, I think the saying is?'

The man spotted the crowbar and the rope and frowned. 'Can I help?' the man asked, uncertain of Gates's intentions.

'Probably not.' Gates rushed towards him and before the man could get away, Gates had cracked the crowbar across his temple, splitting the skin to the bone.

The man crashed to the floor, but he wasn't unconscious. He groaned and moved his hand to his forehead where he had been struck.

Gates was relieved. He didn't want to strangle anyone who was already unconscious. That wasn't the thrill. They needed to be awake, they needed to struggle and know that he was murdering them. That was the rush. The man wasn't in the least bit attractive but he would have to do. Gates knew he was running out of time and once captured, these opportunities would never arise again.

Looking over at the till, Gates saw that there was a CCTV camera looking down at him from high on the wall. He gave it a little wave. He hoped that DI Ruth Hunter would get a first-hand look at what he was all about.

'Hello, Ruth,' Gates said with exaggerated mouth movements, hoping she and the other officers could lip-read what he was saying.

He looked at the man, blood cascading down his face and dripping onto the floor. His victim groaned and tried to move again. That poor little man with his poor little life. Opening up this little shop at the break of dawn. He added nothing to the world. A waste of space. A waste of air. A waste of the earth's resources that he consumed. Killing him would release him from the pain and misery of the life that he felt compelled to live. It would also rid the planet of one more of the leeches that infested their society.

Gates propped the man up against a shelf of biscuits, his face now awash with blood. This really wasn't what he had planned. He felt like an alcoholic with a pint of shandy. Taking the rope in his hands, Gates looped it around the man's neck and began to pull as he slowly squeezed the life out of him.

Despite the shortcomings, there was still a sense of euphoria and elation. Those were the perfect words for it. But the thrill wasn't as overwhelming as it had been before.

Maybe he would have to try again.

CHAPTER 26

The rumble of the recycling lorries clattering outside told Ruth that it was time to get up. The bed was so warm, and Sian was lying facing her but still asleep. Ruth watched her for a moment, then got up and shuffled to the kitchen where she clicked on the kettle.

A robin fluttered outside and landed on the snowy windowsill. The garden and then the fields that stretched beyond were covered in thick snow. Ruth didn't remember snow being forecast. It might look beautiful, she thought, but driving into work was going to be a pain in the arse. The robin flapped away and Ruth went over to the advent calendar that Sian had bought her. She made a mental note to pick up one each for Sian and Ella on the way home from work. Better late than never. She drifted away into memories of Christmases when Ella was young. The pink Hannah Montana advent calendar, the excitement of wrapping Ella's presents on Christmas Eve and the joy of being woken at some ungodly hour the next morning. Of course, Sarah was with her in all those memories and Ruth was hit by a spike of sadness.

An odd rustling noise from the living room caught her attention. It sounded like someone was moving around in there, but she knew that Sian and Ella were still in bed.

Pulling her dressing gown around her, Ruth ventured out into the tiny hallway and looked into the living room. Someone *was sitting on the sofa. At first, she could only see their smart shoes and expensive suit trousers.*

Overwhelmed by the shuddering feeling of dread, Ruth moved through the doorway. There was a man sitting on the sofa. She recognised his blonde hair, designer glasses and detached expression.

'Good morning, Ruth.' His voice had a Germanic accent.

It was Jurgen Kessler.

'What the hell are you doing here?' Ruth asked, feeling herself shaken.

'I've come to tell you about Sarah. I thought you would know that?'

'Wait. How did you get my address?'

'Don't you want to know what happened to Sarah? I can show you on my phone. I have pictures of her,' Kessler said, standing and pulling his phone from his suit jacket.

Out of the corner of her eye, Ruth saw a figure on the sofa behind her. She turned for a moment. The black, dead eyes of Kerry Gates looked back at her. Her white, dead cadaver was lying across the sofa as though she was in a morgue.

Ruth woke with a start. Her pulse was still racing. She took a deep breath, held it and let it out slowly. The dreams of Kessler, though rare, were torturous.

Sian stirred, opened one eye and immediately saw Ruth's expression. 'Nightmare?'

Ruth nodded. 'Oh yeah. One of those where you celebrate waking and realising the horror is over.'

Sian moved over and hugged her. 'Bless you. Not surprising is it?'

WAKING UP TO THE METALLIC clicks of radiators expanding as Amanda's central heating fired up, Nick stirred on the sofa, pulled back the blanket and sat up. He had slept relatively well, all things considered. He moved his shoulders to remove some stiffness from his neck and stood up. It had been a long time since he woke up on a sofa without the plunging feeling of self-loathing, hangover, urine and half-remembered blackouts.

After the AA meeting, Nick had returned to Amanda's home and checked on her. She had been out for the count. Relieved that she hadn't been sick or decided to get more alcohol, Nick made a cup of tea, watched ten minutes of *Gogglebox* and decided to go to sleep. He knew the lengths that an alcoholic would go to get booze. When he was in the grips of alcohol's magnetic pull, he had snuck out of Auntie Pat's old home at Pen Y Brin, which was in the middle of nowhere, and walked six miles in the rain before stealing cans of cider from a petrol station. The craving and need to get alcohol was that overpowering.

At eleven the previous evening, Ruth had called to tell him about her encounter with Gates. He knew she was lucky to be alive but tried to keep the conversation upbeat. She might have been his boss, but he cared about her.

It was nearly seven when Nick laced his brown brogues. He quickly checked on Amanda, who stirred but continued to sleep, then made himself coffee and toast. As he waited in the neat kitchen, he gazed up at the montage of photos on the wall. Amanda had certainly travelled the world. A hot-air balloon ride over a South African desert, tandem sky-diving in Australia and white-water rafting in New Zealand. It wasn't a surprise. Amanda was an addict and could probably become addicted to anything. It wasn't a coincidence that there were lots of adrenaline junkies in AA.

A sound came from the bedroom upstairs and Amanda appeared bleary-eyed in the kitchen doorway.

'Morning,' Nick said. 'I've made coffee.'

'Don't look at me. I look like shit,' Amanda protested, putting her hands over her face.

'Just admiring your photos.' He pointed to a picture of some tiger cubs playing in some grass. 'Where was this taken?'

'It's a tiger sanctuary in Sumatra.'

'And Sumatra is ...?' Nick frowned.

'Indonesia, you thicko. The cub's eyes are closed for the first ten days. And then when they open, they're this amazing blue.' She pointed to the photo. 'When they grow up, they go amber.'

'Thank you, Amanda Attenborough.' Nick smiled. This was fun, but he knew that they would have to address the elephant in the room. 'Any idea why you picked up?'

Amanda winced. 'No. I don't know. I've ruined everything, haven't I?'

Nick shook his head with a knowing smile. 'Most of the people in AA relapse at the beginning. It takes a while. I've known stubborn bastards take five years before they finally get the idea that they can't drink. They go out every few weeks, try again and are surprised when two days later they're drinking vodka for breakfast.'

'You don't hate me, then?'

'No. Don't be stupid. Alcoholism isn't a lifestyle choice.' Nick patted his pocket. 'I've got your bank cards and money. I've checked and you've got food.'

'I'm under house arrest?'

'Definitely.' Nick grinned.

Amanda walked towards him and buried her head in his chest. 'I love you, you know that?'

'I love you too,' Nick replied quietly, surprising himself. 'And don't go out.'

'Don't worry. I have no desire to drink any booze. I feel sick.'

'It's not that. It's just with your breath, hair and no make-up, you'll scare the children,' Nick quipped.

Amanda hit him playfully. 'Fuck off, Nick.'

'Take the day off. Drink water and watch TV.' Nick turned and went, feeling a glow of contentment.

CHAPTER 27

Ruth found herself feeling out of control as she watched the CCTV footage of Gates in the convenience shop that morning. Along with the rest of CID, she had had to watch Gates murdering an innocent man after mouthing her name at the camera. However illogical, she felt that somehow she was responsible for what he was doing.

As she headed out to have a ciggie on the concrete steps outside Llancastell nick, her mobile rang. It was a number she didn't recognise.

'DI Hunter?' she said.

'I assume you got my message from this morning?'

It was Gates. Ruth knew the voice immediately. This time she didn't feel the lurch in the pit of her stomach. She didn't know why, but she wasn't surprised that he had made contact. She expected something like this, so it was a relief that it was happening.

'How did you get my number?' Ruth asked calmly.

'You gave it to me, Ruth. Don't you remember? When you talked to me outside my house in Pentredwr.' Gates's tone was one of mock offence that she hadn't recalled doing so.

'What do you want?' Ruth said softly.

'I'm a little bit confused, you see, Ruth,' Gates said in his usual overfamiliar tone.

'What are you confused about?' Ruth was playing along.

'Where do we go from here?'

What does he mean by that? She didn't know if he was being deliberately cryptic or did he genuinely want to talk about what he should do. Either way, she needed to keep him talking.

'It's probably best that you come in. Then we can talk about it,' Ruth said. Gates had nothing to lose by remaining on the run and that made him incredibly dangerous.

'What are we going to talk about, Ruth?' Gates asked.

'I think you need to be understood, Andrew. You want people to know why you did what you did. That's important to you, isn't it?' Ruth was going on what Professor Douglas had said about Gates being abandoned.

'Not just me. Everyone needs to feel understood. And we all have our own stories. You have yours, Ruth. And that's why I understand you.'

Ruth would not be drawn into talking about herself. 'You can't keep running. We will find you eventually. And you know that.' There was no element of threat in Ruth's voice; it was just a matter-of-fact statement.

'Yes, I know that. If I'm honest, I'm exhausted with it all. It's not really the right time of year to be doing all this. At first, I thought it might be fun, but it's not what I expected. Do you ever get that?' he asked.

'What's that?' Ruth didn't know what he was driving at but wanted him to keep talking to her.

'The one from this morning. From the shop. I had looked forward to it. But I felt ... disappointed. It wasn't enough. It did nothing for me ...' Gates stopped talking mid-thought.

It was chilling for Ruth to hear him talking about taking a life with the word *it* and such utter disregard for another human being.

'If you're tired, then just come in. It's warm, dry, there's food. Everything is taken care of. You can sleep.'

Gates didn't seem to be listening. 'I need more, Ruth. Something bigger. Something more exciting. I can't explain it.'

Ruth knew exactly what he was talking about. Gates had a dark addiction to murder. And, as with any addiction, he was becoming immune to the thrill of killing. He needed to take it a step further to get his fix, and that was a terrifying thought. She just hoped that his growing fatigue of being on the run would stop him.

'You can explain it to me,' she said, trying to appeal to his ego. 'There will be lots of people who will want you to explain.'

'I know.' Gates took an audible breath. 'I could always kill myself, but I think the world would be missing out, don't you?'

Knowing Gates's ego, Ruth wasn't surprised at his comment. 'Where do you want me to meet you, Andrew?' she asked.

'I'm only doing this if you come and meet me alone. I don't want guns in my face, helicopters, the whole circus.'

'I'm not going to come on my own, you know that.'

'I need some dignity, Ruth. Put me in cuffs and lead me to the car. I'm not going to attack you and I'm not going to run. I just don't want a machine gun at my head while I lie on wet concrete. It's about some kind of respect.'

'There will be other officers there, but I understand what you're asking.' Ruth needed to keep Gates onside. They needed his full cooperation to retrieve the remains of all his victims and detail all of his crimes. The victims' families needed to bury their loved ones and have some idea of what had happened to them. For that, they needed Gates. 'Yes. But there's no guarantee that you'll turn up.'

'No, there isn't. But you're going to feel pretty stupid if I'm standing there and you're not there to arrest me.'

Gates had a point. North Wales Police couldn't afford another PR disaster.

A moment passed as Gates thought. 'The Pontcysyllte Aqueduct by Llangollen, the south end. It's a beautiful spot. I'll see you at four o'clock sharp.'

Gates finished the call. She knew there was no point triangulating the position to get a fix on Gates's location. He clearly had a vehicle and would be long gone by the time any officers got to the location.

AS NICK SAT BACK IN his chair at Llancastell CID, he realised he had hit a brick wall in his investigation into Harvey Pearson's murder. If the women on Snowdon that day were Canadian, he wondered if they had been visiting the area. If they returned to Canada, it was also unlikely that they would have seen anything about Harv's death once they left the UK. If they were still in the country, how was he going to find them?

Nick had been trawling through passenger lists for the days after Harv's death. Unfortunately, there were far more direct flights from Liverpool and Manchester to Canada than he had expected. There were, of course, the major cities of Montreal, Toronto and Vancouver. However, there were also flights to Canadian cities such as Alberta or Saskatchewan that he'd never heard of. Having received the Advance Passenger Information, Nick still didn't have much to go on. Passenger passport data was collated by the airlines and transmitted electronically to the authorities of the destination country. The national list for flights from Liverpool and Manchester into Canada ran into thousands.

He had a couple of CID officers trawling through CCTV at both airports to see if they could spot four middle-aged women travelling together, but so far, they had drawn a blank. Added to that, the women could have been flying in or out of Birmingham or even London.

Sitting forwards in his chair, he finished his coffee and pulled himself closer to the desk. He could feel that his waistline was growing. Alcohol had been replaced by sugar, especially chocolate. And here was the irony. For years, he had skipped dessert whenever eating out. Each time he had been handed the coffee and dessert menu, he skimmed right past the tiramisu to the only part of the menu that mattered – more alcohol. Irish coffee was always good as it seemed to be a covert way of drinking. Now he was sober, he needed to try to shift a few pounds. He didn't want Amanda thinking he was a fat alky bastard.

Sifting through new emails, he saw that the Odeon Cinema in Llancastell had sent over their CCTV for the time and day that Rosie Chivers claimed to be at the cinema.

Nick clicked on the email, which confirmed that the Odeon had only sold seven tickets for *They Shall Not Grow Old* in screen seven. It was the only screening of the day. Opening the video file, Nick watched the high-angle view of the carpeted corridor on which large lettering showed each screen entrance. Screen seven was at the far end. Rolling the footage forwards, Nick counted as each person entered the theatre. Two elderly couples. Then a middle-aged man on his own, followed by a father and son. Nick rewound the video, played it again and fast-forwarded it, but there was no sign of Rosie Chivers and her friend. She had lied about her whereabouts at the time of Harvey Pearson's murder. Carol Chivers had no alibi. It was now definitely worth checking Claire Sinclair's alibi for that afternoon too. As for the remaining sister, Emily, they were still waiting for her to establish her Christmas shopping alibi.

The hypothesis of the four Chivers sisters on Snowdon was back on.

CHAPTER 28

The winter sky was tinted lavender as snow fluttered in the air over the Pontcysyllte Aqueduct, twirling and skipping on the cold air currents that blew down from the deep valley. Ruth blinked as another wet, icy speck landed on her eyelashes.

It was three o'clock. Ruth and numerous members of the North Wales Police operational team were moving into position as they surrounded the Pontcysyllte Aqueduct. Confused narrow-boat owners and tourists who had come to see the world heritage site were being cleared from the area.

The aqueduct carried the Llangollen Canal across the Vale of Llangollen and over the River Dee. Ruth could see that it was an imposing piece of engineering with its eighteen stone-and-cast-iron arches. At 125 feet, it dominated the landscape, and Ruth could see for miles into the distance. To her left were the snowy peaks of Snowdonia. She looked back and watched as uniformed officers continually turned away a steady stream of cars from the tourist car park.

Before leaving Llancastell earlier, Ruth had been given CCTV footage from a local cash machine in Ruabon. Gates had used Gwenda Chadwick's debit card at around one o'clock, just after he spoke to Ruth on the phone. Her bank's fraud and security team, who were continually monitoring the use of her cards, contacted CID at Llancastell immediately. Twenty minutes later, the bank branch had down-loaded CCTV footage of the person taking out the money. It was no surprise that it was Gates. He was dressed in a bur-gundy walking jacket and a black woollen ski hat pulled low over his ears and his forehead. The trademark tinted glass-es were gone. Gates grinned up at the CCTV camera and waved the money at them. Ruth instructed the bank to con-tinue to keep the cards in service. It had allowed them to keep track of Gates's movements, and at this stage, with-out cash Gates was even more likely to resort to violence or worse to get what he needed. His disregard for human life was alarmingly obvious to everyone.

From the CCTV, they also got a partial number plate of a white Ford Escort van that Gates got into after taking out the money. They had it traced through the DVLA and found it had been stolen from a builder's yard. They could now put the full registration into the ANPR, which would alert them if Gates drove on any of the main routes in the area.

Ruth's radio crackled. 'Three-six from Gold Command. Echo-charlie-three and four are in position, over.'

'Three-six, received,' Ruth replied.

The codes referred to the two police helicopters on standby should Gates try to do anything that required him being tracked from the air.

Ruth then radioed the teams of AROs, who had been positioned out of sight at either end of the aqueduct, to check they were ready to go if anything went wrong. Marks-men were hidden up in the thickly wooded areas on the ad-jacent hills. Everyone was in place and ready to go.

The North Wales Police Media Department had negotiated a twenty-four-hour media blackout to prevent members of the public being drawn to the aqueduct by live news reports.

Now feeling anxious, Ruth wondered how this was going to play out. Had Gates had enough of being on the run and was now willing to hand himself in? On the one hand, Gates had an ego the size of a planet and clearly took delight in thinking that he had made the police look stupid. He had escaped from custody once, as well as luring police to a fake hideout and hoodwinking officers when he returned to kill his wife Kerry. Keeping one step ahead of them clearly got him excited.

However, she also knew that Gates was keen to tell his story to whoever would listen. And to do this, he would need to stand trial and go to jail. There would be journalists, writers and even filmmakers queuing up to add Gates's story to the growing canon of true-crime books, television and films that were now part of a multi-million-pound business. Ruth hoped that Gates's ego would get the better of him and he would sacrifice his temporary freedom for his day in the sun.

The snow turned to sleet, pattering on Ruth's stab-proof jacket. She could feel the tension in her stomach and took a deep breath. She needed this operation to go well.

Her radio crackled again. 'Three-six from alpha-one. Eyeball on unidentified male crossing the canal on the footbridge at the north end of the aqueduct, over.'

Ruth thought for a moment. The north end was the other side of the valley. 'Received. Alpha-one from three-six, do we have a description of unidentified male, over?'

'Three-six. Male is middle-aged, medium build and height, wearing a dark-red jacket and black woollen hat, over.'

It was Gates.

That wasn't what had been planned. Ruth's mind was whirring. Why was Gates coming from the north end? There could be a simple explanation, but it worried her. Why had he changed the plan? Maybe it was his ego showing them that he would do it his way.

'Received. Three-six to all units. Target is heading for the aqueduct from the north end. If target attempts to cross, all units to stand down until target is at the south end, over.' Ruth had arranged to meet Gates at the south end and she wasn't going to deviate from that. It was far too dangerous to try to intercept Gates as he walked across the aqueduct with the massive drop either side.

'Three-six, eyeball on target, now proceeding over the aqueduct.'

Ruth could see Gates in the distance strolling along the towpath, which she had learnt was three hundred metres long. She calculated that it shouldn't take him more than five minutes to get to the end. It was time to move.

Moving out of her hidden position, Ruth walked alongside the empty canal. It was silent except for the wind that buffeted her.

Now at the middle of the aqueduct, Gates stopped and looked around as if he wasn't quite sure if he was going to continue. He looked down at the enormous drop and the River Dee that splashed and swirled around the rocks below. What was he doing? Was he planning on jumping to his death? Surely, he was too arrogant for that ...

The tension rose as Gates hesitated. Then, thankfully, Gates continued to walk towards where Ruth was waiting.

'Three-six to all units. Target is approaching. Stand by, over,' Ruth said.

'Received, three-six.'

Out of the corner of her eye, Ruth could see the black figures of two AROs crouching a few yards down the bank, ready and poised for action if needed. However, Ruth intended to stick to her agreement with Gates. She would arrest him, cuff him and take him to the car. Gates wasn't going to attack her.

As Gates approached the final fifty yards, the wind switched direction blowing sleet directly into Ruth's face. She wiped it away from her eyes, squinting through the ice and water. Gates stepped off the end of the concrete towpath.

'Gold Command to all units. Apprehend target. Repeat, apprehend target!' It was an order from the Armed Response commander and Ruth was furious.

The two AROs trained their Heckler & Koch MP5 submachine guns on Gates who had now stopped.

Ruth turned to face the AROs. 'No! What the bloody hell are you doing? This is not what I agreed!'

'Please step out of the way, ma'am!' the ARO said sternly.

'Armed police! Get down on the ground!' the other ARO bellowed at Gates.

No. This couldn't be happening. This wasn't what she had agreed with Gates. Once he was arrested, he would never cooperate now.

'Lie flat on the ground!' the ARO thundered. Gates nodded, sunk to his knees and then lay flat on the sleet-covered concrete.

'What's going on? I haven't done anything!' came the voice from the figure on the ground, who was roughly cuffed, frisked and then brought to his feet.

Ruth wiped her eyes again and looked at Gates. Except the terrified face that looked back at her wasn't Gates. It was someone else!

'I haven't done anything!' the man pleaded.

'Who are you?' Ruth asked.

The man, wide-eyed with fear, looked at the guns that were still trained on him.

'What's your name, sir?' Ruth asked, realising that somehow Gates had tricked them again.

'Ewan Harris. I ... d-don't understand. What's going on?'

'Where did you get those clothes, Ewan?' Ruth asked, starting to piece things together.

'Some bloke in the pub over there. The Trevor Inn.' He gestured to the north side of the aqueduct. 'He gave me the coat and hat and said he'd give me a hundred pounds to walk over the aqueduct and back. Said it was part of some practical joke he was playing on a mate of his. They're on a Christmas work do or something.'

'When was this?' Ruth asked, wondering if Gates was still in the area.

'About an hour ago. He said it had to be at four o'clock to get the money.'

'Thank you,' Ruth said, forcing a smile and signalling for the AROs to stand down.

It was another operational disaster and Gates was still on the loose.

NICK CAME INTO INTERVIEW Room One where Rosie Chivers was waiting for him. He had contacted her and asked her to come in for a 'voluntary' interview. She was slim, with neatly bobbed blonde hair and a tanned face as though she had been abroad. Fiddling nervously with her long cardigan, she looked up. Nick saw her chest rise as her breath quickened. He didn't know if it was the prospect of a police interview or underlying guilt.

'Miss Chivers, thank you for coming in today,' Nick said in a friendly tone as she sat down and opened the case file.

'No problem.' She smiled and avoided eye contact. 'It's Rosie.'

Nick nodded as he thumbed through the case file. 'Rosie, right.' He let her stew in her nervousness for a few more seconds. 'I'm looking into the murder of Harvey Pearson, which happened on Mount Snowdon on the afternoon of Sunday the ninth of December. We're trying to establish who was on the mountain at the time of the murder. We spoke a few days ago when you told me your whereabouts on the afternoon of the ninth. Is that correct?' Nick looked up at her and gave her a kind smile.

'Yes.' She nodded, but she looked like she was struggling to hold it together.

'According to my notes, you said you were with a friend at the Llancastell Odeon cinema and that you went to see the three-o'clock performance of *They Will Not Grow Old*?' Nick explained. He needed to get her to confirm she saw the film, which was a provable lie. That would put her in a very difficult situation.

'Yes, that's right.' Rosie nodded uncertainly.

'You saw the film?' Nick asked as he looked down as his notes. It was purposefully delivered in a nonchalant manner.

'Yes.' Rosie visibly gulped at her lie.

Nick looked up at her. 'You saw the three-o'clock performance of *They Will Not Grow Old* at the Llancastell Odeon on Sunday the ninth of December?'

Rosie had no choice but to hang on in there. 'Yes. I don't understand?'

'Unfortunately, I've watched the CCTV footage from that afternoon. You didn't watch the film, so you need to tell me right now what you were doing.' Nick's tone became grave.

Rosie leaned forwards on her seat and moved awkwardly. She put her lips together and blew out slowly, trying to control her nerves. 'I can't tell you.'

'I'm afraid you need to tell me where you were, Rosie.'

Rosie's hands were now shaking. Whatever it was, Nick could see Rosie was under a huge amount of stress having to admit where she had been. 'I just can't.' She put her hand to her forehead and then a tear rolled down her face.

'It's okay. Whatever it is, Rosie, you can tell me.'

Rosie closed her eyes. 'I was ... with another man. Not my boyfriend.'

'Okay. I will have to confirm that,' Nick said.

'No, I'm not lying, I promise you. If my boyfriend finds out, it would kill him,' Rosie said as the tears rolled down her cheeks.

CHAPTER 29

Ruth sat on the patio, wrapped in a thick turquoise blanket, smoking a ciggie. A cold breeze blew the fragrance of the countryside in from the neighbouring fields. It was perfectly silent. Until her phone pinged with the noise that signalled she had an email. Tapping it open, she saw it was from Steven Flaherty.

Hi Ruth. Results from the police in Berlin confirm that the fingerprints on the passport belong to Jurgen Kessler. I think we can safely assume that it was Kessler that was trying to get a job at Bournemouth University. I have the CCTV to watch tonight and I'll get back to you as soon as I can. Steven x

Ruth took this in. They finally had a solid lead on Kessler, and he may not know they were onto him. The tiny fragments of hope every few months in the search for Sarah were exhausting, and Ruth could spend the whole night with ideas and scenarios whirring through her head. But she had to be pragmatic. She would wait to see the CCTV and go from there. She would park that part of her mind away for the evening.

Ruth's thoughts turned to the Gates case, which was becoming absurd. The only saving grace was that there had been a media blackout, but it was only a matter of time before the story broke. They couldn't hide the fact that there had been helicopters, dogs and armed units at the Pontcysyllte Aqueduct. Anyone could put two and two together and guess that the operation had been connected with the hunt for Andrew Gates. It had been another failure.

Ruth drank an inch off her large glass of red wine. She was definitely drinking more these days. She looked up at the dark sky and tried to relax. Ella had text earlier to say she was looking at some flats up in Aldford in Cheshire. Then she was coming back to report to Sian and her. Ella had thought it was hilarious that the estate agent taking her was called John Kipper. What a funny name! She had sent emojis of fish at the end of her text. Ruth was glad that she was so much more involved in Ella's life now. When she had moved to Liverpool, and Ruth was still mourning Sarah's disappearance, they had drifted apart. It would be nice to have her living up the road.

Sian came out wrapped in a coat. She plonked down her wine glass and filled it from the bottle on the table.

'You're meant to keep red wine at room temperature, you dope,' Sian said as she sat down. 'And you're not meant to be smoking.'

Ruth gave her the finger. 'Fuck off, Mum.'

Sian gave her a sarcastic smile. 'What did Drake say when you got back?'

'He said it was a fucking shambles ... again.'

'He could do with a better vocabulary. Although I'm not sure what's worse than "a fucking shambles."'

Sian had been based at Llancastell nick with Drake in the Gold Command control centre. 'He had a showdown with the Armed Response commander. And Drake has got to explain wasting thousands more of taxpayers' money on another botched attempt to get Gates. Jones was there for a bit and he was very quiet. He went visibly white when you realised it wasn't Gates. Where's Ella?'

'She's gone to look at a flat in Aldford.'

'Ooh. Very posh.' Sian raised her eyebrows.

Ruth gestured to her phone. 'Estate agent's name is John Kipper. Ella thought it was hilarious.'

Sian smiled and sipped her wine. She took a moment then looked concerned. 'John Kipper? Mr Kipper?'

Ruth shrugged. 'That's what she said.'

'Kipper? As in fish?' Sian asked.

'Yes. What's the problem? The man has a comedy name,' Ruth said.

Sian pulled her phone out of her coat pocket and began tapping furiously at the screen.

Ruth was concerned by Sian's reaction. 'What? What's the matter?'

'I know the name and ...' Sian's eyes flicked over her phone screen.

'Bloody hell. What are you talking about?' Ruth's impatience was turning into concern. Sian wasn't easily spooked.

Sian's face was anxious as she read aloud. 'Suzy Lamplugh, a British estate agent, went missing on the twenty-eighth of July 1986 in Fulham, London. She was eventually declared dead in 1994 with the presumption that she had been murdered.'

Ruth was none the wiser as she nodded. 'Yeah, I remember. I was a teenager and just down the road.'

Sian continued to read. 'The last clue to her whereabouts was an appointment to show a house to someone she had written down as "Mr Kipper." Although it has never been confirmed, many believe that convicted murderer and rapist John Cannan was guilty of her murder. Cannan's nickname in prison had been *Kipper*.'

Ruth couldn't take in what she had heard. It had to be a coincidence, didn't it? Was someone using the name as some kind of dark joke? There must be other people with the surname *Kipper*. The whole experience with Gates was making her paranoid, wasn't it?

Ruth grabbed her phone and rang Ella. It went straight to voicemail. That was even more worrying – it was almost never turned off.

'She's not answering.'

Sian looked at Ruth. 'John Kipper? Neither of us believes in coincidences, do we?'

'It's just a surname, isn't it? You think someone has a twisted sense of humour?'

'Maybe ... How many Kippers have you met in your career as a police officer?'

Ruth was feeling sick with fear. 'None.'

'Me neither.'

The tension mounted and Ruth's mind lurched from rationality to utter fear.

'Gates?' Sian asked, thinking out loud.

Ruth felt her insides whirl and drop. 'I don't know.' But her instinct was starting to tell her that she *did* know.

Standing up and dropping the blanket, Ruth moved for the back door. 'We need to go to Alford. It's all we've got to go on.'

Sian followed and picked up her phone. 'I'll see if I can get someone in CID to triangulate Ella's number.'

A vibration buzzed in Ruth's hand. It was her phone and the sound of a text. In that split second, she prayed that it was Ella texting to say she was okay and she was coming home.

The text message was from Ella. Ruth felt the tension begin to leave her as she opened up the message. 'It's from Ella. "Hiya. The flat is perfect. I've got some photos to show you."'

Sian sighed. 'Thank God!'

Ruth's pulse slowed as she continued to read. '"There's another flat up the road that John's going to show me. He made me send you this photo with me in a Christmas hat! LOL. See you in a bit xx."'

Ruth and Sian exchanged a look and smiled. Maybe the job had just made them hypercautious or paranoid? *Thank God for that*, Ruth thought.

Ruth looked down at the photo as it opened. It was a selfie. There was Ella's big beaming face with a red Santa hat. Ruth noticed that her forehead and nose were a bit shiny. Ella wouldn't like that.

And just over her shoulder, there was a man's face, which must be John Kipper.

Except ...

It was the face of Andrew Gates.

Ruth's world slowed and darkened as if time had stopped. And then she felt physically sick.

Andrew Gates had her daughter.

CHAPTER 30

Amanda had recovered from her alcoholic 'slip.' Nick could see that she was feeling a lot better, although she had spent the last hour apologising and generally beating herself up.

As Amanda tried to step over Nick, who was lounging on the sofa, he playfully put out his leg and held her arm so that she fell slowly on top of him.

'Easy, tiger,' she said.

Nick looked into her eyes and ran his thumb down her cheek and then onto her lips. She looked back, her eyes moving around his face and then back to his eyes. She smiled.

'You okay?' he whispered.

She nodded. 'After what happened to me last year, I didn't think I could ever do this again. But you've made me feel so safe, so secure.'

Nick pulled her close and they kissed, pulling each other tighter. She stood up and without a word led him to her bedroom. She undressed, never taking her eyes from his. She walked over and pressed her naked body to him, her hands unbuttoning his shirt and feeling his chest underneath.

Nick could feel her skin against his. Her hair smelt of coconut shampoo and a hint of cigarette smoke. He didn't care. He liked it. He had always liked the hint of booze, smoke or perfume on a woman. That 'just washed' fresh smell wasn't sexy to him.

For a moment, Nick remembered the last time he had had sex before Amanda. It was while he was still drinking and it had been a clumsy, awkward and unsatisfying experience, some of which had been lost to a blackout.

A moment later, they crashed to the bed and made love with an urgency that he found overwhelming. It was like nothing that he had experienced before. A moment where lust and love had fused together. It seemed to heave waves of emotion over him that were indescribable.

And then they climaxed loudly together in the darkness. It was perfect.

For the next few moments, they kissed, giggled and held each other in the stillness of the night.

'Sober sex is great, isn't it?' Nick said as he recovered his breath.

'Sober sex with anyone is great?' Amanda asked with a wry smile.

'You know what I mean. Sober sex with you.'

They kissed again and smiled at each other. Amanda pulled the duvet up to her waist, lay back and sighed.

'Mind if I smoke?' Amanda asked.

'Bit of cliché, isn't it?' Nick joked.

'Don't worry. I'll wait.'

'I don't mind. After that, I don't think I'll care about anything ever again.'

Amanda rolled over onto her elbow, moved a sweaty strand of hair from her face and winked. 'I love you, Nicholas Evans, you know that?'

'I love you too, Mandy.' Nick smiled. The other day it had just slipped out, but this time he knew he meant those words. There had been so many times when he hadn't. He had worried that he never would.

Amanda grabbed a remote from the side of the bed, pressed a button and the album *What's Going On?* by Marvin Gaye began to play. 'Best album ever made, I swear down.'

'You "swear down"? What are you, twelve?'

'And for the record, if you ever call me *Mandy* again, I will strangle you.' Amanda laughed.

'Threatening a police officer? You should be careful. Water?'

'Please.'

Nick got out of bed and headed for the kitchen. It felt strange to feel this good without something artificially buoying his spirits. As he looked around the kitchen to find something to eat, he gazed at the photos of Amanda's travels and adventures. He felt a twinge of warmth and excitement; it was lovely to think that he was with someone who was well-travelled and had such broad horizons. Some of the women in his past were so parochial, they thought a trip down to London was the height of adventure.

Nick's eye was then drawn to a photo of a group of friends. Four thirty-something women with happy smiling faces. Amanda was in the middle with stylish sunglasses and a beaming smile. The background was snowy and mountainous. It looked like they had been skiing. One of the friends, a dark-skinned woman with black curly hair, had a bottle of beer in her hand.

Nick had never been skiing. Maybe that's something he and Amanda could do. His mind ran away with itself, creating images of him and Amanda in the snow with all the cheese and tackiness of Wham's 'Last Christmas' pop video.

Gazing back at the photo, Nick studied Amanda's friends in more detail. On the far right, a dark-haired girl was carrying a rucksack. At the very edge of the photo, he could see that a red square had been sewn onto the pocket of the rucksack. He then zoned in on the bottle of beer in her hand. Was he envious? Maybe for a second, until Nick realised that he had lost the ability to sip slowly from a bottle of beer or two decades ago.

His eye was drawn back to the red square on the rucksack. It wasn't a square, it was a flag. Nick thought of the Welsh flag and the red dragon. He considered it the best national flag in the world.

Nick inspected the flag on the rucksack again.

Red and white with a maple leaf.

A Canadian flag.

*Jesus Christ! You have got to be kidding m*e!

THE VILLAGE OF TYDDYN Llwyn, close to Porthmadog, had a large holiday resort of over two hundred cabins, static caravans and even villas. It had changed a lot over the years and was far swankier these days, Gates surmised. He had been there with Kerry on their honeymoon. The spring of 1995. Robson and Gerome's 'Unchained Melody'

seemed to play from every radio in the place. But it was familiar to Gates. And that made it ideal.

The resort was completely closed in December and so it was the perfect spot for him to hide out.

Ella had started to annoy him. He had told her that he would slit her throat if she screamed. However, she had insisted on a constant stream of psychobabble so he had replaced the gag.

Gates had selected a huge log cabin at the far end of the park, which had magnificent views over Snowdonia's mountains. It was dark now, and Gates had illuminated the living space with candles so as not to draw any attention. Ella was strapped tightly to a wooden dining chair beside a long dining table. Relieved that she had long since given up struggling, crying or making any form of sound, Gates watched her as she stared ahead out of the window into the darkness.

As Gates began to make a fire, his footsteps echoed off the wooden walls and ceiling. There was a leather sofa and an armchair to one side, and a television mounted to the wall opposite.

'Need to warm this place up, my love,' Gates said with a smile. As he looked around, he thought about how this is what he had intended for the annexe of his home. Not with all the wood, of course, but the kind of smart, modern décor that the Air BnB market would appreciate. Tasteful and comfortable.

Whistling a Beatles' song to himself, Gates went to the kitchen to prepare some food. He would not be feeding Ella tonight. Starvation takes away a person's strength and makes them more manageable. Maybe he would give her something in the morning to lift her spirits? 'Eleanor Rigby'. Sounded like Ella, didn't it?

Being in a Scandinavian-style cabin was ironic, Gates thought. Even though his name was English, his father had claimed Norwegian ancestry. *Gates* was actually derived from the people who lived by the gates of a medieval town. It might be another topic of discussion in the books and articles. He knew that journalists would delve into his childhood to try to explain it all. There had been no obsession with killing insects or animals, which seemed to be a prerequisite of the modern serial killer. Although he did remember a biology class at school where he had dissected a lamb's heart. After the class, he had secretly collected up the discarded hearts into a plastic bag and taken them home with him. For the next week or so, he had played around with the hearts, cutting and examining them, until they began to rot. He convinced himself it was quite normal. He had ambitions to be a surgeon and he was just practising for his future career.

It wasn't until he stole a mannequin from behind a department store and took it home to have sex with that Gates had started to fear that his mind and his sexual desires were abnormal.

Gates knew that kidnapping Ella would achieve what he wanted. The strange, intangible bond he had formed with Ruth was confusing him. There was no sexual element to it. But he knew that he felt too compelled to taunt and trick her to get her attention. When he had Ruth's attention, he felt a sense of calm and peace. Even love. When she deceived him, as she had at the aqueduct, then he became angry, even furious. He had watched from a distance as the man he had paid to wear his jacket and hat, who Gates could only assume was some kind of local drunk, had been arrested. There had been guns in his face and he was forced to lie on the wet ground. No dignity. Ruth had lied to him and broken her promise. That's not what he wanted, and she would yield to him. The only conclusion that he could draw was that Ruth had become some kind of maternal figure to him. There was an innate kindness and compassion to her, even when she had dealt with him. Maybe that was it? Ruth was the polar opposite of his own mother, a cold, emotionally stunted and even cruel woman. More importantly, he could never get her attention.

He had a younger brother who had Downs syndrome. If his mother showed any affection, it was reserved for James. It wasn't a great psychological leap for Gates to realise that he was attempting to play out some fantasy where Ruth was now his mother. A new, better, more compassionate version. And now he needed to rewrite his own life history by controlling 'Mother' and forcing her to give him attention, by any means necessary.

Quite what he was going to do with Ella, he wasn't sure yet. In this new fantasy scenario, she was effectively his sister. And he wanted to keep 'Mother' on side. He needed to give her a call soon. Just to put her mind at rest. Poor her. She must be going out of her mind with worry. It was difficult being a parent, he presumed, even when your children were all grown up.

Then Gates had another thought. Didn't Ella actually pose a threat to the attention he might receive from 'Mother'? She was a sibling and therefore a rival for affection and awareness. Sibling rivalry could get pretty nasty. Violent even. Cain and Abel were brothers and look at how that ended.

Might it not be better if Ella were no longer around? Didn't killing her take her out of the picture once and for all? That was the answer, Gates decided. Killing her did seem to make perfect, logical sense. There was a certain biblical logic to it.

And so the decision was made. He would kill Ella to get her out of the way. Not tonight. Tomorrow morning maybe? At dawn. Yes. Killing her at dawn would be a poetical statement.

IT WAS NOW VERY LATE, but CID was on high alert. Having informed Drake the night before that Gates had Ella, Ruth was now sitting with several CID officers. She was frantic but tried to keep the dark thoughts from her mind. Gates's MO had always been men. Normally ones that he had found attractive. That's what he got off on. Taking Ella was clearly a way of getting her attention, just as Professor Douglas had predicted. It could also be some kind of revenge for the bungled arrest at the aqueduct. Maybe Gates had been watching from a distance? In fact, she was pretty sure that he had been. Trying to hold it together, Ruth was finding it difficult to concentrate on anything.

Tapping at a computer, Sian was on the CID system, sifting through everything they had on Gates. It had been checked before, but maybe they had missed something.

'Everything that Gates has done has been carried out in the Dee Valley,' Ruth said urgently. 'He's a creature of habit. He likes to stick close to areas that he feels safe or secure in. He could have gone anywhere. He could have driven into England. But he's kept in a pretty small area because that's all he knows. And wherever he is keeping Ella ...' At that moment, the words stuck in Ruth's throat. She coughed, but no one would blame her for feeling emotional.

Drake came over and put his hand on her shoulder. 'It's okay, Ruth. Come on, let's have a chat in your office?'

Nodding but lost in thought, Ruth followed Drake into her office and sat down.

Drake took a moment as he rested against her desk. 'I can't imagine how you're feeling, Ruth. My kids are everything. And I'm sure it's the same with Ella.'

Ruth nodded. 'It's my fault this has happened.' The guilt that Ella had been drawn into her dark, evil world made the blame and fear all the harder to bear.

'No. No, it's not. Gates is ...' Drake paused as he searched for the right words. 'We know what Gates is. You are not responsible for what he does.'

'He's got Ella because of me!' Ruth raised her voice. Her whole body seemed to tingle with terror and anxiety. The depths of her stomach were hollow with a dark uneasiness.

'This is what I need you to do, Ruth.' Drake looked directly at her. 'I need you to go home and get some rest, however hard that might be.'

'You're not taking me off this case.' Ruth thundered adamantly.

'You know how this works, Ruth.'

'No. You can't do that to me,' Ruth said, her voice breaking a little. How was she meant to go home and get some rest? She wasn't going to rest until she had Ella back.

'Come on, Ruth. You're an experienced copper. No one is going to allow you to work on a case that you're now so personally involved with,' Drake said.

She knew that what Drake had said was true. Yet the idea of not being involved in an operation to rescue her own daughter made her feel sick and hopelessly out of control.

'I'm sorry ...' Ruth mumbled as a tear ran down her face. She didn't want Drake to see her cry, but it was no use. She was overwhelmed.

'I will keep you posted at every point. I promise,' Drake said as he put his hand on her arm.

'I want Sian to be directly involved in the case,' Ruth said.

Drake paused for a moment, his eyes lost in temporary thought. Although her and Sian's relationship was not common knowledge, and technically not appropriate because of their differing ranks, she suspected that Drake had worked it out by now. He was canny and intuitive. 'Okay. But her work on the case has to be dispassionate and fully professional.'

'Of course,' Ruth said as she got up. 'Thank you, sir.'

'We will find her, Ruth. And we'll get her back safely.'

'I know that, sir.'

Ruth left the office but she was already plotting how she could continue the search from home. There was no way that she was going to sit at home twiddling her thumbs, waiting for her colleagues to find Ella. She tapped Sian's shoulder. 'He's sending me home,' she said quietly.

Sian nodded. 'Okay. I'll be here for a bit.' Their eyes met for a moment. 'We'll get her back, I promise.'

CHAPTER 31

Having not slept well, Nick had gone into Llancastell nick early, only to find out the horrific news about Gates's kidnapping of Ella. Drake had asked him to help the team in the hunt for Ella while keeping any lines of enquiry over Harvey Pearson's murder going too. Nick had tried to call Ruth, but she wasn't answering her phone. He couldn't imagine how she was feeling.

Sipping his hot coffee, Nick looked at the computer screen in front of him. Did he need to worry about the photo he had seen in Amanda's house? Four women on holiday together. One of them mixed race and another with a Canadian flag stitched to her rucksack. *Fuck!* Nick sat back angrily. He didn't believe in coincidences. No decent detective ever did. But how was he meant to focus objectively on what it could mean? He didn't even want to entertain those thoughts. Could Amanda and her three friends have been on Snowdonia on the afternoon of Sunday 9 December? Did they have some involvement in Harvey Pearson's death? Amanda knew that Nick was working on the case, so if they had been there, she would have told him by now. Either that or she was hiding something. That made him more than uneasy. Had Amanda even targeted him to find out about the case? Did that mean that everything that had developed between him and Amanda had been a sham, a pretence? The twist of pain that thought brought was nothing compared to what he would experience if that were true. He feared it would send him back to drink, just to deal with the agony of it. Then he thought of Amanda and how she had been with him. His instinct told him that she wasn't faking any of that. No one could be that cold and calculating, could they?

The simple thing would be to ask her where she was. However, there was no decent way of asking her without flagging up his suspicions. Who were her friends? If any of them were from Canada, had they even been in the UK in December? Was he just overthinking the whole thing and there was a perfectly logical explanation? It wouldn't be the first time that he had got things wrong. His mind wasn't wired properly. Alcoholics' brains were different. That's why he had a sponsor for God's sake! To give him perspective. But he couldn't ring Bill. How would he explain that he had fallen in love with a newcomer but now suspected that she might be a witness to, or even involved in, a murder on Snowdon? Bill would sack him as a sponsee on the spot. And he was well within his rights to, Nick knew. It was Bill who had got him sober and helped him stay that way in recent months.

Feeling that the integral structures of his life were collapsing in on him, Nick felt the despair descend. It was the kind of despair that came with a relapse.

Screwing his eyes shut for a moment to try to stop the incessant burble and chattering in his head, Nick opened his emails. He saw that there was one from Lillie's Little Café in Llanberis. He had been in there to question the owner, Lillie Milton, about whether she had seen the four women on the

9 December. Lillie couldn't remember but said she would check CCTV and talk to staff, who were mostly part-time.

Lillie had emailed him at midnight and attached a file.

Hi DS Evans,

It's Lillie from Lillie's Little Café in Llanberis. You asked me about December 9th. I've done a screenshot of the CCTV of four women who came in for breakfast that day. I'm afraid no one could remember much about them or if they had accents. Sorry to not be more helpful. If you would like to see all the CCTV footage, I could ask someone to help me send it to you, or you could look at it here.

Kind regards, Lillie.

Feeling agitated, Nick clicked to open the image file. A black-and-white, high-angle photo showed a round corner table where four women sat eating. He had been praying to see one or more of the Chivers sisters sitting there.

However, he could immediately see it wasn't them. Two of the women had their backs to the camera, wearing hats and scarves. One of the women facing them was drinking a large mug of tea so her face was obscured. The other woman's face was a little grainy, but even though she was wearing a woolly hat, he could see that she had dark skin. She could be mixed race. And she could be the woman he had seen on the wall at Amanda's house.

Knowing that he had a spare key to her house from the other night, Nick grabbed his coat. Though it sickened him, he knew that he had to go to Amanda's house and search for what he could find. Technically, he knew he should wait for a search warrant, but he didn't care about that. He wasn't thinking straight. He just needed to know the truth. Now.

HAVING SLEPT FOR ONLY three hours, Ruth was drinking strong coffee, feeling lost and emotionally drained. However hard she tried, her thoughts were continually drawn back to what Ella might be going through. She would be frightened, but Ruth hoped it was no worse than that. Gates had demonstrated no indications of that terrible need to torture victims that some serial killers exhibited. But sitting alone, feeling powerless, she could only imagine the worst, with disturbing images flashing across her mind's eye. Why did it do that? Why weren't human beings able to control the dark thoughts that entered their heads? Given what she had witnessed in her own life, her career as a police officer, and in particular with Gates, the human brain didn't seem fit for purpose.

The box of Gates's possessions that she had taken from CID sat on the long dining table. Every document, photo album, ticket and receipt had been laid out in piles. It had taken nearly an hour to organise. Was there something here that would give her a clue to Ella's whereabouts? Perhaps Gates's folded birth certificate or *Certified Copy of an Entry of Birth* as it stated in red lettering at the top of the document. He had been born in Glan Clwyd Hospital on 14 December 1975, which made it Gates's forty-third birthday tomorrow. She thought of the eight birth certificates of Gates's victims, which would now be joined by death certificates in the coming months.

Putting aside her coffee and thumbing through a pile of Valentine's cards from Kerry, Ruth realised that Gates had kept every one that Kerry had ever sent him. It didn't make sense to her. Gates was a psychopath who enjoyed murdering men for sexual gratification. However, he seemed to have had a romantic, loving, even if platonic, relationship with his wife, Kerry. Keeping the Valentine's cards seemed an odd quirk.

As she read through the cheesy messages of love, she noticed that the older cards had a repeated message in them: *We'll always have Tyddyn Llwyn xx*. She assumed it was a meaningful reference to the end of the film *Casablanca* when Humphrey Bogart says goodbye to Ingrid Bergman with the line, *'We'll always have Paris.'*

Trying to focus on looking for clues, Ruth flicked through photographs in old-fashioned Prontaprint packets. Her mind wandered again. Sian had returned home in the early hours and gone back to CID in Llancastell at the crack of dawn. She was glad that Sian was there to give her the inside track.

Suddenly, Ruth's phone rang. Although it could have been Sian, Drake or anyone in CID, she intuitively knew it was Gates. She assumed he would have dumped Gwenda Chadwick's phone after the last time he had called her. It would be easy to pick up a pay-as-you-go, or burner, phone from any supermarket. Triangulation from mobile masts could be effective if a suspect continued to use the same phone or if they knew the suspect's number. They now had neither.

'Ruth.' It was Gates's voice, irritatingly upbeat as though greeting a long-lost friend.

'I want to speak to Ella.' Ruth wasn't going to entertain any of Gates's nonsense until she knew that Ella was okay.

'Of course,' Gates said. There was a moment's silence; Ruth's heart started to beat faster.

'Mum?' It was Ella. She sounded scared but her voice was clear and strong, which suggested that she was still physically well.

'Ella? Are you okay?' Ruth's hand shook as she held her phone. Tears ran down her face as she gritted her teeth.

'Yeah, fine, don't worry, I'm—' Ella said, and then she was gone as the phone was taken away from her.

'You lied to me, Ruth,' Gates scolded.

'That wasn't down to me. I was there to pick you up and take you to the car as I promised. I had no idea about the guns and the arrest. It was an order that came from above my head.' Knowing that Gates had some ideal of Ruth that was wrapped up in his own twisted fantasy, Ruth had to play along. 'I'm sorry, Andrew. Really. That wasn't what I wanted and I know that's not what we agreed.'

'It's hard for me to trust you now, Ruth'

'You can trust me. Honestly. But it's going to be hard for me to help you now you've got Ella.'

'You love Ella, don't you?' Gates question seemed genuine, as if he had only just had this thought.

'Of course. She's my daughter.'

'She's your only child, isn't she?'

'Yes. And if I'm going to help you and listen to what you need to tell me, then I need to come and get her,' Ruth said.

There was silence at the end of the phone. She could hear Gates breathing but couldn't second-guess what he was thinking.

'Andrew? Tell me where you are and I will come and get both of you,' Ruth suggested.

'Both of us?' Gates snapped suddenly. 'I don't want this to be about her. This is about me and what *I* want!'

Ruth was scared that Gates was becoming increasingly erratic and angry. 'It is what you want. But you need to let me have Ella, so we can talk and you can have what you need.'

'Stop talking about Ella! For God's sake. Ella this, Ella that. Is she all you can think about? What about me? What about me, Ruth?' Gates shouted down the phone in anger and twisted self-pity.

'I'm sorry, Andrew. I just ...'

'A child for a child? Is that fair?' Gates bellowed.

She had no idea what he was talking about, but she didn't like the sound of what he was saying.

'What child, Andrew?' As far as she knew, Gates didn't have any children.

'Our child. My child!' Gates virtually spat the words down the phone.

'Do you have a child, Andrew?' Ruth couldn't tell if Gates was revealing something of significance or just not making any sense.

'Maybe it would be better if Ella wasn't here,' Gates said coldly.

'Okay. I can come and get her. After that, it would be just me and you. That's a good idea.'

'No, no. I mean it might be better if Ella just wasn't around *at all*.'

Even though Gates was being vague, Ruth trembled when she tried to analyse what he meant. 'I don't understand what you mean, Andrew.'

'Of course you do, Ruth. Why must I simplify things for everyone? If Ella didn't exist, then it really would just be me and you.'

'Please, I don't want you to hurt Ella. You don't need to do that.' Ruth could feel her voice trembling. The desperation and anxiety were overwhelming.

'You need to come and meet me. On your own. And this time, I mean alone. I think you know what will happen if you break your promise again,' Gates said. For once, his voice sounded grave.

'It will be just me, I promise. Just please don't hurt Ella, I'm begging you,' Ruth pleaded. 'Please.' She would do anything to get her daughter back.

The line went dead. Gates had hung up. Her hands were shaking uncontrollably as Ruth tried to phone back. It was a struggle to hit the right buttons. *Pull yourself together!*

It rang out. She tried again. It rang out again.

When were they going to meet? Her sense of impending darkness was overpowering. She couldn't bear to think of her daughter with Gates. She would risk her life for her daughter's without a moment's hesitation. And if that meant going to meet him with no back-up, no armed officers, nothing, then so be it.

She was no longer thinking and acting as a police officer. She was thinking and acting with all the basic, protective instincts of a mother.

THERE WAS AN UNNERVING silence as Nick slipped quietly into Amanda's house. She had gone to work and would be out until early evening. Snapping on his purple forensic gloves, he felt a terrible pang of guilt and betrayal. He had prayed that morning that there would be nothing to show that Amanda and her friends were on Snowdon that afternoon. He promised his Higher Power that he would spend his life relentlessly helping others, both in his job and in sobriety, if Amanda wasn't involved. He knew it didn't work like that. He prayed for his mother twenty years ago. Promised that he would do anything if she was saved from cancer. It didn't work twenty years ago, and he feared it wouldn't work now.

Trying to put himself in Amanda's shoes, and thinking about how she would have acted that day returning from Snowdon, he began to search the house. Striding to the kitchen, he looked again at the photo of Amanda and her three friends skiing. He peered closely at the face of her mixed-race friend. Her half-smile, dark eyes and black ringlets of hair that protruded from below a white woollen hat. Could that be the women who had sat in the café in Llanberis on the morning of Sunday 9 December? Yes, it could be. And if he needed, the boys in Technical Forensics could take certain features from both images and use one of the algorithms of facial-recognition technology to see if there was a match. But it hadn't got to that point. Yet.

Moving closer to the photograph on the wall, Nick checked what Amanda was wearing: a Superdry ski jacket, gloves, beanie and sunglasses. Now that he thought about it, she hadn't worn any of those things the day she had met him up on Snowdon. He spent the next twenty minutes checking her wardrobe, drawers and cupboards but found nothing that matched the clothes in the photo. There might be a perfectly good explanation. However, Amanda worked with the police and she wasn't stupid. If anything had happened that afternoon, the smart thing would have been to get rid of all clothing. That would get rid of any significant risks of DNA or forensic evidence.

Sifting through jewellery cases and bags, Nick still couldn't find anything of use. He was trying as hard as he could to leave no trace that he had been in the house at all. It was something that he had become skilled at.

Sitting on the living room floor, he opened a box of old photos he'd found in a cupboard under the stairs. Going through photos of Amanda as a child, with her parents, on holidays, made him squirm all the more. This was the woman that he was falling in love with. He picked up one photo, sat back and looked at it. She was an innocent five-year-old girl, sitting on an old-fashioned tractor, smiling without a care in the world. At that moment, the enormity of what was happening, and how it might play out, swept over Nick and a tear appeared in his eye. He took a deep breath.

What the bloody hell was he going to do if she was guilty of something? Hand her over to stand trial for manslaughter, conspiracy to murder or worse? Was he capable of doing that? And if this was all his mistaken paranoia, then he would have to live with the fact that he hadn't trusted her.

Putting the box back where he'd found it, he looked around the hall. He was relieved that he hadn't discovered anything. However, he did know that somehow he had to establish where she had been on 9 December.

Looking up the stairs, his eyes were drawn to a square hatch of wood in the ceiling of the first-floor landing. Access to the loft. His mood sank a little. If she had hidden anything away, it would be up there.

Reluctantly, Nick climbed the stairs, took a chair from the spare room and stood on it. He pushed the wooden hatch and moved it to one side. Clicking on his pocket torch, he peered through the dusty, dark air into the roof space. It was only about twelve-foot square and was lined with boxes and black bin bags. It would take hours to go through this lot.

As he reattached the wooden hatch, his thoughts turned to Ruth and how she must be feeling. Ella was a lovely young woman, and he knew how close they had become in the past two years. He would try to ring or even go see her later.

Suddenly, he heard a key in the front door. He froze. As far as he knew, Amanda was the only person who had another key. What was she doing home? Had she seen his car outside?

He manoeuvred the loft hatch back into position as quietly as he could. He stepped down from the chair onto the carpeted landing, picked it up and headed for the spare room.

'Hello?' Amanda's voice called from downstairs. He hadn't locked the front door behind him, so it was just on the latch. There was no way of hiding the fact that he was there.

'Hi there!' he called back breezily, still trying to concoct an excuse in his head.

'You skiving?' she called back.

He went to the stairs and began to descend. She came across, looked up at him and smiled.

'I just popped in to get something I'd left here.' Nick smiled back.

'Not seeing if I was here for a quickie then?' she asked with a cheeky grin.

This was killing him. 'Actually, now you're asking ...' he replied, playing along.

Then her expression changed as she looked down. 'You always walk around in forensic gloves?' At first, it seemed like a joke, but something in her face gave away her realisation of why he might be wearing them.

'No ... I must have forgotten ...' He knew how weak and unconvincing he sounded as he took them off and continued down the stairs to the hall where she was standing.

Then there were seconds of unbearable silence. Was he going to continue to make feeble excuses and bluff his way out of this? Realising that he needed answers, whatever that brought, he let his face show how he was really feeling.

'Really?' she said in an angry, disbelieving tone.

He looked directly at her. 'No ... That was a lie. I'm sorry. I really am.'

She closed her eyes for a moment as though she couldn't quite believe this was happening. And then a tear came.

'Do you know?' she whispered.

'I think so.' He nodded and frowned. 'You just need to tell me.'

'I wanted to tell you, you know? So many times.' She took a breath as she crumbled before his eyes. He couldn't bear to see her like this. She put her hands over her face as the tears and sobbing overwhelmed her.

He held her as she shook. 'Whatever it is, just tell me the truth. And then we can work out what to do. Okay?'

Through the shaking and tears, she nodded.

GATES RETURNED TO THE cabin with food and some other essentials. He felt a sense of achievement as he put the shopping bags down on the kitchen table. He went to the fridge, took out a bottle of white wine and swigged it. It was getting to be a habit, but he liked how it numbed some of the thoughts that whirled uncontrollably around his mind on an endless loop. The darkest of thoughts. It felt like a washing machine, he thought to himself. That endless tumbling of ideas, over and over again. And his thoughts were getting darker.

Going into the bathroom, he looked at himself in the mirror. He hadn't shaved since being on the run, and now his stubble was starting to look like a short beard. If it continued to grow, it would help disguise him even more. He wore the glasses that he had stolen from the man he had murdered in the shop. Plus a baseball cap that he had stolen yesterday. Admiring how different he looked, he smiled and turned off the light. Always one step ahead of the coppers. They were so stupid.

He ducked his head into the living room where he had left Ella tied to the chair the night before. He had slept in way past dawn. When he woke, he had decided to postpone killing Ella for at least a day or two. He wanted to speak to Ruth again and use Ella as a bargaining tool. He couldn't do that if she was dead.

Gates had allowed Ella to use the bathroom that morning at knifepoint. He didn't want to share the cabin with someone who had soiled themselves or stank. Also, that would be inhumane and degrading. That's not what this was about.

'We're relocating this morning, my little darling,' Gates said as he waved over at Ella. She didn't respond, which he thought was rude. He would let it go – this time.

Gates wanted to move on. A change of scene. He was also acutely aware that staying put in the same cabin would make their chances of capture much higher.

As he went around the cabin, his thoughts turned to Heidi, the daughter that he and Kerry had lost so early on in their marriage. And this was where it happened. Not this exact cabin, but this park. It had been God's will, he supposed. For whatever reason. In those days, they still called it 'cot death.' Now, it was sudden infant death syndrome. The doctors couldn't tell him and Kerry why Heidi had died. She had gone to sleep in their small holiday cottage and just never woken up. And it had crushed them both. He believed that Kerry had never fully recovered.

It had only been during the night that Gates had realised Ella must be virtually the same age as Heidi would have been if she had lived. How wonderful it would have been to have watched a daughter grow up and be there every step of the way. Maybe if Heidi had lived, he wouldn't have gone down the dark path that he was now treading.

For now, his priority was to see Ruth. He had her full attention and that made him happy. It might be best to wait another day, to let her fear really grow. Then his power over her would be absolute. She would do and say anything to get her Ella back. Stupid little Ella. A girl that had had all the love and attention of a mother throughout her life. No doubt she hadn't appreciated it. They never do. Girls like Ella don't appreciate anything until it's gone and it's too late. Spoilt. Why had God chosen Ella to live her life, full of love and opportunities, when he had taken Heidi so young? How was that fair? Ella hadn't had an unhappy day in her life.

Gates could feel his anger growing. He glanced over at Ella from the kitchen and then looked over at the knife block, which contained six sharp kitchen knives. Maybe if she lost an ear or a finger, she might appreciate life a little more? Maybe she would appreciate her mother who had done everything for her? Maybe she needed to be taught a lesson?

The clouds drifted across the azure sky and behind the peak of Snowdon. It was morning and Llanberis was quiet. It was always quiet this time of year, thanks to the unpredictable weather and short daylight hours.

Amanda looked up. The sky and temperature boded well for their ascent of the mountain. The climb had been a last-minute thing, but her friend Kristin's mother had been diagnosed with breast cancer a few months ago. They all wanted to do something. Kristin's mum, Jackie, had been the mum that they had all gravitated towards as teenagers and then young adults. She was a free spirit, a child of the sixties, with a calm, non-judgemental wisdom that seemed so different from their own parochial parents. In fact, Amanda had wanted Jackie to be her mother.

Even though they hadn't registered for a particular cancer charity, nor were they being sponsored, Amanda insisted that they all wear something pink in support of Jackie, Kristin and the battle that all women must fight against cancer.

Starting the day with breakfast at Lillie's Little Café, Amanda, Kristin, Nyree and Olivia laughed and chatted as only old friends can. They had gone to school and sixth-form college together. They had shared their first experiences of drinking and throwing up, of boys, lost virginities and break-ups, drugs, exams and holidays. They went to university or college and got jobs, but always kept in touch. Kristin had got married and moved to Canada; the hen night had been a legendary party in Newquay with a stag do from Essex.

And, of course, they had all rallied around Amanda when she had been raped six months earlier.

Setting off at nine-thirty from the Pyg Track car park, Amanda watched as the sun broke through the clouds and the surrounding snowy terrain was brought into sudden and sharp focus. She had been through so much in recent months. To be in this heavenly landscape with the three people that mattered most to her filled her with such joy. As they chatted loudly against the noise of the wind, a valley became visible to the left, ringed by the snow-capped mountains. The lake below was dark blue, deep and cold. In the distance was the strip of green pines that formed a rigid boreal layer. And up above them, as they climbed, rose the grey of millions of tonnes of volcanic rocks and sediment, only softened by the untouched snow.

As they walked towards the point where the Pyg and Miners' tracks met, two men strode past them from behind.

'Morning, ladies,' the older, well-built man said with a cheesy grin.

'Hi there.' The younger man had given them a little wave.

Amanda and her friends slowed a little to let them gain some distance. They didn't want to discuss their lives in earshot of two strange men. Amanda already had the older man down as a pompous twat.

However, it seemed the two men had other ideas as they stopped and turned back down the mountain.

What the hell do they want? *Amanda thought. She had become noticeably more wary of men since she had been attacked.*

'So sorry to interrupt ... I'm not sure if you ladies are interested, but I'm having a party over in Llancastell tonight. We thought you might like to join us for a few drinks after a

hard day's walking?' the older man said, removing his sunglasses and wiping sweat from his brow.

'No, thanks,' Amanda said in an unfriendly tone. He had that 'rugger bugger' air of entitlement that she hated so much.

'Come on. It'll be fun. We don't bite,' the younger man said as he laughed.

Olivia gave a forced smile. 'We're old friends. And we just want to catch up. But thanks for the offer.'

The older man came closer, a little too close. It made Amanda feel instantly uneasy. 'Come on, girls, live a little, eh?'

'Sorry. We're spending the evening together. Just the four of us,' Nyree said in a spiky tone.

And then Amanda saw it. Something in the man's eyes, the expression around the eyes and the mouth. It came back to her like a punch to the stomach.

She was standing two feet away from the man who had raped her.

'I'm sorry, have we met? I'm sure I recognise you from somewhere?' the man continued to grin as he looked at Amanda, who was frozen to the spot, her heart pounding hard. She couldn't breathe. She was having a panic attack.

Kristin frowned. 'What is it, Mand? You okay?'

'I'm ... no ... I'm ...' Amanda said as she gasped for breath.

'I've got a good memory for faces. It's ...' the man said, trying to remember her name.

'He's ... the man that raped me,' Amanda said wide-eyed. She couldn't believe this was happening.

Her statement was loud enough for the two men to hear. The younger man looked at his brother in bewilderment.

'What?' said Nyree.

'Are you sure?' Olivia asked.

'Yes. It's definitely him,' Amanda said, her voice trembling.

'Oh my God! Are you fucking joking?' Kristin asked, turning to look at him.

The man backed away. 'Hang on a second, I think you've got your wires crossed here ...'

Reaching down and grabbing a fist-sized rock with her shaky hand, Amanda knew it was him. You didn't forget something like that. Retreating, the man looked at Amanda as if he didn't believe she was going to attack him. Then she swung her arm and cracked the rock to the side of the man's head.

'You fucking raped me! You bastard!' Amanda yelled, the cry resonating off the valley walls around them like some kind of battle cry.

The man was dazed and dropped to his haunches as he removed his ski hat and wiped blood from his temple. He looked up at Amanda as if she was mad.

The younger man put his hands up defensively. 'Wait, wait – what the hell are you talking about?'

'He fucking raped me and told me to relax because "I might enjoy it,"' Amanda bellowed through her clenched teeth. She wasn't sure what to do next. Her anxiety had been replaced by utter rage.

The older man stood up and took a few steps back, blood on his face, and laughed. 'Oh, that does sound like me, actually. I didn't rape you. You were flirting with me all night. And that's what happens to slags like you.'

Amanda gritted her teeth and her eyes welled. Her fingertips dug into the rough surface of the rock as she squeezed it in her hand. She wanted to beat him to death.

'You're a disgusting prick!' Olivia yelled at him.

The younger man frowned. 'What the fuck, Harv?'

'That's what they're like. All over you one second, taking drinks. Then they pretend they don't want to shag. It's a fucking joke. And this hashtag-MeToo business is a fucking joke!'

The younger man looked horrified. 'I can't believe you've just said that ... There's always been something wrong with you!' He turned and started back down the track.

'Where are you going, Jack?'

Amanda moved forwards a few paces, her three friends now beside her. She didn't know what was going to happen next, but she wanted him to suffer.

The man put his hand to his head again and looked at the blood.

'That really hurt. I could have you arrested for assault, you know?' the man continued to wipe blood from his face and eye.

Kristin opened the pocket where she'd sewn a Canadian flag and pulled out a sheath before removing a six-inch hunting knife.

Nyree and Olivia gasped at the blade, but the man simply laughed. 'What? You're going to stab me?' the man said chortling still.

Kristin moved forwards with the knife. Amanda followed her and the man backed away further.

'This was going to be a gift for my husband, but I think this is a much worthier purpose. First, you're going to get on your knees and beg for her forgiveness, and ours too, for being a pathetic low-life piece of scum,' Kristin said through gritted teeth.

The man smiled, shook his head as he continued to move slowly backwards. 'No chance.'

'Apologise to me, right now!' Amanda spat the words at him.

'I've nothing to apologise for,' the man said, looking around as if conscious of the decreasing distance between him and the edge of the ridge behind. The four women now lay between him and escape.

'Get on your knees, now!' Olivia yelled.

'I'm not going to apologise for being good in bed.'

That is it! Fuck him! Amanda sprung forwards and kicked him full in the stomach. 'Apologise to me now, you pathetic wanker!'

The man staggered backwards, lost his footing, and took a step back to right himself, but there was no ground left. He fell.

They watched in horror from the edge of the ridge as his body bounced over and over until it slammed onto the ground below. Everything slowed in Amanda's head as she watched him tumble and roll over the rocky grey terrain.

And then there was silence as they all gazed down.

'Fuck!' gasped Amanda. The enormity of what had just happened hit her.

Olivia gestured to the ridge. 'We need to get down there.'

Kristin put away her knife and, ever the practical one of the four, was the first to begin to edge down the steep ravine. Amanda followed, inching down step by step, trying to process what she had done. What if he was dead? Then what?

The wind picked up and swirled around them noisily. Amanda couldn't think straight. If he was injured, what were they going to do? Had anyone seen what had happened?

Amanda nervously glanced up but couldn't see anyone else around. Thank God! Her foot slipped on some ice and she skidded down a few feet. Regaining her balance, she could see that Kristin was already at the bottom of the gulley and heading for the man who appeared to be unconscious. She had gone down with precision and no fear. That was what fifteen years living in the Canadian wilderness and being a rescue volunteer did for you.

'He's breathing, just about.' Kristin called up to them as they all got to the lower reaches of the slope. She pulled him onto his back.

They all gathered around him. The man's face and neck were covered in blood and there was a nasty gash to the side of his head where Amanda had hit him.

'His breathing is very shallow, pulse is slow. There could be internal bleeding,' Kristin explained.

'What do we do? I didn't ...' Amanda asked. She hadn't meant to kill him. It was all her fault.

'You were provoked. This man raped you and then laughed about it in your face. He deserves to die!' Kristin said angrily.

'Kristin!' Olivia exclaimed, shocked.

'Are we going to get help?' Kristin asked.

There was silence as the four women looked at each other. Amanda knew that morally they should try to help him if he was still alive. But what if he recovered and did it again? She knew they were all thinking the same thing.

'What are we going to say happened?' Olivia said seriously.

'If he recovers, he will say that Amanda attacked him, we threatened him and Amanda kicked him over the edge,' Nyree said in a very worried voice.

'Olivia, what could that mean?' Kristin asked. Olivia was only a family solicitor, but she was still legally trained.

'I don't know! Manslaughter? We could all get a prison sentence. Amanda could be charged with attempted murder. I don't know ...' Olivia frantically explained. 'But I do know it'll be a nightmare for all of us.'

Amanda and the others took in the consequences of his recovery.

'That can't happen, can it?' Kristin said, looking at them all.

Amanda didn't know exactly what Kristin meant, but she feared they were heading down a very dark road.

'We can't leave him here to die. It could take days.' Olivia was horrified.

'Then we do it now,' Kristin said, moving her gloved hands to Harvey Pearson's throat and starting to apply pressure.

'Don't be stupid! We can't kill him!' Olivia yelled.

'Shut up, Olivia!' Nyree barked.

'Do you want to go to prison, Olivia? What are your kids going to do? Do you want Amanda to spend a decade in prison for attacking the man who raped her?' Kristin yelled back at her.

'I agree. We have to do it. It makes me feel sick, but Amanda can't go to prison. That's not going to happen,' Nyree said.

Amanda put her hands over Kristin's. *'We all do it together.'*

The others followed suit, hand on hand. Amanda closed her eyes as she felt her friends' hands against hers. She felt physically sick.

And after a minute, it was done. He was dead. They sat staring out at the view in shock and disbelief.

Amanda looked up at the sky. The world seemed to have changed colour. What just happened didn't feel real. But none of them would ever be the same again.

CHAPTER 32

Feeling increasingly frantic, Ruth continued to search Gates's personal things, looking for something that would give a hint to where Ella was being kept. It could well be fruitless and a waste of time, but she needed to keep busy. She needed to feel that she was doing something useful. The anxiety sat in her stomach like a nagging, cancerous growth.

Winter sunlight dappled the floor and table where she sat, and she could feel the warmth of the sun on her feet. Sitting back to clear her mind and focus, she cast her gaze to the half dozen or so photos of Ella around the room. Aged six, when she had just learnt to ride a bike by the pond on Clapham Common. An off-guard moment at Bestival in her mid-teens, when she flatly refused to ever have her photo taken. A moment later, Sarah had photobombed the shots and Ella had gone off in a teenage strop. The three of them spent that afternoon drinking watered-down cider and jumping around to Rudimental.

Feeling choked by the memories, she dabbed the beginnings of tears from her eyes and wiped her nose on her sleeve. She forced herself to focus on what needed to be done and sifted through more photographs that smelt stale, like the old paperback novels she read as a kid.

Ruth ran through what she knew and what might be guessed at. So far, Gates had been drawn to places that he knew well or he had some form of attachment to. Where he lived, where he had killed and buried his victims, even the aqueduct, were all along the Dee Valley. It was a pattern that Gates hadn't deviated from so far.

Taking a wedding photograph out of an envelope, Ruth was astonished to see that Kerry was heavily pregnant. How was that possible? Where was the baby? Was that the child that Gates had made a vague reference to? 'A child for a child,' Gates had said. It made her shudder. But there was something about Gates's phrasing, 'our child,' that seemed relevant. It was clearly at the forefront of Gates's mind at that moment.

Ruth traced her finger over Kerry's bump on the photograph. What had happened to the baby that Kerry was carrying? Had the baby died being born? Had the child died after that? She remembered no photographs of any children at the Gateses' home. In fact, it had been something that had struck her, and she had drawn a mental conclusion that they were one of the unfortunate couples who couldn't have children. But it seems that something else had happened.

Shuffling through the photos from that period, she looked for signs of when the pregnancy was no longer visible or any sign of children. There were photographs of Kerry without a pregnancy bump but the photos weren't dated. There weren't any photographs of a baby or a child. Moving through the bits and bobs, she came across a folded piece of paper. She opened it and saw a professional pencil sketch of Gates and Kerry together. It was the sort of thing that you might have done at the seaside, especially a few decades ago. It had a date scrawled in the bottom-right-hand corner

– *10/6/95, Porthmadog.* Shuffling through the papers that she had already looked at, she came across something that seemed like an official wedding photograph. It was electronically dated on the back in small black numbers – *5/6/95.* The sketch had been made five days after the wedding, on what might have been their honeymoon. However, the sketch was only of their heads and shoulders, so there was no clue as to whether Kerry was pregnant.

Did the missing child have any bearing on where Gates and Ella were? Ruth's copper instinct said that it did. Rising from the table to get more coffee and go outside for a smoke, Ruth knocked the table. The first few chimes of a clockwork toy played. Its tune sounded eerie in the silence of the house. Gazing into the box, she saw a pink-coloured jewellery box that she had disregarded in favour of the papers and photos. It had the word *Princess* written on the front in ornate, swirling writing.

Picking the box up gently, she opened it. A tiny plastic ballerina started to pirouette clockwise and the tune began again. Small trays and compartments, all of which were empty, had been covered in soft pink felt. As she went to close the box, Ruth noticed that the mirror on the underside of the lid wasn't fitted properly. Edging the mirror away from the pink lining, she could see that something had been placed behind. A document.

Opening it, she saw it was a birth certificate for a Heidi Laura Gates. The date of birth was the 7 June 1995. Three days before the sketch she had just looked at. Kerry Gates had given birth to a baby girl called Heidi on the 7 June 1995. Behind that was another piece of paper of a similar size. *Certificate of the entry of death.* Heidi Laura Gates had died on the 11 June 1995, aged just four days old. Cause of death was sudden infant death syndrome.

Ruth scanned to the bottom of the certificate. The place of death was listed as Tyddyn Llwyn.

Grabbing her laptop, Ruth typed in the address. The listings came up to show that there was a large holiday park – Borthrodyn Holiday Park – there, near Porthmadog. Under the availability tab, it just read *Closed For Christmas.*

Is that where Gates was hiding Ella?

WHAT WERE THEY GOING to do? Nick was struggling to process what Amanda had just told him. He was crushed by the enormity of it. He could see the pain on her face as she sat on the sofa looking at the floor. None of the clichés, no words, nothing could explain quite how he had felt when he heard about that day on Snowdon.

The irony was that it had been a complete coincidence that Amanda came to AA the day they met. Not surprisingly, she had drunk to the point of blackout every day after Harvey Pearson's murder. Or manslaughter. So Nick was wrong, coincidences do happen.

Trying to put together everything in his head, they had sat in silence for nearly twenty minutes. The woman he loved had been raped by a man who, when confronted, had laughed in her face. If Nick had been there that day, with that knowledge, he would have killed him too. Right there, on the mountain top, with his bare fucking hands. Chucked his dead body down the ravine.

He gritted his teeth just thinking about it. If that was what his old 'friend' Harvey Pearson was capable of, then the world was a far better place without him.

However, Nick was a police officer. Amanda had kept the truth from him. She had effectively lied to him since they met. But did he blame her? Not really. *By the way, my friends and I killed the man whose murder you're investigating.*

Was Nick going to arrest her? No. He couldn't do that. He could have lived with Harvey being attacked and falling to his death as divine retribution for his words, actions and utter lack of humanity. It was the collective decision to end his life once they realised that he wasn't dead that tortured him.

Nick also had to factor in Jack. He knew that his brother had been confronted and accused of rape on Snowdon. He had left him, and Harvey had been murdered. Jack must have suspected that the two incidents were in some way connected but had decided to keep quiet, even lying about which track they were on. But how long would he maintain that silence?

To say that Nick had put his sobriety in jeopardy was the understatement of the year. And the thought of a huge glass of vodka to press pause on the endless chatter in his mind felt overwhelmingly appealing. However, he played it forwards and saw himself in a detox or rehab centre in a month's time. He just needed to get to a meeting.

Amanda shifted uncomfortably on the sofa and looked over at him.

'What do we do?' she whispered.

'I don't know. I really don't know.' Nick began to feel his emotions getting the better of him. He was lost.

He had allowed himself to fall in love with her. And she was everything he thought he wanted. All the cheesy romance of songs and films suddenly made sense for the first time. He had always thought that stuff was nonsense. However, he had felt it. Deep in the pit of his stomach, down in the middle of his empty soul. He remembered a quote from his GCSE English Literature class. Shakespeare, he thought. *Love was like a sickness and its cure together. Like rain and sun, like cold and heat.* He had never taken any notice of the words.

'Do you need to arrest me? Do I hand myself in?' Amanda shook her head at the thought of it.

Nick made a decision.

'No. Harvey Pearson's murder will just go down as one of those unexplained murders that you read about in the newspaper every few years.'

'How ...?' Amanda bit her lip as the tears came again.

'I have to forget everything you just told me. And I have to bury anything that links you or your friends to Snowdon that day.'

'You can't do that. You're a bloody police officer, Nick!' Amanda looked at him in disbelief.

'That man raped you with no moral conscience. And when confronted, he thought it was funny. He could have gone on to do that again. And I've seen rapists progress to far worse.'

'Don't you think what we did was wrong?'

'I don't know. But I do know that none of you should go to prison for someone like Harvey Pearson.'

'What happens if someone finds out what you've done? You'll go to prison.'

'Then you'd better not tell anyone.' Nick's tone was serious. He was putting his liberty in her hands.

Then more silence came as thoughts rushed in and out.

'What about us?' Amanda asked.

'I don't know.'

'Maybe I should just move away and make a new start?' Amanda said.

He wasn't sure if she was just testing the water to see if he would agree with her suggestion.

'I just need some time, you know?'

'Yeah, of course. We both do.'

'I need some time and I need to keep sober. And so do you.'

Amanda nodded.

CHAPTER 33

The atmosphere inside Incident Room One was sombre. The room was crammed full: every chair was taken, and latecomers were sitting on tables or propped against the back wall. Everyone wanted to help find Ella. Ruth was one of their own. Normally the room would have been full of chatter, but this was serious and everyone just wanted to get on with tracking down Gates and getting Ella back safely.

Sipping lukewarm coffee, Sian felt exhausted. Caffeine didn't seem to be hitting the spot, but her adrenaline was keeping her going. It had been a long night, but she had managed a couple of hours of sleep at home. She had supported and comforted Ruth as much as she could. She couldn't get the thought of Ella being with Gates out of her head. She looked over at the case board, where photos of Gates's eight victims had been pinned with names, dates of birth and other details. It made her feel physically sick to think of a photo of Ella up on that board. She wouldn't let that happen.

Looking tired and drawn, Sian watched as Drake got up and went to the front of the room. He waited for the room to settle. 'Morning, everyone. As most of you know by now, Ruth Hunter's daughter was kidnapped by Andrew Gates yesterday afternoon. Ruth is at home on compassionate leave, although I will be keeping her up to date with any developments. Gates is very dangerous and has no regard for human life. It goes without saying, but we need to do our best work in the next twenty-four hours.' Drake looked over at Merringer. 'Luke, what have we got?'

Sian watched as Luke stood and looked at the papers he was holding. She knew that he found it difficult to talk to such a crowded room. He went over to the computer and pulled up an image of a white Ford Escort van that had been burnt beyond all recognition.

'Boss. The white Escort van that Gates had been driving was found burnt-out in Capel Curig, just outside Betws-y-Coed. A 2011 white transit van' – Merringer clicked to an image of the transit van – 'registration alpha-lima-six-one, foxtrot-bravo-delta, was stolen half a mile from where the Escort van was found.'

Sian scribbled down the make and number, but her mind was elsewhere. She had become so close to Ella and Ruth in recent months. They had become a little family. Ruth had joked that they were the archetypal 'blended family.' A lesbian couple with a daughter from a failed heterosexual marriage.

'The owner discovered it had been stolen at around midnight last night. We know that Gates seems to be able to steal vans of a certain era without much trouble. ANPR cameras have been alerted, as have the armed patrols in the area.' Merringer sat down.

Drake rose again. 'We're hoping to get helicopters in the area as soon as possible. Anything else?'

Sian looked at the notes of the intel she had been following up on. 'We're rechecking all known family and friends. Nothing so far. Nothing on Gwenda Chadwick's bank cards or phone. Surveillance still on his home at Llantysilio in case he decides to retrieve anything he's left behind. Uniformed officers are making regular checks on the house in Pentredwr.'

'Do we think he will stick to his original MO and try to kill again?' Merringer asked.

'He's got the taste for it, so there's no reason to think that he won't,' Drake said.

There was a slight commotion as a uniformed officer came in and headed straight for Drake. They talked earnestly for a moment as Drake nodded and Sian could see that he was looking energised.

'Right everyone. Gwenda Chadwick's mobile phone has been active for the past half an hour. Using the GPS and mast triangulation, it seems that it is in a vehicle travelling east on the A5 and that vehicle has just crossed the border into England.'

Bingo! thought Sian. At last they had a concrete lead on Gates and presumably Ella's whereabouts.

IT WAS GONE FOUR O'CLOCK by the time Ruth began to cut through the centre of Snowdonia Park. The heathland was desolate, daubed with a smattering of snow on the higher ground.

Without thinking, she clicked on the radio. 'Santa Baby' by Kylie Minogue was playing and its chirpy, sultry tone immediately grated her. It couldn't be less appropriate, for fuck's sake! She angrily pushed the button again and there was silence. Just the whirr of the road beneath her as she thought and processed and hoped. Was this just a wild goose chase? She didn't have anything else to go on until Gates called her with a time and place to meet. That's if he did call back. And Ruth wanted to be one step ahead of Gates for once.

Wintry trees lined the roadside like dancers poised to start their show. Their leaves had long gone, and their skeleton limbs seemed sinister. The sky had turned a gun-metal grey, although in the distance it was turning to black. She hated the winter. Trees were lifeless with the odd dead leaf hanging in the wind. The skies were at best dismal and at worst fierce and angry. She didn't even like snow. It didn't glisten in the sun. It was crushed by muddy boots leaving brown scars.

The sound of her phone broke the darkness of her thoughts. It was Sian.

'Hi. We've got a fix on Gwenda Chadwick's mobile phone,' she said.

'Where?' Ruth asked. She hoped Sian was going to say somewhere near Porthmadog, which would confirm her hunch about where Gates was holed up with Ella. There was a momentary glimmer of hope.

'The last position was somewhere near Market Drayton on the Shropshire-Staffordshire border. We have no ID on the vehicle yet,' she explained.

There was part of Ruth that wanted to spin a handbrake turn and head for Market Drayton at high speed. However, it didn't feel right. She was still convinced that Gates was going to stay in places and areas that he knew. That was his MO so far. Despite the new intel, she felt compelled by her instinct that Borthrodyn Holiday Park was where Gates was hiding. If she was wrong, then at least there would be a huge police operation following Gwenda Chadwick's mobile phone. She was on compassionate leave and wouldn't be allowed anywhere near the operation anyway. Terrified that Ella could get caught up in an armed police operation against Gates, she knew she needed to check the Borthrodyn link herself.

'Okay, thank you,' Ruth said.

'How you bearing up?' Sian asked.

'You know. Hanging on in there. Just ...' Ruth said.

Sian paused for a moment. 'Are you driving somewhere?'

Ruth wasn't sure how or if to answer. 'I'm checking something out.'

'I don't like the sound of that. Where are you going?' Sian sounded worried.

'Kerry and Andrew Gates had a baby girl called Heidi in 1995. Kerry was pregnant at their wedding. They went to Borthrodyn Holiday Park for their honeymoon.'

'Where the hell is that, and why is it relevant?' Sian snapped.

'Porthmadog. On the second day they were there, the baby died from SIDS. It means that Borthrodyn is somewhere very significant for Gates. He sticks to where he knows and feels comfortable.'

'What about the mobile-phone signal?' Sian asked.

'I don't know. Drake won't allow me to be anywhere near a police operation tracking Gates. I can't just sit at home looking at the walls.' Ruth thought for a moment. 'Gates called me earlier.'

'You're meant to hand that information on to CID straight away!' Sian reprimanded her.

'I couldn't. Gates told me that he wanted me to come and meet him alone. He implied that he would harm Ella if he found any hint of police anywhere.'

'I'm assuming that he didn't give any clues as to where and when?'

'No. But he said something about "a child for a child." As if he saw Ella and Heidi as comparable in some way. I'm clutching at straws because it's all I've got.'

'What are you going to do if they are there?' Sian asked.

'I'll call it in. Don't worry, I'm not going to go all Jodie Foster in *Silence of the Lambs*.'

'Promise?' Sian said with a tone of distrust.

'I promise. I'm not stupid. I'll ring you when I get there.'

CHAPTER 34

Rapping on the front door for the third time, Nick crouched and looked through the brass letterbox of Amanda's front door. She hadn't answered her phone. And now she wasn't answering the door. He was in a panic. What if she had done something stupid?

Suicide was a constant spectre within AA. Those with some form of alcohol problem account for a third of all suicides in the UK. Amanda had been through so much in the past few months. The attack and then the murder. It would be enough to drive anyone to the brink of a breakdown or something more drastic. Of course, she could have just self-medicated herself into a stupor.

Fuck it. He pushed the key into the door and turned it. He would risk her anger for letting himself into her house unannounced. Glancing through the ground-floor rooms, she was nowhere to be seen. He bound up the stairs, two at a time, and went into the bedroom. The bed had been stripped but Amanda wasn't there. Nothing in the spare room either.

Then something occurred to him. Pacing back into Amanda's bedroom, he looked at her dressing table. It was clear. No jewellery, no perfume, moisturiser. Nothing. He frowned as he went to the wardrobe. It was empty.

Taking a breath, he sat on the bed for a moment collecting his thoughts. She had gone. And she hadn't taken a small suitcase as if she was going away for a few days or even a week. It had all gone.

He took a pillow from the centre of the bed and smelt if for a second. Marc Jacobs Decadence. Her beautiful face loomed in his mind. She smiled and he looked into her big brown eyes. There was a pang within his torso that stabbed at him.

Walking slowly down the stairs, he noticed that the stylish architectural photos that had been on the wall were gone too. Then he noticed that the living room was the same. There were a few things left. The bulky stuff. The television, sofa and the table and chairs. In his desperation to find Amanda, he hadn't noticed that her life was no longer here.

He couldn't believe it. In the space of four hours, she had put her stuff in her car and vanished. Where? The only consoling thought was that if she was driving off somewhere to harm herself, she wouldn't have bothered to spend all that time packing up her things.

Walking into the kitchen in a slight daze, he saw a note on the kitchen table. He must have missed it when he raced through the ground floor a few minutes before.

He took a moment before picking it up to read. He knew in his head that Amanda going somewhere else for a new start made logical sense. It was best for both of them. What he knew, what she had told him, was too much for them to be together, wasn't it?

But the weight of his heart told him a completely different story. He loved her with all of his being. They had connected in a way that had revived his belief that he wasn't an emotionally-retarded sociopath.

Reaching for the note, he began to read:

Hi Nick,

You'll have guessed that I've packed most of my stuff and gone. My friend's husband is going to come and collect everything else in the next few days.

I hope you understand that I have to move away. What we've shared together has been amazing and I do love you. But there is so much dark baggage that I fear that we wouldn't survive it. And we might be okay for a while, but I think that eventually it would catch up with us. Does that make sense?

You're an amazing person, you should know that. I know that sobriety is the only way for me, and you taught me that.

Take care of yourself,

Amanda x

Nick was crushed as he placed the letter down. What she had written made perfect sense. He didn't want it to make perfect sense though.

Turning abruptly, he put the key on the table and left. He couldn't bear to be in the house any longer.

Twenty minutes later, he moved slowly around the Co-op looking at the Christmas offers on mince pies, pigs in blankets, crackers and chocolates. Slade's Christmas anthem played loudly as he went to pay for a pizza and six Diet Cokes. He had never felt more alone. He knew he needed to get himself to an AA meeting. He would feel better being amongst his tribe. He always did.

Walking across the car park, the icy wind bit into his face and hands. He eased himself into the car and put the key in the ignition.

Looking over at the shopping bag on the passenger seat, he spotted it sitting there. Crystal clear, shiny and beautiful. A new litre-bottle of vodka. It was almost as if he hadn't remembered buying it. As if another part of him had pointed to the bottle behind the tills and made the decision for him.

He reached over and took the bottle in his hand.

IT WAS FIVE O'CLOCK by the time Sian, Merringer and Drake arrived at the service station just outside Market Drayton. Drake had liaised with the police in Staffordshire, but it was agreed that North Wales Police would lead the operation.

With a mobile phone clamped to his ear, Drake was in the back of the unmarked BMW while Merringer and Sian were in the front.

Looking out at the black clouds that were rolling in, Sian's thoughts went to Ella and what she must be going through, the overwhelming terror and desperation she would be feeling. Even though she wasn't religious, she cast her thoughts into the sky and prayed that Ella would be returned safely. She would do anything for that. Hail Marys, Our Fathers, chants, the lot.

Brightly coloured signs advertised Costa Coffee, Burger King and M&S as families came and went into the main building for toilet breaks and food. A father came past wearing a red Santa hat and holding his daughter's hand as they headed for the warmth of the service station. It made Sian's feelings of helplessness so much worse.

Drake hung up the phone. 'They've triangulated Gwenda Chadwick's phone again. We've got it located somewhere in this area but uniformed officers from Staffordshire have done a sweep and can't see any white transit vans.'

'He could have switched vehicles?' Sian suggested.

'If they're in here, they're not getting out now,' Drake said, determined.

Two Armed Response Units had been placed on the entry and exit. All vehicles coming in and out were being searched thoroughly. Officers from Llancastell CID were searching the service station itself. A helicopter was on standby a mile away, as were armed officers from Stoke-On-Trent's CID. It felt to Sian that all bases were covered. But they'd been in this position before and Gates had seemed to be one step ahead of them at every juncture.

'Sian, Luke. Have a scoot around and see if you can see anything.'

'Yes, boss,' Sian replied as she got out and pulled the collar of her coat up against the light rain that had just started.

'And Sian,' Drake said as she popped her head back in the car. 'Be careful. Don't take any risks.'

'Boss.' Sian nodded.

Zipping up their jackets, they both began to survey the car park. The wind picked up and litter blew noisily past them and up the grass bank.

'You okay?' Merringer asked.

'Fine. Let's just get the bastard this time.'

Sian's radio crackled. 'All units, search of service station complete. No sign of suspect or target.' CID officers had found nothing, which seemed to imply Gates was outside somewhere, possibly in the car park.

'Shit!' Sian said as they moved forwards, scanning left and right for an indication of anything out of the ordinary.

'Anything?' Merringer asked.

'Nothing. Where are they?' Sian prayed that they hadn't missed them.

Something in the corner of Sian's eye caught her attention. A dark-blue van was parked on the far side of the car park, right in the corner. It might have been just her suspicious thinking, but given the spaces closer to the service station, the van looked like it had been parked there to keep out of the way or out of sight.

She clicked her radio. 'DC Hockney to Central. PNC plate check requested on a vehicle, licence sierra-charlie-five-two, yankee-oscar-tango.'

Merringer looked over at the van and the writing on its side. Pulling out his phone, he tapped the words into Google as he read aloud, 'Williams Builders, over twenty-five years' experience from design to build ... Branches in Rhyl, Colwyn Bay, Llundudno ... and Betws-y-Coed.'

They shared a look.

'Betws-y-Coed?' Sian said.

'The burnt-out Escort van,' Merringer said, confirming Sian's thoughts.

Changing course quickly, they moved across the car park while trying not to draw attention to themselves. The van was now thirty metres away to their right. Pretending to have a conversation with Merringer, Sian stole a look over his shoulder. There was no one in the driver or passenger seat.

Sian's radio crackled. 'Central to DC Hockney. PNC plate check complete. Vehicle is a dark-blue Citroën Relay van. Registered to Williams Builders Ltd in Rhyl.'

'Control, received,' Sian replied.

Gesturing to Merringer that they needed to take a closer look at the van, Sian moved across the wet parking bays. There was a clanking sound coming from somewhere.

By the time they got twenty yards away, it was clear that the clanking sound was coming from the back of the van. Something or someone was moving around in the back of the van and knocking against the metallic side door.

Sian craned her neck as she listened closely. Another sound. The whimper of a woman or a girl. There were no words, just a noise as though someone was trying to speak but couldn't.

'Can you hear that?' Sian asked Merringer as her pulse quickened. If someone was tied up and gagged in the back of the van, then they would be moving around trying to get free, banging the door and trying to shout for help through their gag.

'Someone's in there,' Merringer said.

It was Ella. Sian knew it was her and her heart suddenly pounded. What she didn't know was if Gates was in the van too. She couldn't take that risk.

Sian and Merringer scuttled out of sight as she clicked her radio and said quietly, 'All units from DC Hockney. There is a dark-blue Citroën van in the far-right-hand corner of the car park. Licence sierra-charlie-five-two, yankee-oscar-tango. We believe suspect and target could be inside the vehicle. Request back-up.'

CHAPTER 35

It was dark by the time Ruth arrived at Borthrodyn Holiday Park. As it was closed this time of year, she had parked some way along the country road from where the entrance to the park was positioned. She had assumed that any light, especially car headlights, might warn Gates that someone was around.

However, the darkness of North Wales was something that Ruth still hadn't got used to. She had spent nearly half a century in London, where the lights of the city went on for ever and the sky was never dark. Tonight, she had certainly underestimated the utter blackness of night-time. In her mind, the cabins and caravans would be black shapes against the sky and the pathways would be highlighted by the moon. They weren't. She peered into the darkness, which seemed to press at her from every side. It was blacker than inside a coffin, as her grandfather used to say.

Closing her eyes, she willed her daughter to be all right. What she would give to have her in her arms at that very moment. Anything and everything. *Please God, bring her back to me.*

As she tripped again, Ruth took the torch she had brought with her from her pocket. It had a Swiss Army knife attached to the strap. Sarah had bought it for her when they went to Glastonbury in 2005. 'Torch, bottle opener and corkscrew – that's all we'll need,' Sarah had joked.

She clicked on the torch and used her hand to dampen the light as much as she could. She stopped and listened intently for any sound. There was absolute stillness. No air stirred the grass or trees. An eerie feeling of tranquillity heightened her senses in the dark.

In those frozen seconds, she heard the crunch of dried twigs underfoot. It came from the wood behind her. Then there was nothing. Straining her hearing, she froze and listened again. Nothing. Just her imagination?

Continuing to walk cautiously forwards, she soon came to the far border of the park, which was marked with a ten-foot wire fence. As the moon slid from behind the clouds for a few seconds, Ruth could see that, beyond the fence, the land fell away downhill very steeply. Where it ended, there was an enormous sheer drop, which she assumed to be a beach or the sea below. The moonlight dappled the dark sea that stretched away, but then as the clouds returned, the whole view was plunged into a murky darkness again.

Turning back, Ruth surveyed the holiday park. The stillness of the air seemed to suck every sound into the nothingness. She narrowed her eyes looking for the smallest hint of light or movement. Still nothing. Dejected didn't quite describe the extent of her feelings. She had trusted her instincts, and they had let her down.

Her phone buzzed in her pocket and she unlocked it, no longer worried about the light from her screen. It was a text from Sian:

We've found a van. I'm sure Ella's in it. Not sure where Gates is. Waiting for AROs. I'll ring as soon as I know anything. Love you xx

At last they had some good news. Tracking the phone had proved to be the right decision. A feeling of utter helplessness swept over her. The very thought of Ella tied up inside a van that was surrounded by armed police officers horrified her. All she could do now was drive home and await further news.

Letting the full beam of her torch flood over the park, Ruth set about returning to her car. There was a distant noise from the far-right-hand side of the park. It sounded like a door closing. Maybe it was nothing.

And then as the wintry breeze swirled, she could smell something familiar. Cigarette smoke. But not ordinary cigarette smoke. Menthol cigarette smoke. And there was only one person she had come into contact with recently that smoked menthol cigarettes.

Andrew Gates.

THE CAR PARK AT THE far end of the service station was now deserted. Police officers had been quietly moving cars and members of the public away from the area of the van for about ten minutes. Sian watched as the teams worked in a low-key and calm manner. They didn't want to alert whoever was in the van to their presence.

A call had come through to Drake minutes earlier. The GPS trace on Gwenda Chadwick's phone had been pinpointed to the end of the car park where the van was parked. They were certain now. Gates was in that van with Ella.

Sian, Merringer and Drake had put on their Kevlar stab vests from the back of the car. Sian liked the tight feeling around her torso. It made her feel safe and protected. Other officers from Llancastell CID and one of the ARO units moved into positions behind bins and long four-foot hedgerows that ran along the top of the empty parking bays. It was silent except for the distant noise of traffic. Sian could feel the tension in her stomach and her adrenaline pumping. She had never been on an armed operation of this scale before. She just wanted to get Ella out safely.

The sky above her was dark except for a blinking red dot as an aeroplane went over them obliviously. Passengers tucking into food and drink, watching a movie, unaware of what was going on thirty thousand feet below them. Her face and ears stung in the cold wind. Wriggling her toes, she tried to get the circulation going as her feet began to numb. Close by, she could see the new electricity pumps for electric or hybrid cars. A green Union Flag was emblazoned on the side of the pumps to show off their eco-friendly status.

Drake smoothed some drizzle off the bald crown of his head. He was the senior-ranking officer and leading the operation. He looked at her for a moment. His eyes and expression were calm. For about five minutes now the movement and noise from the van had stopped. 'I can't hear anything, can you?' he asked her.

Sian shook her head. Was it worrying that the movements and whimpering had stopped? Had Gates done something to Ella to keep her quiet? Or had Ella injured herself while trying to free herself? 'No, boss. Nothing for a few minutes.'

Drake frowned as he craned his neck to listen. Still nothing. His frown turned to a look of concern. He silently gestured to the four AROs, dressed in their black Nomex boots, gloves and Kevlar helmets over balaclavas, to approach the van. Carrying Glock 9mm pistols, they edged in a low crouched position towards the side of the van where the sliding door was positioned. They stopped and squatted, two either side of the door.

Sian calculated that there must have been a dozen firearms within a fifty-yard radius of the van. No one was taking any chances with Gates.

Drake clicked his radio. 'Three-seven to all units. Officers in position at target vehicle.'

The radio crackled back. 'Three-seven received.'

Drake gestured to Sian and Merringer. They moved in unison over the icy parking bays. It was now radio silence.

Suddenly, the noises from within the van started again. Someone was moving around. A noisy metallic bang is if someone had kicked the side panel. The whine of a female voice. More movement.

We need to move now, Sian thought, her anxiety twisting her insides.

Drake gave the AROs the signal to get the sliding door of the van open. Still crouching, the ARO took a K-tool, which can remove the core of a lock in seconds, and with his black-gloved hands working skilfully, pulled the metallic lock out of the door without a sound.

They were on.

Sian held her breath as Drake signalled to the AROs to make their move. She flinched as the side door was pulled open. *Crash!*

The AROs sprang into action, weapons trained in front of them.

'Armed police!' they bellowed. 'Armed police!'

Sian couldn't see what was going on for a moment. There was a terrible female scream. Her heart pounded in her chest.

The AROs moved back. As Sian approached, she could see a naked couple on a mattress cowering under a blanket. They looked terrified.

'Sir, there's no sign of the suspect or target,' an ARO said.

'For fuck's sake!' Drake growled to no one in particular.

Where was Ella? How had they got this so wrong?

Going around to the back doors of the van, Drake opened them angrily. He began to root around as Sian joined him.

A moment later, Drake pulled something from under a tool bag and showed it to Sian.

It was Gwenda Chadwick's mobile phone.

CHAPTER 36

For the last ten minutes, Ruth had tried to follow the direction of where she thought the cigarette smoke had come from. It was virtually impossible, but she was guessing somewhere to the right of where she had been standing. She had been right all along. Gates was in the park somewhere, and so was Ella.

Using her torch as little as she could, she crept down beside one of the static caravans, heading for the right-hand side of the park. The aluminium and hardboard structures groaned quietly in the wind. If she hadn't been so pumped full of adrenaline, it would have been creepy.

Ducking in and out of the rows of statics, she had no idea if she was making progress. For all she knew, she was heading in the wrong direction.

Then as she turned into another row of caravans, she spotted the faintest flicker of light up ahead. She couldn't work out what it was. As she approached, she could see the glass window of a caravan that had an orange glimmer on it. Then as her eyes focussed, she realised what it was. The orange flickering in the glass was a reflection. Someone in the opposite caravan had a candle burning. It was throwing out a shimmering orange pattern of light.

It was Gates. She knew it. She just hoped Ella was all right.

The clouds parted again and the moonlight now made everything visible. *Bloody divine intervention*, she thought.

Moving quietly down the side of the static caravan, she put her hand on the cold wooden balustrade and handrail of the decking out front. She pulled herself up on her tiptoes to get a better look. There was definitely more than one candle. The glow permeated the whole interior of the caravan.

Suddenly, a shadow crossed in front of the light, moving past the window. The figure then stopped in a small kitchen and picked up a kettle from the hob. The candlelight silhouetted the figure, throwing huge shadows on the wall behind.

The figure turned into the light. She saw a face in the orange glow.

Andrew Gates. Now bearded and wearing a baseball cap, but she would know him anywhere.

Ducking down, Ruth's mind raced. Where was Ella? How was she going to get her out of there? Her head said she should move away and phone for back-up. She looked at her phone. It was the far end of the park and there was no signal. That made her mind up for her. She was going in. She refused to leave her daughter in that kind of danger and terror any longer.

Crouching below the level of the balustrade, Ruth crept back along the side of the caravan. Her pulse thudded loudly in her eardrum.

She spotted a side door with a silver lever handle. It was a way in. Then there was a large window that ran along the rest of the caravan and was where most of the candlelight was coming from.

Scurrying along on her hands, she peeked through the wooden spindles. Someone was on a chair facing into what looked like the main living space.

Ella. Her beautiful daughter. Her mouth was gagged and her hands tied behind her back.

Ruth's whole body shook for a moment with the shock of seeing her daughter like that. It was a maternal instinct. She took a breath to steady herself. *Keep it together, Ruth. Focus.*

Scurrying around to the front of the caravan, she could see there was another entrance. Hoping Gates was preoccupied in the kitchen area, she tiptoed up the short stairs to the door. They creaked noisily and she froze for a moment. Taking the last two steps in one movement, she reached the door.

She crouched and moved the handle down quietly, trying to ease it open. It was locked. *Jesus! Now what?*

Time was running out. Her eyes flitted around, looking for something to use. On the decking beside her was a smooth grey ornamental rock the size of a fist. She grabbed the rock and then took off her coat. Her heart was beating so fast that she didn't even feel the cold December night air. Placing her padded coat against the glass, she tapped the rock against the coat and glass, building the force of each tap. It was a trick she had learnt years ago in Streatham CID. Feeling the glass eventually crack, she pulled the coat away and put it back on. Some small pieces of the door's glass had dropped to the other side but had made no noise. A carpet or a doormat, she assumed.

She swiftly pulled the shards of glass from the door, placing them carefully onto the decking. Pushing her arm through the small hole she had created, a spike of glass scratched and then cut her forearm. She didn't have time to care.

Gritting her teeth, she continued to move her arm downwards. The cut was getting deeper, but she focussed on what she needed to find. Then her finger felt it. A cold metal key. *Thank God!* She turned it quietly. It clicked as she unlocked the door. *Great.* Step one was done.

Pushing the door open, she saw Ella looking directly at her, wide-eyed. Ruth put her finger to her lips even though she knew Ella wasn't stupid. Edging across the floor, she reached Ella and removed her gag. She looked at Ella's hands which were tied behind the chair's back. Without undoing the rope, there was no way of getting Ella free. Ruth fumbled with the knots for a moment.

'Do you want to use this?' a voice said loudly.

She spun to see Gates standing a few feet away with a large kitchen knife.

'I came on my own,' Ruth said, trying to buy time and sound as calm as she could.

'But you weren't going to stay to say hello, were you? And that's not polite, Ruth, is it?'

Ruth put her hand in her coat pocket and quickly located the Swiss Army knife. However, she couldn't seem to open anything on it with one hand. 'I thought you wanted to talk?'

'I think we're past talking, aren't we?'

'Are we?' Ruth used her thumbnail to ease the corkscrew out of the knife, ready for action. She just needed to distract him for a moment. And then it came to her. 'Do you want to talk about Heidi, Andrew?'

Gates's face and body immediately stiffened and he glared at her. 'What? Heidi? What the hell do you know about Heidi?' he thundered, gripping the knife tightly in his trembling hand.

Just the reaction that Ruth wanted. Gates was now distracted.

'I thought you might want to talk about her. It's so sad what happened,' Ruth continued.

'How dare you talk about Heidi!' Gates roared as his eyes blinked.

'It happened here, in this park, didn't it?' Ruth asked.

'How do you know all this?' Gates asked, thrown by what Ruth was asking him.

In that split second, Ruth made her move. Bringing out her clenched fist, she had positioned the corkscrew so that it protruded between her forefinger and middle finger. She lunged forwards and swung it upwards at Gates's throat before he could react.

The corkscrew penetrated the soft tissue under his chin, went up into his mouth and through his tongue.

Gates screamed as he clutched his jawbone and spat blood.

Spinning swiftly, she kicked him between his legs with every ounce of energy that she had. Gates groaned like an animal and crumpled to the floor.

'Mum!' Ella gasped.

'It's all right. I'm getting you out of here.'

Seizing the knife that he had dropped, Ruth quickly cut the ropes and pulled Ella to her feet. They staggered towards the door.

Turning to look back at Gates, Ruth wondered if she should finish Gates off there and then? It wasn't her nature. It went against everything that she held dear. But he was a murdering monster.

'Mum!' Ella pulled her and they made their escape.

'Are you okay?' Ruth asked as they leapt down the stairs and sprinted into the darkness.

'I am now. How did you find me?' Ella asked.

'Long story.' Ruth pulled out her phone. There was a signal and she rang Llancastell. 'This is DI Hunter. I'm at the Borthrodyn Holiday Park. I have my daughter Ella with me. Andrew Gates is injured and I need any officers in the area to attend now.'

After about a minute of running, Ruth and Ella slowed for a moment to get their breath. They looked at each other and hugged.

'I thought I'd lost you,' Ruth said, squeezing her daughter tightly.

They needed to get to the car, and then Ruth could get Ella away safely.

The darkness around them suddenly disappeared. As Ruth looked up, the ground before them was flooded with light. It confused her for a second until she saw Ella turn around.

Headlights.

A van was speeding up behind them. It was Gates.

Ruth kicked herself for not incapacitating Gates when she had the chance.

Ruth pulled Ella by the shoulder. 'This way!' They headed left and then back right, but Ruth was now disorientated. Which way were the exit and her car?

The lights of the van appeared behind them again.

Running at full pelt, and checking continually that Ella could keep up, Ruth looked at where they were going.

Ahead of them was the ten-foot wire fence that she had seen earlier. They were going the wrong way. They were trapped.

Gates sounded the van's horn like a madman. Despite his injuries, he was getting off on chasing them down.

Ella pointed to a small gate within the fencing. They turned, sprinted and went through it. Ruth wondered if the fence would stop Gates's van.

She soon had her answer as he smashed through it at high speed, sending poles and fencing flying into the air. He was now only a hundred yards behind and would soon be on them.

Heading down the steep hill, trying to maintain her footing, all Ruth could see ahead of them were the clifftops and the sea beyond that. Now where? Gravity pulled them as they ran downhill, now out of control. Ruth hadn't realised how steep it was. Her feet banged on the frozen ground below, knocking the air out of her as she went.

Twenty seconds later, the van was only mere feet behind them. In front, the cliff edge was only fifty yards away. Jump to their death or get smashed by Gates's van. Not much of a choice.

The van's engine roared as Gates floored the accelerator and pumped the horn again. As they sprinted, Ruth could sense the van bearing down on them. She expected her heels to hit the bumper any moment now. Would she prefer they jumped and took their chances rather than let Gates use them as playthings?

Out of the corner of her eye, Ruth saw Ella's hand reach out and grab the shoulder of her jacket. She then stumbled as Ella yanked her sideways. They lost their footing and tumbled over each other across the icy grass. For a second, Ruth wasn't quite sure what had happened.

Sitting up, Ruth watched as Gates slammed on the brakes, trying to stop the van. The wheels locked and skidded on the grass, which was frozen solid. The van slid down the steep slope picking up speed. It was out of control.

Ruth realised that the van was about to go over the edge. Gates's luck had run out. He was going to plummet to his death and there was nothing he could do about it.

Ella shot her a look as the women watched Gates sliding towards certain death.

The van slowed a little as the ground levelled out by the clifftop. The front wheels dropped over the edge with a metallic clunk. The van continued moving forwards.

And then it stopped.

Half the van remained on the clifftop.

Ruth couldn't believe it. *You've got to be bloody kidding me!*

'Wait there!' Ruth shouted to Ella as she clambered to her feet and jogged over to where the van was precariously positioned. The driver's door opened very slowly.

Ruth slowed as Gates swung his legs out of the driver's door. She watched as he tried to edge himself out. There was no way he could climb along the side of the van without it tipping over and dropping into the sea below. Part of her hoped that Gates would do exactly that.

Pausing for breath, Ruth arrived at the van and looked at him. He looked over and waved. 'Looks like I'm stuck,' he said as blood dripped from his mouth. He sounded as though he had been out for a leisurely drive.

'Yeah, it does,' Ruth called back.

'If you put your weight on the back of the van by sitting on the bumper, I think you can stabilise it. Then I can try to climb back through the inside of the van,' Gates said in a breezy tone and then spat out a mouthful of blood.

Ruth couldn't believe Gates's utter delusion. He had just tried to kill them.

'I don't think so,' Ruth replied.

Gates frowned in disbelief. 'You can't just leave me here!'

Ruth shrugged. How could she possibly help save Gates? Her priority was her and Ella's safety.

'I think it's best that we just wait for help. I've called for back-up. Just make yourself comfortable and sit tight,' Ruth said.

Gates looked down at the drop and sea below. 'We can't wait. The van might tip over at any minute. You're a police officer. You need to do your job and help me get out of here.'

'Do I?' Ruth couldn't help the thrill she was getting from Gates being trapped with no power.

'You need to do as I say, Ruth, or I'll ...' Gates paused. He was filled with rage.

'Or you'll what?' Ruth said calmly.

'Or I will organise from prison for someone to hunt you, your daughter and everyone you love down and kill them all in their sleep.' Gates met her eyes. She could tell he meant what he said.

And in that moment, Ruth knew that while he was still alive, Gates would always be a threat to her life and those she loved.

Ruth nodded. 'Get in the van and I'll go around the back.'

Gates smiled at her. 'Thank you, Ruth. Thank you. Things are better when you do what you're told.'

Ruth looked down at the bumper. Was she prepared to help him live?

She opened the doors carefully and could see Gates looking back at her from the driver's seat.

'That's it. Sit on the back of the van and I can make my way out,' Gates shouted to her.

Ruth shook her head. 'I don't think so.'

She turned and began to walk back to where Ella was standing.

'What the hell do you think you're doing?' Gates screamed. 'Where are you going? You can't just leave me.'

Ruth raised her hand as if to wave goodbye, reached Ella and put her arms around her.

In that moment, Gates made a move from the driver's seat, swinging his leg over into the back of the van. The van tipped forwards, then back, like a seesaw.

Gates moved again impatiently. There was a low metallic groan as the van tipped and slid very slowly forwards.

'No! Help me out of here!' Gates screamed.

The van stopped as its back wheels, axle and tow bar caught on the clifftop.

Ruth and Ella watched in horror as Gates gave a 'Ha!' and began pulling himself up the now vertical van. He found footing on the side door and pushed himself up again. His hand was now level with where the back doors of the van were hanging open. With another concerted effort, he might be able to pull himself out.

For a moment, Gates's head appeared from behind the doors. Somehow, he was going to escape. He looked over at Ruth and Ella and gave his best smug grin.

'Why don't you do the world a favour and just die!' Ella cried emotionally.

'No thanks,' Gates replied, emerging from the van.

Another groan came from the axle below. Gates looked down as the wheels turned and he and the van plummeted out of sight.

Ruth raced forwards as she heard the deep sound of a metallic crash and then a splash as she peered over the edge of the cliff.

The van lay mangled on some jagged rocks that were covered by shallow water as the tide came in. Beside that, Gates's body lay prone on his back on a flat rock. His head had been split in two like a melon.

He was dead.

CHAPTER 37

It was Christmas Day. Nick lay on the sofa drinking tea and watching irritatingly chirpy television. He had already stuffed himself with an enormous bacon sandwich.

He had to concentrate on the things he should be grateful for. He was still sober – *just*. It had been two weeks since he poured a litre of vodka down the sink. So, four months of good sobriety was something to be very grateful for. He had even had a semi-truthful conversation with his sponsor Bill. He admitted that his relationship with Amanda had gone too far and that it was his fault. He got a bit of a bollocking. In fact, Bill's exact words were, 'Yer head's up yer arse, yer wee twat!' Nick got the gist of what he was saying.

At midday, he was going to drive over to Llanberis and have Christmas dinner with Auntie Pat, Cerys and baby Alex. He and Cerys would mock each other and they would laugh and have great food. Having a baby there would make it even more special and festive.

Yet however hard he tried, Nick's mind was still drawn back to Amanda. He couldn't help it. He was addicted to the very thought of her. The what-ifs and could-have-beens. What was she doing? Was she thinking of him or was he out of sight so out of mind?

The only way he knew how to deal with this repetitive thinking was to take life a day at a time. It was a well-worn mantra, but really there was only one day he could control: today. He couldn't do anything about yesterday or tomorrow. If he woke and concentrated on the next twenty-four hours, then life felt manageable.

Clicking the channel, he watched an advert for a sweet liqueur being poured over ice in slow motion. The liquid glistened in the light as it splashed into the glass. Behind the glass, an open log fire roared with Christmas stockings hanging down from the mantelpiece.

Bloody hell, Nick thought. Alcohol was never that glamorous when he drank it. But then again, swigging cheap Russian vodka from the bottle when you've just been sick and fallen down the stairs is probably as far from glamorous as you can get.

Getting up and heading to the kitchen to make more tea, Nick heard a noise. At first, he thought it was birds outside. And then it came again. A rapping sound on his front door. Someone was knocking.

Who the hell was knocking on Christmas morning? Neighbours inviting him around for a Christmas drink? Not likely, since he had drunkenly insulted them while lying hammered in his front garden two years ago.

Tying up his dressing gown, he smoothed his hair and beard and opened the front door.

It was Amanda. She smiled awkwardly.

Nick didn't know the right thing to think or feel. All he knew was that a powerful wave of relief and joy crashed over him. He could barely breathe as his heart banged through his chest.

'Happy Christmas, Nick,' Amanda said quietly. She moved a hair that had fallen in front of her eyes behind her ear nervously.

'Oh my God.' Nick shook his head and then gave a half-laugh.

'If you want me to go away, then I completely understand,' Amanda said, gesturing to her car and taking two steps backwards.

'No, no. Please ... come in.' Nick took a breath as he felt a tear forming in his eye. *Don't cry, you prat*, he scolded himself.

Nick closed the door and turned to look at her.

'I knew when I woke up this morning that I needed to see you,' Amanda fiddled nervously with her hair and then swept it from her face.

'I'm so pleased to see you.'

'Are you?' Amanda flashed a glimpse of a smile. She obviously had no idea how Nick would react when she left the house that morning.

Nick took her hand and put it to his chest where his heart was pounding. 'Feel.'

Then Amanda reached for his hand and placed it on her chest. It was banging just as fast.

'What are we going to do?' Amanda asked.

'I know the sensible thing for us to do. But the thought of not being with you makes me miserable. Actually, it's making me ill,' Nick admitted.

'I love you ... you do know that?' Amanda gasped as tears streamed down her face.

It was too much to bear. He grabbed her to him and hugged her tightly. They pulled back to look at each other and he wiped the tears from her face. Then they kissed, softly at first and then deeper, like they needed each other to survive. He ran his hands through her hair as she gasped.

He stopped and put his hand to her face. 'This is the best Christmas present ever. Swear down.'

'Swear down? What are you, twelve?' Amanda laughed.

'Stay here. With me. For as long as you like.' Nick was running ahead of himself but he didn't care. He didn't want to be without her ever again.

'You might not want me to.' Amanda looked a little serious.

'Why?' Nick held his breath. What was it? He didn't want anything to come between them.

'I'm pregnant, Nick.'

AS SHE POURED MORE Buck's Fizz, Ruth realised that she was already tipsy. She didn't care. In fact, she fully intended to be drunk and merry for the next few days. 'It's Beginning to Look a Lot Like Christmas' by Michael Bublé was playing from the living room. There's nothing quite like a total Christmas cheese fest. Especially after what they had been through only weeks ago. Although the thought that Gates hadn't revealed the whereabouts of the remaining bodies still lurked in Ruth's mind when she let it.

Ella was under a duvet on the sofa with silver tinsel wrapped around her neck. She had been staying with Ruth and Sian since her kidnapping. Although Ella claimed she was okay, Ruth knew that there had been some nightmares and panic attacks. Promising that she was still intending to buy a flat, Ella said she would start looking again in January. As far as Ruth was concerned, Ella could stay for ever.

Sitting in front of the log fire, Sian was in pyjamas opening a large present. She squealed in delight at the designer gift set Ella had bought her and hugged her.

That reminded Ruth. She had ordered Sian something online that still hadn't arrived. It was only a small gift, but it was annoying.

Opening her emails on her phone, she saw a message from the company she had ordered it from giving a delivery date of 27 December. She shrugged. It was Christmas Day and nothing was going to annoy her.

An email from 23 December that she had somehow missed caught her eye. It was from Steven Flaherty. The email was titled: *Nothing on the CCTV – Just a quick update.* Breathing a sigh of relief, Ruth put away her phone. Not that long ago, no news would have worried and disheartened her. Today, it was a relief not to have any drama. She would open the email another day.

Watching Sian and Ella lying on the sofa together, giggling at some video that Ella had found on her phone, Ruth knew that she had all she needed. At least for today.

THE CHRISTMAS-DAY AA meeting was busy. People were dressed in Christmas jumpers, hugging and laughing with the knowledge that a sober Christmas for them was a good one.

Nick and Amanda sat on the front row to one side. As the meeting started, a middle-aged woman read a passage from The Big Book. Nick reached surreptitiously for Amanda's hand and they interlocked fingers.

"'A complete change takes place in our attitude to life. Where we used to hide away from responsibility, we find ourselves accepting it with gratitude. Instead of wanting to escape some perplexing problem, we experience a thrill of challenge in the opportunity it affords for another application of AA techniques, and we find ourselves tackling it with surprising vigour.

"The last fifteen years of my life have been rich and meaningful. I have had my share of problems, heartaches and disappointments, because that is life, but I have also known a great deal of joy and a peace that is the handmaiden of inner freedom. I have a wealth of friends and, with my AA friends, an unusual quality of fellowship. For, to these people, I am truly related. First, through mutual pain and despair, and later through mutual objectives and newfound faith and hope. And, as the years go by, working together, sharing our experiences with one another, and also sharing a mutual trust, understanding and love – without strings, without obligation – we acquire relationships that are unique and priceless.

"There is no more 'aloneness,' with that awful ache, so deep in the heart of every alcoholic that nothing, before, could ever reach it. That ache is gone and never need return again.

"Now there is a sense of belonging, of being wanted and needed and loved. In return for a bottle and a hangover, we have been given the Keys of the Kingdom."'

The reading was over and room responded, 'Thank you, Sophie.'

There was a moment as everyone quietened to invite anyone to share what they wanted.

Nick felt Amanda's hand tense for a moment.

'Hi, my name's Amanda, and I'm an alcoholic. And Merry Christmas to everyone here.'

'Merry Christmas, Amanda,' the room replied.

Enjoy this book?
Get the next book in the series
'The Devil's Cliff Killings' #Book 4
https://www.amazon.co.uk/dp/B086H35P5G
https://www.amazon.com/dp/B086H35P5G

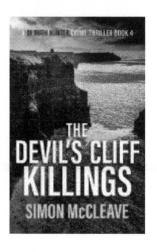

The Devil's Cliff Killings
A Ruth Hunter Crime Thriller #Book 4

Your FREE book is waiting for you now

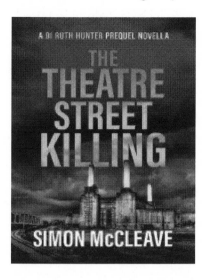

Get your FREE copy of the prequel to
the DI Ruth Hunter Series NOW
http://www.simonmccleave.com/vip-email-club
and join my VIP Email Club

AUTHOR'S NOTE

Although this book is very much a work of fiction, it is located in Snowdonia, a spectacular area of North Wales. It is steeped in history and folklore that spans over two thousand years. It is worth mentioning that Llancastell is a fictional town on the eastern edges of Snowdonia. I have made liberal use of artistic licence, names and places have been changed to enhance the pace and substance of the story.